# AMERICAN FIRSTS

INNOVATIONS, DISCOVERIES, AND GADGETS
BORN IN THE U.S.A.

By
Stephen J. Spignesi

# AMERICAN FIRSTS

INNOVATIONS, DISCOVERIES, AND GADGETS
BORN IN THE U.S.A.

By
Stephen J. Spignesi

NEW PAGE BOOKS
A division of The Career Press, Inc.
Franklin Lakes, NJ

AMERICAN FIRSTS
EDITED AND TYPESET BY NICOLE DEFELICE

Cover design by DesignConcept
Printed in the U.S.A. by Book-mart Press
Graphical elements © 2004 *www.clipart.com*

To order this title, please call toll-free 1-800-CAREER-1 (NJ and Canada: 201-848-0310) to order using VISA or MasterCard, or for further information on books from Career Press.

The Career Press, Inc., 3 Tice Road, PO Box 687,
Franklin Lakes, NJ 07417
**www.careerpress.com**
**www.newpagebooks.com**

CAREER
PRESS

New
Page
BOOKS

**Library of Congress Cataloging-in-Publication Data**

Spignesi, Stephen J.
    American firsts : innovations, discoveries, and gadgets born in the U.S.A. / by Stephen J. Spignesi.
        p. cm.
    Includes bibliographical references and index.
    ISBN 1-56414-691-X (pbk.)
        1. Technological innovations. 2. Inventions. I. Title.

T173.8.S668 2004
609.73—dc22

2003060314

# DEDICATION

For my cousin Angelyn,
with love and gratitude

**There is surely a piece of divinity in us,**

**something that was before the elements,**

**and owes no homage to the sun.**

—Sir Thomas Browne, *Religio Medici*

# CONTENTS

# American Firsts

# —Contents—

# —Contents—

# INTRODUCTION

## The Two Wings of the Worker

*Creativeness is the basis of evolution. With what then is it possible to strengthen the acts of creative power? Only with cheerfulness. Joy is a special wisdom. Cheerfulness is a special technique. This enhancement of vigor arises out of a conscious realization of the creativeness of elements. Truly, creative patience and cheerfulness are the two wings of the worker.*

—*New Era Community*, Passage 163
**The Agni Yoga Society**

Try to imagine a world without telephones, airplanes, or air-conditioning; without anesthesia, computers, movies, or skyscrapers.

Try to imagine doing business without cash registers, barcodes, e-mail, or express delivery service; without photocopying, telephone books, or typewriters.

Try to imagine being sick and not having access to CAT scans, MRIs, the blood bank, or angioplasty; or that cortisone, cardiac bypass surgery, tetracycline, novocaine, or even Band-Aids did not exist.

Try to imagine living your life without your bifocals, your contact lenses, your blender, or your blue jeans; without your can opener, Cheerios, ironing board, deodorant, dental floss, or electric razor; without your fluoride toothpaste, frozen food, birth control pills, panty hose, or paper towels; without your toaster, sneakers, or tampons.

And after you drag yourself through the mental hell of imagining such an appalling existence, take it one step further and imagine living your life without *toilet paper*.

Now stop imagining.

All of these things are real and all of these inventions, developments, and breakthroughs—and hundreds more achievements equally significant—are all American Firsts.

What, specifically, is an American First?

It is something that changed the world, and which came into being thanks to an American.

American Firsts include technology brainstorms, medical advancements, systems and procedures that improve efficiency, devices and tools that increase personal safety and fight crime, new and different food products, and, lest we forget, great games, sports, snacks, and toys that make life *a whole lot of fun*.

America is the birthplace of the coolest inventions on the planet. All the recorded music in the world owes its existence to our invention of tape recording. (And it is quite something to hear Czech and Finnish musicians playing the American creation jazz!)

Blue jeans sell for ridiculous sums of money on the black market in countries where people cannot simply walk into a Gap.

The microwave oven was quickly embraced by harried cooks all over the world.

And every foreign skyscraper exists because *we built one first.*

Add to these wonders the *fun stuff*—from bubble gum to Scrabble; crossword puzzles to potato chips; Ferris wheels to Fig Newtons; Jell-O to Jacuzzis; Monopoly to roller coasters; Silly Putty to volleyball— and it is obvious that this would be quite a different world without American Firsts.

On any given day, any given American may utilize hundreds of American Firsts as they meander through their hours. If every American First blazed in a glowing neon red color, everyone in this country (and countless people around the world, for that matter) would be walking around with retinal burns.

Need and curiosity, opportunity and chance, desire and creativity—all of these combined with the pioneer spirit to create a breed of people who wanted to know more, do more, travel farther, and make life better—at first, for themselves and their families; and later, for their city, state, country, and the rest of the world.

One of the most valued of all skills is problem solving. That simple term defines the motivating passion of inventive Americans, and it describes the American Zeitgeist in a nutshell.

Americans are not now, and never have been, complacent.

When travel took too long, we invented the automobile—and we also learned how to fly.

When scientific and business calculations became too complex for existing devices, we invented the computer.

When we understood how our arteries became clogged and caused heart disease, we invented angioplasty and cardiac bypass surgery.

When we decided to go into space on a regular basis, we invented the space shuttle.

Oh, and also let us not forget that when it quite simply got *too damn hot*, we invented air-conditioning.

In this book you will meet ordinary people, brilliant scientists, passionate inventors, amazing thinkers and, yes, eccentrics, oddballs, nuts, and zealots.

What they all have in common, however, is an open mind.

A mind open to thinking differently; to paying attention; to capitalizing on mistakes; to considering untried, untested, and, yes, sometimes bizarre ideas in the hope of making life—for everyone—better.

Today, more than 200 years after America invented herself, American society is the most eclectic and intriguing culture in the world.

America is known around the world and across the landscape of history as the first nation in the history of mankind to declare the equality of man in writing.

Enormous, amorphous, and multifaceted, America is a powerful global presence that exports food, technology, medicine, science, and culture to the rest of the world.

The blended nature of the American people reflects the American melting pot at its most innovative and imaginative. And the countless American Firsts that exist—and this book can only discuss a fraction of them—has done a world of good with the undeniable result being a better world.

The title of this Introduction, as well as its opening quote, is drawn from a yogic text that defines creative patience and cheerfulness as the "two wings of the worker."

The ones responsible for our American Firsts surely possessed both of those attributes in abundance.

After all, considering what they were accomplishing, and the place where they were doing it, how could they have not?

> Stephen Spignesi
> July 4, 2003
> New Haven, CT

*Sometimes people call me an idealist.*
*Well, that is the way I know I am an American.*

**—President Woodrow Wilson**

# A

## Activase®

Debut: 1987
Inventive Americans: Robert Swanson and
Dr. Herbert Boyer and the Genentech scientific team

The year: 1953. An ambulance screeches to a stop in front of St. Raphael's Hospital in New Haven, Connecticut. The man inside the ambulance is having a serious heart attack. He is 64, and smokes three packs each day. They rush him into the emergency room, give him oxygen and morphine, and monitor his vital signs. If he does not recover on his own, then they watch him die. The only tools doctors had to treat heart attacks in the 1950s, according to one medical journal, was the "stethoscope and the electrocardiograph."

The 1960s saw the development of cardiac care units (CCUs), followed by the use of the cardiac defibrillator, improved cardiac diagnostic imaging techniques, and new drugs. The 1970s saw increased use of balloon angioplasty.

In the 1980s, though, the most important cardiac drug of all time was released and changed the way heart attacks were treated.

Activase is a Tissue Plasminogen Activator (usually referred to as "t-PA"), a thrombolytic drug that almost instantly dissolves blood clots in patients having a heart attack or stroke. (Officially, t-PA is recommended for "acute myocardial infarction," "acute massive pulmonary embolism," and "acute ischemic stroke," and it should be administered within 30 minutes of the onset of the attack, and no later than three hours after the patient's first symptoms.)

Since its debut in 1987, Activase has been increasingly used as the first measure in treating heart attack or stroke victims when they show up at the emergency room. Activase is the type of drug that at one time was referred to as a "miracle drug." Its powers are, admittedly, amazing. Usually, a heart attack or stroke is caused when a blood clot blocks the flow of blood to the heart or the brain, respectively. Activase, and drugs like it, quickly clear the obstruction and, if administered quickly enough in three measured doses, can clear the clot and restore blood flow before permanent damage is done to the heart or brain.

Activase was developed at Genentech, a biotech/pharmaceutical research company that was founded in 1976 by Robert Swanson and Dr. Herbert Boyer. The company was formed to make use of recombinant DNA technology, a new medical breakthrough pioneered by Boyer and Dr. Stanley Cohen.

Prior to developing Activase, Genentech cloned human insulin and human growth hormone using their new technology.

In 2000, Genentech received FDA approval for TNKase™, a t-PA drug that can be administered in a single dose in just five seconds.

# Air Bags

Debut: 1973
Inventive American: General Motors

You're driving along on the highway, doing 60–65, when the driver of the SUV in front of you suddenly slams on his brakes to avoid hitting a deer in the road. You respond instantly by slamming down on your brakes, but it's too late. For a millisecond, you remember an old high school physics class in which the teacher taught you something about speed and weight combining to increase force.[1]

One of your classmates had asked why hitting a pothole at 45 miles per hour does more damage to the car than striking it at 10 miles per hour.

You hurtle towards the rear of the SUV and you see a bumper sticker that reads "This Car Climbed the Rockies."

And then you hit.

You crash into the rear of the SUV at 45 miles per hour. In a maelstrom of noise, metal, and sunlight, your air bag inflates in a fraction of a second. You survive. Your car is a mangled mess, no longer drivable, but you survived. You get to live on and experience the joys of dealing with insurance companies, doctors, and lawyers.

The air bag saved your life.

This is one of those American Firsts that has not only made people's lives easier since becoming standard equipment, it has saved lives and prevented injury.

The air bag is an automotive passive restraint device designed to instantly inflate when the car is in a collision. The bag prevents passengers from being thrown into the steering wheel or windshield.

According to General Motors:

> Today's air bags are inflated with a high-tech combination of electronics, computers, and chemistry. Sophisticated sensors predict the likely severity of a crash. When a crash of sufficient severity occurs, the sensing system triggers a release of gas in the air bag inflator. The bag literally bursts from its storage site (beneath the air bag cover) at high speed. The entire deployment process is faster than the blink of an eye. The inflated air bag helps cushion the occupant's impact with the vehicle interior. The gas used to inflate the air bag is forced out of the bag when the occupant hits the bag, and it quickly dissipates through small pores and/or vents in the air bag fabric.

An air bag will deploy if a car is traveling between nine and 16 miles per hour at the time of a collision.

Today, air bags are also installed on the passenger side of the vehicle, and many car manufacturers also offer side air bags.

Because of the risk of injury to infants and young children, air bags in many newer models are equipped with an on/off switch.

# Air-conditioning

Debut: 1902
Inventive American: Willis Haviland Carrier

Living, working, sleeping, eating, driving, playing, and all other facets of normal life are unpleasant and sometimes impossible when temperatures reach the high 90s and the humidity percentage is close to those numbers as well.

How did we live before air-conditioning? And how do people around the world in stifling climates manage to function *without* air-conditioning? Many men and women in Middle Eastern countries wear long garments that cover almost their entire body, and they walk steadily through treeless deserts seemingly unfazed by the blistering heat. Maybe their internal thermostats are set to a higher tolerance than those of us in the western world who start whining if the temperature in our houses goes above 76 degrees. Nowadays, air conditioning in America is perceived to be almost as important as central heating and running water.

When Willis Carrier invented the practical air conditioner in 1902 and had it installed in a printing plant, he was earning $10 each week at the Buffalo Forge Company and had earned his master's degree in Engineering the prior year. He was awarded a patent for his "Apparatus for Treating Air" in 1906, and this new technology grew exponentially as improvements were made and Carrier and his colleagues gained a deeper understanding of the relationships between temperature, humidity, and dew point.

The earliest air-conditioning installations were in department stores and movie theaters. These establishments saw their business skyrocket during the hot summer months when the movie that was playing or the sale that was running was second in importance to the fact that the buildings were air-conditioned.

After people experienced air conditioning in public places, they wanted the same comfort for their homes and, in 1924, home air conditioning units hit the market. Central air-conditioning for homes followed later. And then we demanded A/C in cars and we were obliged.

Cool, eh?

# The Airplane

Debut: 1903
Inventive Americans: Orville and Wilbur Wright

It has been said that flying dreams are the most common. In the early 20th century, we learned to fly in reality. This was, in essence, a fulfillment of a fantasy we had been living for eons in our dreams.

When we learned to fly, we took control of our world.

No longer was distance between places an obstacle—to business, social interaction, conflict, research, or any other of the myriad pursuits that are an integral part of the human condition.

Communication and travel shrunk the world. Wireless communication gave us the power to talk to almost anyone, anywhere, at anytime. Air travel gave us the power to go there.

On December 17, 1903, 32-year-old Orville Wright and his 36-year-old brother Wilbur, took turns making four controlled flights in their self-made biplane at Kitty Hawk, North Carolina. Orville made the first flight of 12 seconds and traveled 100 feet. Wilbur then flew 175 feet, followed by Orville's 200-foot flight. Wilbur made the fourth and final flight that day of 852 feet, which lasted 59 seconds.

History is replete with stories of men building machines in which to fly, and so the Wright Brothers' airplane was not really the first flying machine. It was, however, the first machine to allow controlled flight by man; thus, it is the milestone achievement and a true American First that gave us the skies.

# Alcoholics Anonymous

Debut: 1935
Inventive American: Bill Wilson

You open your eyes. The digital clock on your nightstand reads 6:15. You blink your eyes and this sends a blaze of pain through your skull. You move your head slightly in a futile attempt to ease the agony of the knife buried in your brain and this brings a wave of nausea. You try to remember the previous 10 to 12 hours. You know you went out with Ron and Mike. You know you went to a bar. You know you started on tequila boilermakers at 8:30 and the last thing you remember is talking to a girl named Lily as you stood waiting in the line outside the bathrooms. She had a rainbow tattoo on the small of her back. She pulled up her shirt to show you. Then all is blank until now. How many shots of tequila did you have? Eight? Eleven? How many beers? Eight? Eleven?

You sit up. The nausea returns. You stand up. The nausea gets worse. You rush to the bathroom. The headache makes you whimper. You throw up. Then you have diarrhea. It doesn't help.

You sit on the edge of the bed. Even your eyes ache. You have to be at work in two hours. You take a deep breath and open the drawer of the nightstand next to your bed. You reach in and grab a bottle of vodka. You look at the bottle a moment, perhaps briefly reconsidering drinking in the morning. The moment passes. You unscrew the top, tilt the bottle to your lips, and drink deeply. You gulp the vodka down in three or four swallows—what is that? Four or five shots?—and you instantly feel the warmth spread throughout your stomach. Within seconds you feel better. You take another small swig to top off this fermented breakfast of yours and then you put the bottle away. There will be time for more later. You get up, take a cold shower, drink three cups of black coffee, take a Vicodin, and get dressed. By 7:30 you feel almost human, and you manage to make it to work on time.

While still feeling the effects of the vodka and the Vicodin, your boss calls you into his office. Today is your last day, he tells you. You go home immediately and drink all afternoon. The following morning is a repeat of the previous morning, but you don't shower and go to work this day. Instead, you get up, throw up, drink coffee, and then you attend your very first Alcoholics Anonymous meeting. The meeting takes place at high noon in the basement of a Catholic Church on Humphrey Street. All eyes are on you when it's your turn and, in a small voice, you say, "Hello. My name is Glenn and I'm an alcoholic."

"Hi, Glenn."

One day at a time.

Do not drink *one day at a time*, and you will be able to beat alcoholism.

That, in essence, is the guiding principle of Alcoholics Anonymous and, in 1935, Bill Wilson ("Bill W."—no last names) developed a set of 12 steps to help members get through those oh-so-long days, one at a time.

Is alcoholism a disease? The answer is yes, according to the medical community, but there are many who reject that conclusion. The practice of defining addictions as diseases is controversial. Drinking is a voluntary act, the argument goes; how can someone "catch" a disease by seeking it out through their own actions? Under these criteria, is heroin addiction a disease? Smoking? Drinking coffee? All of these practices involve a psychophysiological dependence on a substance, as in alcoholism, and yet no one but the alcoholic is deemed officially "sick" by the medical establishment.

Whether or not you accept the definition of alcoholism as a disease, there is no doubt that it needs to be treated and the AA program works.

AA has over 100,000 groups and 2,000,000 members all over the world. Its innovative "12 Step" program has been successfully applied to other addictions, including drugs, food, gambling, and sex.

These are the 12 steps of Bill W.'s Alcoholics Anonymous program.[2]

1.  We admitted we were powerless over alcohol—that our lives had become unmanageable.
2.  We came to believe that a Power greater than ourselves could restore us to sanity.
3.  We made a decision to turn our will and our lives over to the care of God *as we understood Him.*

4. We made a searching and fearless moral inventory of ourselves.

5. We admitted to God, to ourselves, and to another human being the exact nature of our wrongs.

6. We were entirely ready to have God remove all these defects of our character.

7. We humbly asked Him to remove our shortcomings.

8. We made a list of all persons we had harmed, and became willing to make amends to them all.

9. We made direct amends to such people wherever possible, except when to do so would injure them or others.

10. We continued to take personal inventory and when we were wrong promptly admitted it.

11. We sought through prayer and meditation to improve our conscious contact with God *as we understood Him*, praying only for knowledge of His will for us and the power to carry that out.

12. Having had a spiritual awakening as the result of these steps, we tried to carry this message to alcoholics and to practice these principles in all our affairs.

# Amazon.com®

Debut: 1995
Inventive American: Jeff Bezos

Have you ever bought anything from Amazon.com?
Thought so.

Amazon, like eBay, has defined a standard for effective commercial use of the Internet. Originally nothing but a bookseller, Amazon now sells music (they bought CDNow.com), clothes, computers, and countless other commodities. They have also expanded the Amazon environment to include lists of books by users, recommendations, and access to used books.

The ease of use of the Amazon Website and the "community" feel of the site is key to their success—which, like eBay, taps the enormous reach of the Internet to create a virtual neighborhood among users.

Amazon was launched by Jeff Bezos in 1995 in a garage, and now does over $3 billion a year in sales. He used doors as desks and his instructions to the temp agencies to which he turned to for staff were: "Send us your freaks."

Today, Amazon is a major threat to brick and mortar stores such as Barnes & Noble and Waldenbooks; the chains have responded to the challenge by establishing high-profile Web presences with sites that, truth be told, mimic a great deal of what Amazon developed.

Amazon is now well established all over the world as the Web place to go for books. Quite a leap from that garage, eh?

## ANESTHESIA

Debut: 1845
Inventive American: Dr. Horace Wells

*Before:*

You are a 30-year-old man and you have a malignant vascular tumor on your left jaw. The year is 1832. Your doctors have determined that if the tumor is not removed, you will die. When you consider that anesthesia has not been invented yet, and that the doctors will have to cut open your face to remove the tumor, you actually consider dying from the cancer a viable option.

*After:*

You are a 19-year-old Union soldier and you have just had the bottom half of your right leg severely mangled by a Confederate bullet. The year is 1862. The limb must be amputated. You take a giant swig from a bottle of whiskey and then the doctors lay you down and place a glass dome over your face. Inside the dome is a cloth soaked with ether. The use of this liquid in this manner is a new technique developed in 1842 called anesthesia.

You inhale the sweet, metallic vapors, and you quickly feel yourself drifting into a realm in which voices are somewhere in the distance and your body floats through the haze.

You hear the doctors talking. "Grab it just above the knee."

You hear the clanging of surgical tools. "Saw faster or you're going to shred the skin."

You are awake but you do not feel pain. After a period that could have been minutes or hours, you fall asleep. When you awaken, a blood-soaked white bandage covers the stump of your right thigh. You are in pain, but opium and alcohol help you deal with it. All in all, your surgery went well.

*Today:*

You are a 50-year-old woman in the hospital for a mastectomy. You lie in bed the morning of the surgery, relaxed and comfortable from the pre-op narcotics and tranquilizers administered to you by your nurse.

You are wheeled into the operating room where an army of masked, gowned, sterile medical professionals are preparing for your operation. The anesthesiologist introduces herself and puts an IV into your arm.

When the surgeon is ready to begin, the anesthesiologist tells you to count backwards from 10. You make it to seven and the next thing you know, you are in your hospital bed with a morphine drip attached to your arm and a patient-controlled button in your hand that allows you to give yourself more pain medication if you feel you need it. In 24 hours, you will be taken off the morphine and given oral narcotics that will handle the rest of the post-surgical pain. All in all, your surgery went well.

The invention of anesthesia brought about the end of surgical pain. Ether was first used in 1841 by Dr. Crawford Long of Georgia. In 1845, Dr. Horace Wells demonstrated the use of ether during surgery for Harvard Medical School students. A year later, Wells was credited with the discovery/invention of using ether as an anesthetic.

Anesthesia has been called the most important invention of the past 2,000 years. It has evolved exponentially since its initial use to the point now where one of the most important doctors in surgery is the anesthesiologist. Surgery today is, for all intents and purposes, pain-free. Post-surgical pain is a reality, of course, but that occurs *after* the anesthetic wears off.

Modern anesthetics are also "clean." They are very powerful and require smaller doses of chemicals to be administered into the patient. Most of these drugs leave the bloodstream very quickly too, allowing patients to return home only a few hours after most outpatient surgeries.

# Angioplasty

Debut: 1964
Inventive American: Charles Dotter

As is often the case with modern medical techniques that mimic much less delicate mechanical processes, angioplasty can justifiably be described as using a router to clean a pipe. The "pipe," however, happens to be a coronary artery and the "gunk" being cleaned out consists of deposits of fat. But the principle is the same.

Angioplasty was an American First, but there should be a caveat attached to this statement: American Charles Dotter first used catheter angioplasty in the peripheral vessels in 1964, but the technique was not embraced by American doctors. In fact, it was ridiculed and rejected.

More than a decade later, it took the European medical community, specifically Eberhart Zeitler and Andreas Gruentzig, to use and improve the procedure, and now it is widely accepted as a major medical breakthrough.

And for all the shortsightedness of U.S. doctors, an American can still rightfully take credit for it.

# The Apgar Scale

Debut: 1952
Inventive American: Dr. Virginia Apgar

The Apgar scale is a quick and easy means for medical personnel to immediately evaluate the overall health of a newborn. It is used at one minute after birth, and then again at five minutes after birth. The test assigns a numerical value of 0, 1, or 2 to five key physiological elements: heart rate, respiration, muscle tone, reflex response, and color. A score of between 7 and 10 means the infant is in good to excellent health; between 4 and 7 means the infant may need close observation and possible assistance; below 4 is a serious danger sign and the infant will need immediate, possibly life-saving help. A difficult or premature delivery can suppress a baby's Apgar score temporarily.

The test was developed by New York Columbia-Presbyterian Medical Center obstetric anesthesiologist Virginia Apgar and is now used all over the world.

# The Artificial Heart

Debut: 1982
Inventive American: Dr. Robert Jarvik

People still make jokes about the old TV show *The Six Million Dollar Man*. "We can rebuild him," they told us in the opening and, by golly, they did, with the end result being what was termed a "bionic man." Critically injured U.S. astronaut Steve Austin had his legs, right arm, and left eye replaced by atomic-powered electromechanical devices that gave him super strength, speed, and vision.

Ludicrous, right?

Hardly.

If anything, *The Six Million Dollar Man* was too restrained in its depiction of replacing human parts with bionic parts. Today, many human parts and organs can be replaced or appended to human parts—and one of the most important medical breakthroughs was the American First of Dr. Robert Jarvik's artificial heart. In 1982, it was installed in dentist Barney Clark, who lived 112 days with the Jarvik-7 replacing his human heart.

Today, Dr. Jarvik is working on the Jarvik 2000, an artificial heart the size of a thumb.

The days of the true bionic man are here.

# The Assembly Line

Debut: 1901 (Olds); 1913 (Ford)
Inventive Americans: Ransom Eli Olds; Henry Ford

The Oldsmobile was the first American automobile assembled on an assembly line, so Ransome Eli Olds should get credit for this innovative system of manufacturing, which he first implemented in 1901.

But it was Henry Ford who, more than a decade later in 1913, first used the conveyor belt assembly line in his Michigan plant, which laid the groundwork for the completely automated assembly systems used today. Ford's production process fully assembled a Model T in one hour and 33 minutes.

Today, the assembly line is used all over the world in literally every manufacturing industry, from Oreo cookies and computers to coffeemakers.

# AstroTurf®

Debut: 1965
Inventive Americans: James Faria and
Robert Wright (for Monsanto)

AstroTurf is fake grass. It was developed in 1965 by two engineers at Monsanto as an alternative playing surface for sporting events.

Natural grass doesn't stand up to heavy play, the use of cleats, and excessive rain, for example. AstroTurf was a synthetic playing surface designed to eliminate the problems of playing on natural grass, while still providing the feel of a natural playing surface.

AstroTurf quickly became the standard for stadiums and other playing venues, from the high school and college level to professional venues. Players complained that the nylon fibers used for the fake grass caused "burn" injuries when slid on, and cleats could not be used on AstroTurf, but it was valued all over the world as an alternative to planting and maintaining a real playing surface .

In 1988, FieldTurf was released, and it was touted as a superior alternative to AstroTurf. FieldTurf was as close to natural grass as had yet been developed, it could take 40 inches of rain without canceling play, and players could wear cleats.

AstroTurf is still the dominant surface, but as AstroTurf contracts and warranties expire, many educational institutions and sports venues are replacing their AstroTurf with FieldTurf.

# The ATM

Debut: 1939 (Simjian); 1968 (Wetzel)
Inventive Americans: Luther George Simjian; Don Wetzel

ATMs—Automatic Teller Machines—are everywhere. Their ubiquitousness speaks to how society has changed over the past several decades. Today, the notion of "outdoor banking" is considered mundane; it is often a routine part of many people's day.

Simjian and Wetzel are credited with designing and inventing what was to become the modern ATM, but it was Chemical Bank that launched the first ATM service in 1969 when they installed a machine at its Rockville Center, New York branch. ATMs became widespread during the 1970s and are now as common as gas stations.

Today, most ATMs all over the world are linked so that anyone can use any ATM, even if they are not a customer of the bank that offers it. This is not free, however, and if someone uses an ATM other than their own bank's, they are charged a fee for the service. ATM service fees have grown exponentially into a very lucrative revenue stream for banks. In 1999, U.S. banks' profit from ATMs was $4 billion,  almost half of which was from "double-dipping"—charging customers twice for using a single ATM. The customer's own bank imposes a fee simply for performing an ATM transaction, and the "off-us" bank—the bank that owns the ATM machine that the other bank's customer used—now charges a fee for using their machine. That is how ATM users pay twice for one transaction.

There has been constant debate about the fairness, even the legality, of charging customers twice for ATM transactions, but so far, in most cases, the "off-us" fees have survived court challenges.

Banks claim that processing another bank's ATM transactions costs them money so they should be entitled to recoup. This makes sense, but the fees are often usurious. For instance, some banks charge up to $4.50 to withdraw $20 from an ATM, a transaction which, according to federal reports, costs the bank 27 cents to process.

Connecticut and Iowa have banned the surcharges, but these prohibitions are being challenged in the courts by the banking industry.

K.D. Weinert, Planning Director for the Fund for Public Interest Research, concluded his article, "A Brief History of ATMs" (available at *www.StopATMFees.com*) with the following cogent point:

> *What the future holds for ATM fees is uncertain. What is certain, though, is that even the original promoters of the ATM could not have imagined what a profit machine their invention would be 25 years later. After all, in how many businesses could you get away with charging money for a service you once gave away, without markedly improving the quality of the service (even the latest ATMs can do little more than the "accept deposits," "transfer money between accounts" and "withdraw up to $300" that the ATMs of the late 1970s could do)...and despite the price of the underlying technology having dropped to a fraction of its original cost?*

So much for making money the old-fashioned way...by earning it.

I never use ATMs. I go inside my bank and I do business with a teller. I know them, and they know me. For many of us, that still means something.

# Audiotape Recording

Debut: 1940
Inventive American: Marvin Camras

I know what my speaking and singing voice sounds like. I have heard myself interviewed on TV and radio many times over the years and, in my younger halcyon days, I was in bands, played piano and sang in bars, and tape-recorded many of my performances. So, I (like others who have had the opportunity to watch or listen to themselves) know what my speaking and singing voice sounds like.

But many people do *not* know what their true voice sounds like, and these many people, when they eventually *do* hear their own voice on a tape recording, recoil in horror at what they actually sound like. This can be especially disconcerting for someone who would like to make singing a career. Hearing yourself on tape warbling an off-key, atonal ditty that you had been certain was Pavarottiesque when issuing forth from your vocal chords can almost immediately deflate any and all hopes of singing at Carnegie Hall—or on *American Idol*, for that matter.

At first, the tendency is to blame either the tape, the tape recorder, or the person doing the taping.

"That's not what I sound like! There must be something wrong with the tape you used. It must be defective. I *know* I sound better than that!"

So then they usually move on to take two, only this time the singer really makes an effort to give it everything he's got. He consciously makes sure he's on key; he enunciates; he hits the notes from above (as a choir director once taught me); and he does everything in his power to channel Matt Monro, or even Marilyn Monroe, for that matter, when belting out his signature tune. ("Time in a Bottle?" "American Pie?") Oftentimes, the results are the same.

The enormous popularity of karaoke has given many people a chance to sing along with professional accompaniment and this is often the final nail in the coffin, rather than being an experience that enhances latent talent. There is nothing worse than hearing "Let's Stay Together" sung (with full band and horns, of course) by someone who is as far from Al Green as Sinead O'Connor is from an audience with the Pope.

Marvin Camras's cousin wanted to be an opera singer. In 1940, Camras used magnetized piano wire to record his cousin's performances. (It had been earlier proved that sounds could be recorded magnetically.) The wire did record the sound of his cousin singing, but the wire twisted as it wound through the recording machine and the playback was unintelligible. Camras then modified the recording head of the machine so that the sounds were recorded symmetrically around the wire. This worked and Camras was able to produce a recording on which his cousin could hear what he truly sounded like. Shortly thereafter, the cousin abandoned his idea of becoming a singer and moved on to another career.

Based on his success with his machine, Camras went to work for the Armour Research Foundation where he developed improved recording machines, some of which were used by the U.S. military for training recruits and duping enemy ships into thinking they were being attacked.

Camras was less than thrilled with the results from using wire for magnetic recordings (it was fine for mimicking depth charge explosions, but awful for other, more mundane uses), so he began to experiment using tape which he coated with iron-based ferrous oxide paint. After much trial and error, he came up with the perfect paint for the tape and quality sound recording was a reality.

Camras's magnetic-based recording technology quickly became the foundation for almost the entire entertainment and computer industries.

For his monumentally influential invention, Camras was inducted into the National Inventors Hall of Fame in 1985.

# B

## THE BACKSTROKE

Debut: 1912
Inventive American: Harry Hebner

Can a swimming stroke be considered an American First? Yes, it can when it is an American who is credited with inventing it.

Olympic swimmer Harry Hebner was almost disqualified at the Games for improper swimming when he first used his new stroke. He kept his medal, though, after the judges ruled that the only requirement in a backstroke race was that the swimmer remain on his back for the duration of the competition. There were no specifics about arm movements or timing, and the alternating arm pulls of Hebner's backstroke were deemed legal. Hebner's stroke was quickly recognized as the best backstroke ever developed; not only is it still in use today by swimmers, it has not been changed since its debut.

# Band-Aids®

Debut: 1920
Inventive American: Earle Dickson (for Johnson & Johnson)

The Band-Aid is one of those products that has suffered because of its own success. The idea of the Band-Aid—an individual, sterile, adhesive bandage—was so welcome and quickly became so popular (after an initial slow start) that the term "Band-Aid" is now no longer used by many people as a trademarked name, but rather as a generic term for any individual adhesive bandage—like Kleenex, Xerox, and other similarly ubiquitous products.

In the 1860s and 1870s, more than 90 percent of surgical patients died after their operations. Doctors operated with their bare hands and "surgical packing" consisted of sawdust from the floor of the operating room.

A British surgeon named Joseph Lister knew that germs were the culprit, and, in 1876, he gave a lecture in Philadelphia about germs. In the audience were Joseph Lawrence and Robert Johnson. Joe Lawrence believed Lister, and went on to concoct a disinfectant rinse that came to be called Listerine, in Lister's honor.

Johnson went on to start a company with his brothers to manufacture sterile bandages.

In 1920, Earle Dickson, a Johnson & Johnson employee, came up with the idea of affixing pieces of the Johnson bandages to surgical tape to create individual, self-applicable bandages.

Thus, the Band-Aid was born.

Johnson & Johnson have tried valiantly to remind the public that Band-Aid is a trademark. In their earnest commercials, wounded and bleeding kids sing that they "are stuck on Band-Aid brand..."—which comes off as ridiculously awkward. A kid with a cut finger is *not* supposed to be shouting (actually, *singing*) to his mother, "Mommy I need a Band-Aid brand bandage!"

It's all about the money, of course, and Johnson & Johnson justifiably want to protect the name of their product. But the product's success has permeated the culture and any individually wrapped bandage is now, to J & J's chagrin, known as a band-aid.

# Bar Codes
## (The UPC—Universal Product Code)

Debut: 1949 (patent granted on October 7, 1952)
Inventive Americans: Joseph Woodland and Bernard Silver

Bar codes are everywhere these days. They are automatically printed on almost every manufactured item—even though there are still many retail outlets that do not use bar code scanning devices. Someday, though, everyone will, the thinking goes, and so the code is printed on more than 95 percent of consumer items.

A bar code consists of 12 numbers separated by double lines at the beginning, middle, and end of the sequence. A laser/optical scanner reads the pattern of the numbers and instantly identifies the item and its correct price. Bar codes have been a boon to the retail industry, as well as the United States military, which requires that every single item it purchases have a scannable bar code. Bar codes allow speedy checkouts at stores, continual inventory updating, and accurate information about purchasing patterns.

But did you know that there is a Satanic conspiracy theory about bar codes?

Bar codes were invented in 1948 by Bernard Silver, a graduate student of Drexel Institute in Philadelphia, and Joseph Woodland, his partner. They initially worked with ultraviolet ink, but eventually settled on the pattern matching system in use today.

What possible Satanic meaning can there be in black lines that stand for numbers?

The secret lies in the three separator bars mentioned previously. The three separators in the standard bar code consist of two thin lines that look exactly like the bar code pattern for the number 6. Thus, according to the conspiracists, every bar code has a large 6-6-6 in it, the Biblical sign of the Antichrist. Another paranoid theory is that the government eventually plans to have bar codes placed on every citizen, either on the back of the wrist or on the forehead, for constant monitoring of the populace.

Interestingly, it was recently announced that laser bar code technology has advanced to the point where bar codes can now be imprinted directly onto meat and eggs and be read without damaging the product. This means that, yes, bar codes can now safely be placed on human flesh.

Imagine a future in which you order a ticket to a baseball game at home on the Internet using your own personal bar code ID number. When you get to the stadium, you hold out your hand, and an optical scanner reads the bar code tattooed (or whatever) on the back of your wrist. The master database (which everyone will be sharing by then) confirms that you did, indeed, purchase a ticket, and you get whisked through the entrance in the time it takes to swipe a bag of chips across a grocery store cash register scanner.

Science fiction? Not really. We're pretty close to this scenario already.

# The Bathysphere

Debut: 1930
Inventive Americans: William Beebe and Otis Barton

A bathysphere is a reinforced, pressurized spherical deep-diving chamber in which people are lowered by a cable to study the oceans at depths at which diving is impossible.

The bathysphere was designed and invented by William Beebe and Otis Barton and was first tested in 1930 when Beebe descended 1,426 feet in a five-foot-wide sphere. In 1934, the two men successfully descended approximately 3,000 feet in their invention.

Today, the bathysphere has been superseded by the bathyscaph, a free-diving, self-contained vessel consisting of a flotation hull with a manned observation capsule fixed to its underside. The bathyscaph can reach depths of more than six miles.

# The Bifocal Lens

Debut: 1775
Inventive American: Benjamin Franklin

Some people need a certain amount of correction for distance vision that differs from the amount of correction they need for close vision. This problem has plagued man seemingly since we first opened our eyes. Yet, it was the American Founding Father

Benjamin Franklin who came up with a solution to this ubiquitous problem: the bifocal eyeglass lens. Bifocals combine convex and concave lenses and correct both nearsightedness and farsightedness. Bifocals eventually evolved into trifocals and, today, bifocal vision correction is even available in contact lenses.

# The Blender

Debut: 1922 (Poplawski); 1935 (Waring)
Inventive Americans: Stephen Poplawski; Fred Waring

If you see a blender in a movie or TV show, you can be fairly certain there will probably be a "turn on the blender with the top off" joke coming up relatively soon. Why do we find this funny? Who knows? But we do.

Stephen Poplawski is credited with being the true inventor of the blender, but it was big band leader Fred Waring who is best known as the father of the blender. In 1922, Poplawski attached a spinning blade to the bottom of a container and used the electric device to make mixed fountain drinks at a soda fountain.

Thirteen years later, Fred Waring and his partner, inventor Fred Osius, took Poplawski's idea, made some improvements and changes over several years, and, in 1937, began marketing the Miracle Mixer for $29.75. The name was eventually changed to the Waring Blender, which is still sold today.

The blender was immediately popular. People began using the blender for pureeing foods, and also for making frothy mixed drinks in bars. It is said that Dr. Jonas Salk even used the Waring Blender when concocting his polio vaccine.

# The Blood Bank

Debut: circa 1935
Inventive American: Dr. Richard Charles Drew

It is sad that sometimes the people who can most help humanity die at an early age. Who knows what Dr. Richard Charles Drew may have come up with if he had lived past the age of 46?

Dr. Drew, while working at the Presbyterian Hospital in New York in 1935, conceived the idea of storing blood plasma for surgeries and emergencies, something which had never before been tried. This revolutionized medicine and Drew went on to become the first director of the Red Cross's blood bank division. Ironically, Dr. Drew's blood was not welcome at any of his own blood banks. He was black and no white person at the time would even consider being transfused with "black blood," even though it was as red as theirs.

Today, the overwhelming majority of hospitals around the world have their own blood bank, and blood drives are used as a way to keep banks stocked.

# Blue Jeans

Debut: 1873
Inventive Americans: Levi Strauss and Jacob Davis

Blue jeans were originally invented as work pants, not as a fashion statement. Levi Strauss sold dry goods in San Francisco and, because a large part of his clientele were the gold miners drawn to California with dreams of striking it rich, he was regularly in need of sturdy work clothes. In 1873, his partner, Nevadian Jacob Davis, came up with the revolutionary idea of using steel rivets in addition to stitches at the stress points of canvas work pants.

The idea immediately caught on and now blue jeans are sold everywhere in the world and are available in a staggering array of colors and styles. Authentic American blue jeans once sold for hundreds of dollars on the Russian black market before the fall of Communism.

# The Brassiere

Debut: 1913
Inventive American: Mary Phelps Jacob

No, the brassiere was not invented by a man named Otto Titzling. The bra was invented by Mary Phelps Jacob because she simply did not have anything else to wear.

If you define a brassiere as a garment to support the breasts, then the ancient Romans *should* be credited with creating the first bra. However, there is a major difference between Roman bras and the bras of today. The early Roman bra was designed to lift the breasts *out* of the dress and support them as they lay exposed to the world. Many modern women are not averse to showing cleavage, but they draw the line at parading through the grocery store bare-breasted.

Mary Phelps Jacob invented the bra when she needed something to wear beneath a gown and none of the existing undergarments of the time gave her the support the garment required. Women wore corsets back then, and they were bulky, uncomfortable, and did not work for many types of dresses. In Mary's case, the sheer gown she had bought had a plunging neckline and the whalebone inserts of her corsets were visible. After a little thought, Mary designed the first bra using nothing but two silk handkerchiefs and some pink ribbon. She fashioned two cups out of the handkerchiefs, used the ribbon to tie them and, voila, no more corsets!

Thanks to Mary Phelps Jacob, the corset was issued its death sentence and women (and lingerie manufacturers) everywhere cheered.

# The Bread-Slicing Machine

Debut: 1927
Inventive American: Otto Rohwedder

Sliced bread is such a simple yet wondrous enhancement of daily life that an actual phrase—"the greatest thing since sliced bread"—was coined to emphasize just how fantastic something was in comparison to sliced bread.

It took Otto Rohwedder 15 years to perfect a machine that would evenly slice a loaf of bread and then wrap it up. Toast lovers everywhere salute Otto and his valiant efforts.

# Brillo® Pads

Debut: 1915
Inventive American: Milton B. Loeb

Brillo Pads were originally developed to clean aluminum cookware, but it wasn't long before it was discovered that they had countless other uses—or that they could be marketed to busy housewives who did not have time to scrape dried mashed potatoes off their pots.

Brillo Pads are made of fine gauge steel wool and are imbued with a tallow-based soap. Brillo also offers soap-free pads, and smaller "junior size" pads that are used once and thrown away.

# Bubble Gum

Debut: 1928
Inventive American: Walter E. Diemer

Walter Diemer probably should have majored in something other than accounting in college. Granted, his degree did get him a terrific job with the Fleer Chewing Gum Company in Philadelphia, but after he finished his day's work, he would turn to his pastime of tinkering with gum recipes.

One day in 1928, he accidentally created a gum that made bubbles when air was pumped into it. Until then, chewing gum had been thin and fragile, and a wad of chewed gum would never have been able to be stretched into a bubble. It would immediately break.

Diemer had found a way to maintain gum's chewability and yet be thick enough to blow bubbles. One day, he made up a five-pound batch of the stuff and took it down to a local grocery store and sold it by the chunk. The entire five pounds sold in one afternoon.

Diemer's bosses were very pleased with his fortuitous discovery and, because he was an employee of Fleer, they claimed the copyright on the invention. Diemer never received a penny in royalties for his creation. Reportedly, he didn't care, though. He was so pleased to have created something that brought so many people so much joy that the money was irrelevant.

And he probably made a pretty good living as an accountant anyway. And I'll bet he sat at his desk blowing bubbles all the livelong day.

# C

## The Calculating Machine

Debut: 1885
Inventive American: William Seward Burroughs

William Burroughs was only 28 years old when he invented the world's first calculating and listing machine, and when he died at the young age of 41, more than 1,000 of his machines had been sold. By 1926, that number had grown to one million machines sold.

Burroughs came up with the idea for a machine that would add columns of numbers while working as a bank clerk at the Cayuga County National Bank in Auburn, New York, near his birthplace of Rochester. He witnessed and experienced firsthand the tedium of maintaining bank records using nothing but pencil and paper (and lots of erasers, of course).

Burroughs designed and built a machine that would do the job, but it had one fairly serious problem: The answers the machine provided were not always right. Apparently, the force with which one pulled the handle of the machine could change the answers. Using even the most generous and forgiving criteria possible, there is no way of considering this initial version of Burrough's machine as anything but a failure. After all, if a machine's raison d'être is to correctly add numbers and it adds them wrong, then it doesn't really fulfill its purpose, right?

Burroughs knew he had a problem and immediately set to work on an improved machine, which he patented in 1893. This new version added correctly, and it quickly became an indispensable piece of office equipment. The electronic calculator has made the mechanical adding machine something of an office dinosaur, yet they are still around and, yes, they do add correctly when you pull the handle.

In 1897, Burroughs retired from his company, the American Arithmometer Company, due to poor health and died the following year. By then, the company had become the Burroughs Adding Machine Company. William Seward Burroughs was inducted into the National Inventors Hall of Fame in 1987.

# Caller ID

Debut: 1982
Inventive American: Carolyn Doughty (for Bell Laboratories)

Caller ID is now offered by almost every telephone service in America and it has been a boon to the privacy-minded and the stalked. Sure, you can block your number so someone's Caller ID can't read it, but there now also exists services which refuse blocked calls. If a person with a blocked phone number calls someone with this Privacy Manager service, the call does not even ring through to the called person's phone. It is intercepted by a computer that plays a recording telling the caller "the person you are calling does not accept blocked calls." The caller is then given the opportunity to unblock their number, or hang up. Either way, the person being called is protected: They will either know the number of the caller or they will not get the call.

The technology for Caller ID has been around since 1982, thanks to a creative and foresighted Bell Laboratories employee named Carolyn Doughty.

# The Can Opener

Debut: 1858 (Warner); 1925 (Lyman)
Inventive Americans: Ezra Warner; William Lyman

The modern hand can opener that fits any size can and uses a sharp edge to pierce the top has only been around since 1925, but prior to that, two versions were invented that both used a chisel-type device to remove the top.

The tin can had been around for half a century by the time someone got around to figuring out an easy way to open them. Peter Durand invented canned food for the British Navy in 1813. The cans, however, were made of solid iron, and Durand committed quite an inventor's faux pas by not giving much thought to how to get the food out of the can. His instructions read, "Cut round the top near the outer edge with a chisel and hammer."

In 1858, Ezra Warner created the first true can-opening device—a tool that looked like a bent bayonet. William Lyman's invention in 1925 was the first to use a rotating wheel, but it only fit one size can. This was soon corrected, and this rotating opener is the one used today.

All the incarnations of handheld can openers were true American Firsts.

# Carbon Dating

Debut: 1947
Inventive American: Willard Frank Libby

In the first *Star Trek* movie, the hot bald female android repeatedly referred to members of the crew of the *Enterprise* as "carbon units," or "carbon-based units," or something close to that. (And by the way, I am asking, no...I am *begging* all you *Star Trek* devotees, you legions of Trekkers out there that may be reading this, not to write me with a 61-page explication of the linguistical vagaries of the different life-forms in the *Star Trek* films. I'm probably not 100 percent correct in my citation, but I only referred to it to make a point for this entry, not to anger *Star Trek* fans. Honest. And you'll notice I referred to you as Trekkers, not Trekkies. That was done out of respect. *Ich ein Trekker*.)

The hot android was right. Humans—and all other life-forms—*are* carbon based, and that was the scientific truth on which the technique of carbon dating was developed. (Carbon is also found in the overwhelming majority of inanimate objects as well.)

When a living thing dies, the unstable radioactive isotope of carbon called carbon 14 in it begins to decay at a specific, unchanging rate. By calculating in whatever it is you want to date the amount of the element carbon that it originally possessed and then comparing the amount of carbon remaining in it with the amount of carbon in the environment, you can date the piece with extraordinary precision.

It worked for the Dead Sea Scrolls; the jury is still out for the Shroud of Turin. (Carbon dating tests on the Shroud of Turin placed the object circa 1260–1390, yet many believers are certain that it is the burial shroud of Jesus Christ and, therefore, actually from the first century. The primary argument *against* accepting the Shroud carbon dating testing results is that the Catholic Church refused to provide the testing laboratories with a large enough piece for accurate dating. One scientist I read suggested that a piece the size of a *handkerchief* was needed for the test, but the Church only provided a piece the size of a *postage stamp*—which was then further cut up for testing by three different labs. The debate continues.)

Since its debut, carbon dating has become the most important tool science possesses for accurately dating everything from mummies to coins. So far, the tests have been accurate within a span of 50,000 years; that is, testing continues on artifacts and fossils older than 50,000 years with inconclusive results.

Willard Libby was a scholar, a scientist, a teacher, a chemist, a writer, a Nobel Prize winner, and he was one of the elite few who worked on the Manhattan Project to develop the atomic bomb. In 1952, he published his book *Radiocarbon Dating*, which detailed his breakthrough method.

Willard Libby, born in Grand Valley, Colorado, died in 1980, having given science the most accurate and useful means of measurement since the invention of the ruler.

# The Cardiac Pacemaker (internal)

Debut: May 7, 1958
Inventive American: Wilson Greatbatch

One of the first patients to receive one of Wilson Greatbatch's internal cardiac pacemakers was a young man with a heart block who had collapsed and almost died at his job at a rubber factory. Heart block is when the electrical signals from the upper chambers of the heart do not reach the lower chambers, causing irregular or rapid heartbeats, and shortness of breath. Heart block can lead to unconsciousness and, in some cases, death. After receiving a pacemaker, he became a hairdresser and lived another 30 years. Greatbatch offers this and other pacemaker success stories as the reason he became an inventor. When two surgeons described the potentially fatal condition of heart block to him, the first thought that came to his mind was, "I know I can fix it."

Greatbatch was trained as an electrical engineer and worked as a radioman during World War II. After his honorable discharge, he attended Cornell University on the GI Bill and eventually ended up teaching electrical engineering at the University of Buffalo, where he also worked at the nearby Chronic Disease Research Institute. One day, while trying to design a machine to record rapid heartbeats, he used the wrong transistor and was astonished when the circuit he had created pulsed at the precise rate of a human heartbeat.

From there, it was merely a matter of perfecting a device that would take control of the heart's rhythm by applying painless shocks at the ideal rate of 72 beats per minute. There were some initial problems with the first devices because Greatbatch and his colleagues did not allow for human bodily fluids getting inside the device and shorting it out. Once that was corrected, and a 10-year lithium battery was invented, Greatbatch's cardiac pacemakers gave heart block patients a life expectancy similar to a healthy population of the same age. (Prior to the 10-year battery, patients had to undergo surgery every two years to replace the batteries in their pacemaker.)

In September 2003, Wilson Greatbatch turned 84 years old. He is still active, and his current research involves energy and the HIV virus.

Greatbatch was inducted into the National Inventors Hall of Fame in 1986.

# The Cash Register

Debut: 1879
Inventive American: James Ritty

Before the cash register was invented, merchants made change out of a box or out of their pocket. In 1879, 43-year-old tavern keeper James Ritty invented the "Incorruptible Cashier," the first mechanical cash register. (Isn't it interesting, and possibly a sign of the times, that Ritty did not christen his invention the "Accurate Cashier," but, instead, made a point of stating that it could not be "corrupted"?)

Ritty's machine used paper tape, hole punchers, and a recording dial to keep track of transactions.

John Patterson bought Ritty's patent in 1884 and used it to launch the national Cash Register Company, now known simply as NCR.

The first electric cash register was also an American First and was developed by Charles Kettering in 1906 while he was working for NCR.

# The CAT (Computerized Axial Tomography) Scan

Debut: 1975
Inventive American: Robert S. Ledley

Dr. Robert S. Ledley invented the ACTA—the Automatic Computerized Transverse Axial diagnostic X-ray scanner—which was the world's first whole-body computerized tomography (CT) machine. Interestingly, Dr. Ledley is not an internist or a surgeon, either of which would find great value in a whole body Xray. Dr. Ledley has a D.D.S. (Doctor of Dental Science) degree from New York University and an M.A. from Columbia University.

The CAT scan revolutionized our ability to see inside the human body and is now used routinely for everything from diagnosis to radiation therapy mapping.

Dr. Ledley holds more than 20 different patents and was a professor of physiology, biophysics, and radiology at the Georgetown University Medical Center. Today, he is the president and research director of the National Biomedical Research Foundation. He is also editor-in-chief of four highly regarded, peer-reviewed scientific journals.

# ChapStick®

Debut: Early 1880s
Inventive American: Dr. C.D. Fleet

ChapStick is sold all over the world and is a highly lucrative product. Ironically, the American who created it received a total of five dollars for the rights to his invention.

In the early 1880s, Dr. C.D. Fleet of Lynchburg, Virginia softened and shaped wax (probably beeswax) and other ingredients (perhaps menthol, or mint—the historical record is silent on the specific ingredients of Dr. Fleet's concoction) into a tubular shape and then wrapped it in tinfoil. He sold this preparation to his patients and other denizens of Lynchburg as a lip salve to be used to heal and prevent chapped lips.

By 1912, Dr. Fleet had had enough of selling lip balm. He was not making enough money from sales of his product, so he sold his recipe to Lynchburgian John Morton for five dollars. Morton and his wife produced ChapStick in their home kitchen and they were extremely successful. A.H. Robbins bought the ChapStick brand in 1963 and now offers a variety of ChapStick products, including sunblock and flavored.

Believe it or not, the following is true: There is a ChapStick addiction subculture. Apparently, there are people who become addicted to the feeling of having slick, lubricated lips and some "addicts" reapply ChapStick every 30 minutes all day long. There is ongoing debate on the Internet as to whether or not Chapstick contains addictive ingredients (it does not), and there are even support groups for people who simply cannot live without ChapSticked lips. Dermatologists have acknowledged that there may actually be something to the idea that a physical dependence can arise from overuse of ChapStick, or any other lubricating lip balm for that matter. This dependence does not have to do with the ingredients of ChapStick, however, but rather the level of moisture a person gets used to and then demands for their lips. If a ChapStick user (abuser) applies it so often that, to them, ChapSticked lips feel comfortable, normal dryness of lips will be perceived as uncomfortable and unpleasant.

We have not yet come across any Chapstick 12 Step programs, but it's probably only a matter of time.

# Cheerios®

Debut: 1941
Inventive Americans: General Mills

In 1941, "Cheerioats" debuted as the first ready-to-eat oat cereal. This was a big deal because, prior to this cereal, oats had to be boiled before being eaten. They were an immediate success and, four years later, General Mills changed the name to Cheerios. Today, there are eight varieties of Cheerios: Cheerios, Team Cheerios, HoneyNut Cheerios, MultiGrain Cheerios, Frosted Cheerios, Apple Cinnamon Cheerios, Berry Burst Strawberry Cheerios, and Berry Burst Triple Berry Cheerios. Always enormously popular (they have long been an infant's first "finger food"), Cheerios significantly expanded its market reach when it was discovered in the 1990s that oat bran lowered cholesterol. This prompted a new Cheerios "heart healthy" ad campaign and now regular Cheerios features a heart-shaped bowl full of the cereal on the box, and the Honey-Nut box has a text line that reads, "may lower cholesterol."

Cheerios are now sold all over the world.

# Cheerleading

Debut: November 2, 1898
Inventive American: Thomas Peebler (at Princeton)

Yes, it is true that fans first began cheering for athletes and teams at sporting events in Britain in 1883, but the cheering was unorganized, randomly begun, and did not have the rules and regulations that define professional cheerleading of today—a recognized sport that was a definite American First.

Thomas Peebler is responsible for the sport of cheerleading as we now know it. He was the Princeton Pep Club member who recruited six students to cheer at a Princeton vs. University of

Minnesota football game on November 2, 1898. The six cheerleaders were all men. My, how times have changed. Interestingly, it was World War II that greatly increased the number of women cheerleaders. With all the boys fighting "over there," women were tapped to take their place as cheerleaders for sporting events.

Today, cheerleading is a combination of dancing, gymnastics, and, of course, pom-poms, and is so popular, national competitions are broadcast on ESPN.

# Cheese in a Can

Debut: 1966
Inventive American: Nabisco

Admit it: you've eaten this stuff, right?

Easy Cheese is viewed by some folks in other countries as a metaphor for everything that is regrettable about American culture—and American cuisine: bland, mass-produced, processed foods that eliminate as effectively as possible many of the memorable elements of the original. Fine cheeses become cheese in a can; wonderful cuts of beef become the McDonald's hamburger; handmade dessert delicacies become Ring Dings and Twinkies.

Perhaps the argument can be made that American culture does have its superficial elements. The obvious response to that is, "So?" Look at what we Americans have done in a little more than 200 years. So we've made some foods easier (and admittedly less "gourmet") but so what? Americans are busy. Anything that helps us save time is a blessing.

Cheese in a can was invented by the Nabisco Company in 1966. It is called Easy Cheese and it is manufactured in Wrightstown, Wisconsin. It is real cheese, lasts a really long time, and does not need refrigeration.

How does it taste?

It tastes fine and is commonly eaten on crackers or used to make a quick cheeseburger. Granted, it's not Swiss, Parmesan, or imported Brie, but so what?

All things in life come with trade-offs.

# The Chia Pet®

Debut: September 8, 1977
Inventive American: Joseph Enterprises, Inc.

The Chia Pet is one of those American Firsts that make visitors from other countries furrow their brows.

What is it? What is it used for? The answers do not dispel their puzzlement. A Chia Pet is a piece of pottery in the shape of a head or an animal that grows greens.

Are the greens edible? Interestingly, Joseph Enterprises, the owner of the Chia Pet trademark, never applied to the FDA for licensing Chia Pets as a food product so they cannot claim the greens to be edible. Yet, they are a form of watercress and it is a fact that many Chia owners do, indeed, eat in salads the greens that sprout from the Chia Professor—or the Chia Pig.

Chia Pets are only sold around the holidays because, Joseph Enterprises tells us, they are handmade pottery items and it takes an entire year to produce enough Chia Pets for one holiday season.

Each Chia Pet can be replanted and comes with enough Chia seeds for three plantings.

# The Chocolate Chip Cookie

Debut: 1930
Inventive American: Ruth Wakefield

Ruth Wakefield owned and operated the Toll House Inn in Whitman, Massachusetts when she first invented the chocolate chip and then used her new creation to invent the chocolate chip cookie. (No wonder they're called Toll House Cookies!) Ruth broke up bars of semi-sweet chocolate to make the chips and then stuck them in her cookies, in which they melted, creating the cookie delight that today is beloved all over the world. Thanks, Ruth. Weight Watchers probably has a wing dedicated to your memory.

# The Clipper Ship

Debut: 1850
Inventive Americans: Lauchlan McKay and Donald McKay

A clipper ship is a sharp-bowed sailing vessel of the mid-19th century. Its characteristics include tall masts and sharp lines, and it was built for great speed on the open waters.

Donald McKay, a master shipbuilder, working from plans co-conceived with his brother Lauchlan, built the first clipper ship in 1850. It was called the *Stag-Hound* and it had three masts.

The McKay brothers then built the *Flying Cloud*, a blazingly fast ship. On her maiden voyage, she sailed 374 miles in a single day.

The steamship ended the era of the clipper ships, but their beauty and speed still enthrall people more than 100 years later.

# CNN®

Debut: 1980
Inventive Americans: Reese Schonfeld and Ted Turner

The idea of a 24-hour, all-news cable station was not initially met with enthusiasm. In fact, odds were given on how long the Turner/Schonfeld gamble would last. The idea itself was considered a foolish debacle. Who would want to watch the news all day—and night—long?

Fast forward more than two decades and it is clear that CNN was not only a good idea, it was a milestone moment in media. CNN is now a global force. In the movie *Wag the Dog*, one of the characters makes the statement—accepted and believed immediately by all—that a campaign for president could no longer be successfully waged without being on CNN.

CNN defined a new model for television news: the 24-hour news cycle. No longer would people accept a half-hour summary at noon and six, with the rare interruption of the afternoon soap operas for "breaking news."

Today, CNN is available in more than 80 million American households, and has 37 news bureaus and 800 U.S. affiliates. It is seen all over the world and has lately been copied by MSNBC and Fox, both of which launched their own successful 24-hour cable news channels.

Their motto is "CNN—the most trusted name in news."

# Coca-Cola®

Debut: 1885
Inventive American: Dr. John S. Pemberton

The original incarnation of Coca-Cola contained cocaine. Cocaine was a common ingredient of patent medicines in the late 19th century, and it was so beloved and believed to be so beneficial that the early ads for Coca-Cola pitched it as a "brain tonic." Cocaine in early Coke did what cocaine on a little spoon does: It made people more alert and focused; it elevated mood (to the point of euphoria); it eliminated fatigue and had something of an analgesic effect. Who knew it was addictive?

Eventually *everyone* did, and over the past century, the Coca-Cola company has worked very hard to eliminate any traces of cocaine from the beverage. However, cocaine is found in the cola nut (a seed of the coca leaf) and it is therefore impossible to remove it entirely. The amount of cocaine in Coca-Cola is so miniscule, however, as to be unmeasurable; by any and all standards, Coca-Cola is cocaine free. It is not caffeine free, though, because this stimulant is also found in the coca leaf and no attempt is made to remove it for regular Coke. It is removed, though, for production of caffeine-free cola beverages.

Coca-Cola is the world's most recognized trademark. Some estimates claim that 94 percent of the world's population recognizes the Coca-Cola name and/or distinctive Spencerian Script logo.

The original formula for Coca-Cola syrup was concocted by Dr. John Pemberton in his Atlanta, Georgia backyard in early May 1885. (Today, the secret formula of Coke is known as "7X.") He used a three-legged kettle, and his bookkeeper Frank Robinson not only came up with the name, but also drew the first script version of the product's name. The syrup was mixed with water and first sold to the thirsty at the soda fountain in Jacob's Pharmacy in Atlanta on May 8, 1885. It was touted as a brain and nerve tonic, but Pemberton lost money in his first year selling the drink. The story is told that Pemberton saw one of his employees adding carbonated seltzer water to the "tonic," and the Coke we know today was born.

Today, Coca-Cola is the most popular beverage in the world. More than one billion Cokes are consumed every day, and the soda has become known as the quintessential American drink.

Coca-Cola's strongest competitor is Pepsi®. There are differences between the two colas, though, and many people have a favorite. Coke has a heavier, more carbonated taste and feel, and has an orange-based flavor tone beneath the vanilla and cola flavors. Pepsi is lighter and sweeter, and uses a lemon-lime flavor tone beneath its cola flavoring. Also, Coke has 47 milligrams of caffeine per 12 ounce serving to Pepsi's 37 milligrams. Both have about 39 grams of sugar, though.

These days, there is also an enormous, worldwide Coca-Cola subculture. The Coke logo has been licensed for use on a slew of products, and there are collectors all over the world who seek out these items and often pay top dollar for them. A recent search for Coke products on eBay® returned more than 30,000 individual items.

# The Collapsible Ironing Board

Debut: 1892
Inventive American: Sarah Boone

As long as there have been garments, there have been wrinkles. And as long as there have been wrinkles, there has been the need to iron. And as long as there has been ironing, there has been the need for a surface to iron on.

Before African-American inventor Sarah Boone designed and built an ironing board with folding legs, people improvised. They would, of course, iron on the kitchen table, but oftentimes there simply wasn't enough room for larger garments and things like curtains and sheets. For longer items like trousers, sometimes people would find a long board and lay it on top of two widely spaced chairs. This may have provided a surface, but this approach involved a lot of uncomfortable bending.

Sarah Boone took a narrow wooden board, fit a padded cover to it, and attached hinged legs to its bottom so that they could be collapsed when not in use. It was a simple, yet ingenious idea, and her collapsible ironing board, patented on April 26, 1892, was the ancestor of our modern ironing boards. Today, collapsible ironing boards are made of metal and the legs slide on tracks, but the concept is the same and all we tireless ironers owe Sarah Boone a debt of thanks.

# Color Film

Debut: 1850s
Inventive American: Levi Hill

Color photography is one of those fields to which many inventors, researchers, scientists, and artists contributed. Therefore, it is difficult to look to a particular moment and event in history and say, "So and so invented color photography in..."

We can come close, though. American Levi Hill seems to be the first person to perfect a system for taking color photographs. And his system worked.

Unfortunately, Hill's invention was not very well received mostly by the people who had the most to lose from his breakthrough: the makers of daguerreotypes—those black and white images of the time created on light-sensitive metallic plates coated with silver. As news of his advancement circulated, Hill found himself on the receiving end of much vitriol and nastiness. In fact, he actually received threats from members of the New York State Daguerrean Association, if you can imagine the level of menace that might be put forth by a bunch of 19th-century photographers.

In 1856, Hill published a book explaining how he did what he did, and future shutterbugs might suspect that this was the official beginning of being able to take color photos. But it wasn't. The reason? Hill used the opportunity of publishing his book to vengefully lash out against—you guessed it—the members of the New York State Daguerrean Association. The Association responded by suing Hill for libel, they won, and his book was pulled from publication.

Several years later, the technology of color photography was advanced by Scottish, French, and American scientists, but it is clear that the first breakthrough was by an American.

Interestingly, after Hill's book was "banned," his color process became one of those legends that many in a field are aware of, but no one can actually prove. In the 1980s, this changed when an art historian named Joseph Boudreau got his hands on a copy of Hill's book, studied it carefully, and—eureka—was able to reproduce Hill's color photo process perfectly. It was not a myth. Color photography was an American First.

## ABRAHAM LINCOLN'S PATENT REQUEST

One of our all-time greatest and most beloved presidents was also an inventor. Is there anything more emblematic of the American ideal? Even her leaders are creators.

*March 10, 1849*

*To the Commissioner of Patents:*

*The petition of Abraham Lincoln, of Springfield in the County of Sangamon & state of Illinois*

*Respectfully represents.*

*That your petitioner has invented a new and improved manner of combining adjustable buoyant chambers with steamboats or other vessels which has not, as he verily believes been heretofore used or known, and that he is desirous that Letters Patent of the United States may be granted to him therefore, securing to him and to his legal representatives, the exclusive right of making and using, and of vening to others the privilege to make or use, the same, agreeably to the provisions of the Acts of Congress in that case made and provided, he having paid thirty dollars into the Treasury of the United States, and complied with other provisions of the said Acts.*

*And he hereby authorizes and empowers his Agent and Attorney, Z.C. Robbins, to alter or modify the within specification and claim as he may deem expedient, and to receive his patent; and also to receive back any moneys which he may be entitled to withdraw, and to receipt for the same.*

*A. Lincoln*

# Condensed Milk

Debut: 1856
Inventive American: Gail Borden

"Milk is a living fluid," Gail Borden wrote in 1856, the year he patented condensed milk. He continued, proclaiming that "as soon as [it is] drawn from the cow, [it] begins to die, change, and decompose." If there was ever anything that would *discourage* children from drinking their milk, it might be the notion of the white liquid being dead and actually decomposing in their glass.

Gail Borden was not well educated and had no scientific training. He was, however, a creative thinker and a visionary. His eyes were always open and he regularly noticed what was wrong and then came up with ideas on how to fix it.

During a sea voyage in 1851, Borden saw children on board die because the cows that had been brought along to provide milk for the journey were not producing enough to keep the children alive. Yes, before 1856, the "storage containers" for milk were the actual cows themselves.

Borden knew that society needed a way to safely store foods for long periods of time. He decided to try modifying milk for this purpose, which was quite a challenge considering that fresh whole milk had what was probably the shortest "shelf life" of any comestible of the time.

Borden determined that if the water could be removed from milk, then what remained would be condensed milk that should remain fresh for long periods of time. Milk is three-quarters water, so Borden used what was known as a vacuum pan to slowly heat (but not cook) milk so that the water gradually evaporated. The system worked, and, to introduce it to homemakers, he began to sell his condensed milk door-to-door.

Borden's condensed milk was an enormous success, and, suddenly, the milk business began to grow exponentially as "the milk that didn't spoil" became available. The milk was also used by the military during the Civil War, and when the soldiers returned home and told their families about it, the demand increased even more.

Condensed milk was simply a great idea. Two years after receiving his patent, the Committee of the Academy of Medicine proclaimed that Gail Borden's condensed milk was "unequaled" in purity, stability, and value.

Condensed milk made Gail Borden rich and allowed him to start the company that bears his name and which still thrives today, selling all manner of dairy products and, now, other food products as well.

Although milk was the food product that had made him famous, Borden had been vocal and passionate all his life about condensing other foods. When he was in his 20s, one of his most memorable attempts was his creation of the "meat biscuit."

Borden boiled 120 pounds of meat down to ten pounds. (It already sounds revolting, doesn't it?) He then added flour to this "substance," shaped it into individual biscuits, and baked them.

Granted, the resulting item was a handy, hearty biscuit of meat, and *Scientific American* praised the product as an important invention, but no one would eat them. A Navy doctor said they were disgusting, and the Army said not only didn't they sate the appetite, but they caused soldiers to become nauseous.

Good thing he moved on to milk, eh?[3]

# The Contact Lens (plastic)

Debut: 1948
Inventive American: Kevin Tuohy

Let's call this *Steve's Contact Lens Horror Story*.

I wear glasses for driving and TV watching; I do not need corrected vision for reading or working at the computer. I experimented with contact lenses once in my life. I visited a local eye doctor who gave me soft plastic lenses, and instructed me on how to "install" them.

I went back to work, but the lenses didn't feel right. I called the doctor and he told me to remove them, clean them, make sure they were not inside out, and put them back in. I did as instructed and they still did not feel right. They felt like they didn't fit properly, and they were irritating my eyes. They were also giving me a headache.

I called the doctor back again and he told me to switch them. That's right. He told me to put the left lens in the right eye and vice versa.

I again did as told and that was the beginning of the nightmare.

Within an hour, I couldn't see. I wasn't blind, but my eyes hurt so much that I could barely open them to squint. I took out the lenses and drove home, although to this day I do not know how I managed to drive without killing myself and several others.

Once I got home, I called an eye surgeon who was a friend of the family and, based on what I told him, he concluded that I had corneal abrasions in both eyes. He told me to place cold compresses on both eyes (which by now felt like they were on fire) and stay in a dark room. Long story short: I ended up in bed wearing sunglasses in a pitch-dark room, ice packs on my eyes, crying 24 hours a day (not from emotion, but from my eyes constantly watering), for three entire days.

By the third day, I was able to open my eyes enough to see a little (enough to sign a malpractice lawsuit, which I never did), and a few days later, I was fine. The surgeon had told me that if I did not recover within that time, he'd prescribe medicated drops, but other than that, there really isn't much they can do for corneal abrasions.

I never went back to that doctor and I have not worn contact lenses since. To this day, my eyes are hypersensitive to light and I need sunglasses anytime I'm outside, even on overcast days.

Sometimes, it seems that doctors do not know what they are doing.

My story notwithstanding, contact lenses are extremely popular and are worn successfully by millions of people.

The first plastic contact lenses were invented by American optometrist Kevin Tuohy in 1948. The lenses were designed to only cover the cornea. Later developments by Americans and others, resulted in soft, comfortable plastic lenses that are available today in a wide array of colors, as well as in bifocal prescriptions, disposable form, extended wear form, and one-day lenses. There are also novelty contacts available that can give the wearer the eyes of a cat— or a zombie.

# Cornflakes

Debut: 1894
Inventive American: Will Keith Kellogg

Will Keith Kellogg never progressed beyond a sixth-grade education, yet during his 91-year life, he created one of the healthiest foods of all time, gave millions to charitable causes, and was a presidentially-named delegate at a White House conference on the health of children.

After working as a traveling broom salesman when he was in his late teens, Will went to work as a clerk for his older brother John, who was physician-in-chief at the Battle Creek Sanitarium in Michigan. While at the Sanitarium, Will began researching food with the hope of finding an easily-digestible bread substitute that could be made from boiled grains for the Sanitarium's vegetarian patients.

One day, he left a pot of boiled wheat on the stove unattended, and the substance hardened. He rolled it out anyway, and the cereal flake was born. He later boiled corn, and cornflakes were born. He served them to the patients and everyone immediately loved them. When people recovered and were discharged from the institution, they would order the cereal flakes by mail, and Will quickly developed a thriving business.

Dr. John was not interested in the marketing end of the new creation, so Will took over, and the Kellogg company began its successful life. Will expanded the business to Australia and England, and, today, cornflakes are recognized and sold all over the world.

# The Coronary Bypass Operation

Debut: 1962
Inventive American: Dr. David C. Sabiston, Jr.

"Coronary bypass surgery consumes more of our medical dollar than any other treatment or procedure."[4]

The first coronary bypass operation was performed at Johns Hopkins in Baltimore, Maryland in 1962. Dr. David Sabiston bypassed clogged coronary arteries using arteries from the patient's own leg. Blood could then flow to the patient's heart, unimpeded by fatty deposits or constriction. The average coronary bypass operation "lasts" between seven and 10 years before the new arteries similarly clog. A second surgery is then required, although death from a heart attack often occurs before the surgery can take place.

The total cost for a typical coronary bypass operation in America are approximately $25,000, of which the cardiac surgeon receives around a third.

Of all coronary bypass surgeries, 79 percent are performed on men; 97 percent are performed on whites. In 2002, approximately $5 billion was spent on coronary bypass operations in America.

Today, the operation is performed all over the world, although the cost differences are staggering. Canadian surgeons are paid around $1,100 for each coronary bypass operation, which is four to five times less than their American counterparts.

Some physicians and medical researchers believe that many coronary bypass operations are unnecessary and do not prolong life beyond normal expectancy for someone with coronary heart disease. Nonetheless, doctors are ordering the surgeries, patients are willingly undergoing them, and, as stated earlier, these operations are, in a large part, how Americans spend their medical dollars.

# Cortisone Synthesis

Debut: 1949
Inventive American: Percy Lavon Julian

Cortisone is used to treat a staggering array of ailments, including skin conditions (such as psoriasis and eczema), asthma, blood disorders, gastrointestinal diseases (such as ulcerative colitis), arthritis, and other inflammatory disorders. Before Percy Julian successfully synthesized cortisone in a lab, natural cortisone, of which the beneficial uses were well-known to doctors, had to be extracted from the adrenal glands of oxen. The cost? Hundreds of dollars *a drop.*

Synthetic cortisone is now a fraction of a cent a dose.

Percy Julian's grandfather was a slave. This tragic legacy did not stop Percy from getting an education, including a master's from

Harvard and a Ph.D. in Organic Chemistry from the University of Vienna.

His first accomplishment was to synthesize a drug to prevent glaucoma. He then synthesized cortisone (detailed in a paper published in 1949), and later, the male hormone testosterone and the female hormone progesterone.

The United States acknowledged Julian's contribution to medicine by issuing a 29 cent stamp in his honor.

# The Cotton Gin

Debut: March 14, 1794
Inventive American: Eli Whitney

Before the cotton gin was invented, the seeds of the cotton plant had to be removed by hand. Tedious is not an adequate word to describe this work, but because Southerners had slaves to do it, no one really gave it too much thought— except Eli Whitney.

Eli Whitney's cotton gin automated the job and turned the South into one of the most productive regions in America.

His machine was actually quite simple: A screen of wires held the cotton plants, and a drum embedded with tiny hooks was turned as the cotton fed past it. The hooks picked the seeds out of the cotton, duplicating what slaves had been doing with their hands.

Almost immediately after he first demonstrated it, farmers planted untold acres of cotton, and it all needed to be harvested well before Whitney had a chance to patent and protect his invention.

His machine was pirated heedlessly, and, after over a decade of lawsuits and broken contracts, Eli Whitney retired from the cotton business at the age of 39 and moved north to New Haven, Connecticut where he applied his talents to inventing machines and tools.

He never made any money from one of the most revolutionary inventions in agricultural history.

# Crayola® Crayons

Debut: 1903
Inventive Americans: Edward Binney and C. Harold Smith

Binney and Smith owned a paint company in New York. In 1903, they came up with the idea of combining paraffin wax with color pigments, and the crayon was born. Today, there are many crayons on the market, but Crayola essentially owns the business. Every little kid must have a Crayola flip-top box. It's a law. The holy grail of crayons is still, of course, the box of 64 with the built-in sharpener.

The first box of Crayolas contained eight crayons: black, brown, orange, violet, blue, green, red, and yellow.

There are now 120 "core colors" which never change, and, over the years, Binney & Smith has retired and introduced 400 different crayon colors.

The colors of Crayola crayons have changed for political reasons, as well as artistic. In 1952, "Prussian Blue" was renamed "Midnight Blue" in response to teachers' requests. In 1962, "Flesh" was renamed "Peach," in response to the Civil Rights movement. In 1999, "Indian Red" was renamed "Chestnut" because some children thought that the color represented the skin tone of Native Americans when, in fact, it had been named for a reddish-brown pigment found near India. It was changed anyway. Today, Crayola offers a box of what they describe as "multicultural" crayon colors: each color is of a realistic skin tone of the different races.

Some of the most recent additions to the Crayola crayon color list include Pink Flamingo, Caribbean Green, Banana Mania, Outer Space, Eggplant, Pig Pink, and Vivid Violet.

# The Crossword Puzzle

Debut: December 21, 1913
Inventive American: Arthur Wynne (for the *New York World*)

The first book ever published by Simon & Schuster was a book of crossword puzzles. When Dick Simon and Lincoln Schuster graduated from the Columbia School of Journalism in 1924, they decided to start a publishing company. For the previous 10 years, the newspaper *New York World* had been publishing weekly a new puzzle invented by one of their editors. Originally  called "Word-cross," then "Cross-word,"then "Crossword," the puzzles were extremely popular with the reading public and eventually the world had hundreds of them. Simon & Schuster compiled them into a book, which was an immediate, enormous success.

A decade earlier, Arthur Wynne, the *World*'s puzzle page editor, had concocted a diamond-shaped, word fill-in puzzle for one of the Christmas issues of the paper. It was instantly popular and Wynne is now credited as the creator of the puzzle that is now a worldwide phenomena.

(Note: The world's first crossword puzzle is available on-line at *www.quizland.com/cotd/worldsfirst.htm.*)

# Cruise Control

Debut: 1945
Inventive American: Ralph Teetor

This sounds like the punch line of a joke, but it isn't: A blind man invented cruise control.

Inventor Ralph Teetor accomplished more in his lifetime sightless than many sighted people ever do. He was smart, motivated, and creative, and the fact that he had been blind from the age of 5 did not hinder his work ethic. He built a one-cylinder car when he was 12; received a Bachelor of Science in Mechanical Engineering from the University of Pennsylvania; and worked on rotors for Navy destroyers during World War I.

Cruise control probably came about due to car sickness. One day, Teetor was riding with his attorney, who had a tendency to drive in a somewhat herky-jerky manner. (I happen to know someone who drives like that and I simply will not ride with him. Is there anything worse than nausea from car sickness? I myself have been literally incapacitated by it after some abominable rides.) His barrister's constant accelerating and slowing gave Teetor the idea of a device that would completely control the speed of the vehicle and maintain a steady and smooth ride.

In 1945, Teetor, working as president of his family-owned business, Perfect Circle Corporation (they made piston rings for car manufacturers), patented an invention he called Controlmatic. Other early names for cruise control were Touchomatic, Pressomatic, and Speedostat, none of which really accurately described the device's function. "Cruise control" was finally settled on, and the option was first offered for vehicles in 1958. The Chrysler Imperial, the Chrysler New Yorker, and the Chrysler Windsor were the first car models to offer cruise control.

Today, cruise control is a popular option on most cars and has become a favored convenience for long-distance traveling. We can't help but wonder how many speeding tickets have been avoided by drivers assuring a state trooper, "I had the cruise control locked at 55, Officer. Honest!"

# The Cylinder Lock

Debut: 1861
Inventive Americans: Linus Yale, Sr. and Linus Yale, Jr.

We lock up everything these days.

There are doorknob locks and dead bolt locks on and in our houses. There are combination padlocks on our lockers at the gym. There are latch locks on our briefcases, and key and keypad locks on our cars.

The functionality and security of the lock has also been digitized. We now have lockout software for our computers, and PIN numbers for ATMs and checkout terminals. High security venues, in addition to using magnetic card readers and keypads, now also use voiceprints, retina scans, and thumbprints for identity verification, all of which are nothing more than elaborate expansions of the simple key lock.

Some padlocks can take a bullet and not open. Some dead bolts can withstand a battering ram.

But all of this begs the question: Do we feel safer? Security experts will tell you, if you ask, that locks are not guaranteed assurances that no one will get into your house. Locks are deterrents and time-wasters. The logic is that a burglar will case your place, note its dead bolts, security system, and locked windows and decide a break-in is too risky and time-consuming, and move on to your neighbor's place. Your neighbor never installed dead bolts and doesn't have an alarm, and routinely leaves his windows open and only has key-in-knob locks on his front and rear doors. This is why you will come home to find a cop car in his driveway and your house buttoned up tight.

# D

## The Dental Chair

Debut: 1840
Inventive American: Milton Waldo Hanchett

Milton Waldo Hanchett of Syracuse, New York, invented the first professional dental chair in 1840 and patented it in 1848, but the idea of a comfortable chair for dental patients that also made them easier to work on by the dentist was on the minds of many for decades prior to Hanchett's patent.

In 1790, Josiah Flagg cobbled together the first true dentist's chair by attaching a headrest and an instrument tray to a living room armchair.

Fifty years later, Hanchett designed a chair with an adjustable seat, headrest, and back, and patented it in 1848.

The first modern reclining dental chair, the one, uh, beloved by so many patients today, was invented by John Naughton of Des Moines, Iowa in 1958.

# Dental Floss

Debut: 1815
Inventive American: Levi Spear Parmly

These days, the public arena is a cesspool of bad manners. Self-involved cell phone creeps, inconsiderate drivers, toilet-mouthed teens...the list is endless.

Some people floss in public. Add them to this list.

These dullards actually carry dental floss with them, but do not deem it necessary to adjourn to the bathroom to floss their teeth after they have finished eating. This is a disgusting habit, although flossing, in and of itself, is a highly commendable personal endeavor.

The first piece of floss was a silk thread. In 1815, Dr. Levi Parmly of New Orleans, was using silk thread to clean between the teeth of his patients, and he also recommended that they do likewise at home. For several decades, flossing was practiced, but it wasn't until 1882 when a Massachusetts company produced unwaxed silk floss for home use that a product became commercially available. Johnson & Johnson holds the first patent for commercial dental floss, which was granted to the company in 1889.

Advancements led to nylon floss and, today, there exists a wide array of flossing products, including waxed and unwaxed, flavored and unflavored, and dental tape that is used like floss.

# Deodorant

Debut: 1888
Inventive American: An inventor from Philadelphia whose name has been lost to the ages. (Even the Mum company—Mum was the first deodorant—doesn't have a record of his name.)

Prior to the 20th century, everybody reeked. It was a fact of life that everyone stank, and everyone was quite blasé about accepting body odors permeating the air.

If we could time travel to, say, Mozart's Austria and actually meet the gifted genius, we would probably be immediately repulsed not only by him, but by everyone with whom we came in contact. Bathing, for the most part, was infrequent. Powders and perfumes were used in quantity to mask odors, but they probably didn't work that well. Clothes were often covered with food stains, and people's hands and faces were slimy and disgusting. Add to this the fact that the streets were the common disposal sites for the contents of chamber pots and you can imagine the nausea-inducing way of life prior to the invention of indoor plumbing, soap, and deodorant.

It has often been said that people are enamored of their own odors, and revolted by the smells of others. This is probably hard-wired into our DNA for survival: The smell of "others" means the enemy is present.

As we expand our circle of intimates, we begin to accept more alien odors and construct a network of trusted "others."

The invention and widespread use of deodorant and, later, antiperspirant, almost completely eliminated the olfactory factor of socialization. Animals still use it and always will. (What's the first thing stranger animals do when they meet? They smell each other. That would not go over too well in modern human society.)

The first product specifically created to *prevent* rather than mask body odor was called Mum, and it was a cream that was applied to the skin with the fingertips.

Bristol-Myers bought the Mum company in 1931 and, since then, we have been de-smellified (to quote Jerry Seinfeld) by roll-on deodorants, spray deodorants and, after the environmental damage done by spray cans was revealed, pump bottle deodorants.

A recent survey showed that 75 percent of Americans wear deodorant. It is said that most French people do not, and that they must adapt to the American custom of *not* stinking in public when they move here.

Many cultures still consider body odors primal, earthy, and sensual. In many cultures, women do not shave their legs or armpits. Americans shave, bathe, shampoo, and use deodorant. Some people in other cultures call us repressed and accuse us of being ashamed of our natural odors.

Perhaps. But it does make for a more pleasant day, yes?

# The Dewey Decimal System

Debut: 1876
Inventive American: Melvil Dewey

The Dewey decimal system is a system used in libraries for the classification of books and other publications. It uses the numbers 000 to 999 to cover the general fields of knowledge, and subdivides each field by the use of decimals and letters.

It was conceived and developed by Melvil Dewey when he was working as a student librarian at Amherst College. At the age of 25, Dewey came up with a system that, with modifications and enhancements, is still in use today in libraries all around the world.

The beauty of the Dewey decimal system is that it is limitlessly adaptive; books can be added to the shelves without having to reorganize existing titles.

# The Dishwasher

Debut: 1889
Inventive American: Josephine Garis Cochran

The first true dishwasher didn't wash dishes. It just splashed water on dirty dishes by means of a cranked spraying wheel. Joel Houghton thought it was a great invention, though, and he patented it in 1850. Needless to say, it didn't go very far.

The first automatic dishwasher that actually washed dishes was invented by Josephine Cochran of Shelbyville, Illinois in 1889. Her invention consisted of a wooden tub inside of which was a wire basket with rollers in it. The dishes were placed in the basket, a crank was turned, and the rollers rotated the dishes while hot water and soap were sprayed on them.

Cochran demonstrated her machine at the 1893 Chicago World's Fair and eventually, her small company was bought by what is known today as the KitchenAid Corporation.

Today, dishwashers are standard equipment in most kitchens.

# The Disposable Diaper

Debut: circa 1959
Inventive American: Marion O'Brien Donovan

In 1940, 23-year-old Marion O'Brien Donovan quit her job at *Vogue* magazine when she married and started a family. It was quite a change to move from the busy world of New York publishing to the domestic world of caring for a newborn, but Donovan happily stayed at home with her child.

Every mother of that era had to contend with the disgusting chore of changing cloth diapers. What especially frustrated Donovan was her child's tendency to *immediately* wet a freshly changed diaper. And back then, wet diapers equaled wet sheets.

Donovan, who was born in 1917 in Fort Wayne, Indiana, was an extremely bright and creative young woman, and when she saw a problem, she sought a way to solve it. For several years, Donovan quietly worked on an idea she had for a waterproof diaper cover. She cut up countless shower curtains and, working with a small sewing machine at home, she tried many different patterns and designs for some type of leakproof cover a baby could wear on top of his or her diaper.

Donovan's diaper cover made its debut at Saks Fifth Avenue in New York in 1949, with its patent still pending. (She eventually received the patent in 1951.) The diaper covers were a huge success. Mothers were ecstatic that something was now available which would keep the crib sheets dry and not cause chronic diaper rash, a common problem with the only other alternative at the time—rubber baby pants.

As happy and excited as she was about her success, though, Donovan was still not satisfied with the overall diaper-changing situation. She had a bigger dream: a disposable diaper! A diaper that could be removed and tossed away, instead of having to be rinsed, washed, dried, and used again.

As simple as this idea was, the fulfillment of it was the exact opposite.

She knew that the diaper would have to be made of paper, but she had to figure out a way of assuring that the wet paper would not rest against the baby's skin. The successful disposable diaper must achieve two functions: absorb the wetness, and then move it to an inner layer, away from the skin. This is called "wicking," and, after many tries, Donovan found the right combinations and consistencies of papers that would do the job.

Was Donovan's innovative invention as warmly received as her waterproof diaper cover had been?

Hardly.

Donovan visited all the major paper companies with her designs and prototypes, and was routinely laughed out of the office. Her invention was mocked as being something no one really needed, and we cannot help but now wonder, in somewhat more enlightened times, if a blatant sexism was not part of the continual rejection of the idea. After all, the CEOs she pitched her idea to were probably all male, and it is unlikely that many of them did much diaper changing.

It ultimately took 10 years before someone with perception and vision realized the merit and commercial potential of Donovan's invention; in a redemption of the gender, it was a man. Victor Mills took Donovan's idea and used it to create Pampers. Mothers everywhere applauded his enlightened sensibility.

Donovan died in 1998 at the age of 81.

Make of this what you will: Marion Donovan's son James is, today, a renowned urologist.

# The Donut

Debut: 1847
Inventive American: Hanson Crockett Gregory

A ring of dough deep-fried in oil or fat. Mmmm, now that's good eatin'! The donut (or doughnut) was created by Captain Hanson Crockett Gregory, who somehow came up with the idea of frying dough in oil instead of baking it. A century later, Dunkin' Donuts was born, followed by Krispy Kreme Donuts and any number of imitators. Donuts really aren't all that good for you, but they are so popular they can easily be considered a staple of the American diet.

# The Drinking Fountain

Debut: Early 1900s
Inventive Americans: Halsey Willard Taylor and Luther Haws

Halsey Taylor invented the sanitary public drinking fountain after his father died from typhoid fever caused by drinking contaminated public water. During the early 20th century, the available public water source usually consisted of a tin cup tied to a faucet. Everybody drank from the same cup. Around the same time, Haws invented a sanitary drinking fountain that was quickly installed in schools.

Water fountains are found everywhere these days, and are most common in public buildings. The watercooler and bottled water are more prevalent in private offices and places not heavily frequented by the public.

# The Drinking Straw

Debut: January 1888
Inventive American: Marvin Stone

The drinking straw is one of those simple conveniences that completely change the ergonomics of a common, everyday routine. To drink without a straw, we place a bottle, cup, or glass to our lips, tilt our head back, sometimes only slightly, and literally *pour* the liquid into our mouth. As it enters out mouth, our swallowing faculty takes over and the beverage is transferred into our throat, and then down into our stomach. The drinking straw completely eliminates the need to move the head whatsoever while drinking. In fact, I know a man who, because of serious disk problems in his neck, was actually forbidden by his doctor from drinking with anything but a straw. His doctor did not want him tilting his head back and further compressing the disks. Imagine: a simple object designed as a convenience also serves to help the afflicted. And it is an American First as well!

In 1888, Marvin Stone created the first drinking straw by hand-winding a piece of paper and then covering it with paraffin wax. Machine-winding of straws began in 1906. Today, straws are available in paper and plastic, and they come bendable and in swirling configurations and colors.

# The Drive-in Theater

Debut: June 6, 1933
Inventive American: Richard Hollingshead, Jr.

On a warm Tuesday night in June 1933 in Camden, New Jersey, cars lined up to watch a movie under the stars for the first time.

The first drive-in theater was the brainstorm of 28-year-old auto parts store owner Richard Hollingshead, and it was, un-questionably, a gamble. Would people want to watch a movie while sitting in their cars? Would the sound be okay? What if it started to rain while the movie was running? Hollingshead knew, however, that Americans loved their cars. And he also knew that families with small children often avoided going to the movies, and that some people, especially those who had a physical disability of some type, simply could not navigate the aisles and tightly placed seats in ordinary movie theaters. Hollingshead believed that these people, among others, would greatly enjoy sitting in the comfort of their own car and watch-ing a movie. And he was right.

Hollingshead had developed his idea by mounting a projector on the hood of his car and showing movies on a sheet hung on a tree. He placed a radio behind the sheet for sound, and he experi-mented with distance, window placement, and car placement. Soon he had everything figured out, and in May 1933 he applied for a patent for the world's first drive-in theater.

On June 6, 1933, he opened for business, charging 25 cents per car, plus 25 cents per person. Three or more people got in for $1. The first movie shown was a 1932 comedy called *Wife Beware*, starring Adolphe Menjou. His theater held 335 cars and the site was 500 x 600 feet. He used RCA speakers for sound, and ramps so the cars in the rear could see the screen.

All of Hollingshead's concerns soon proved groundless. The drive-in theater quickly became a wildly popular American entertainment option. Parents took the kids, who always wore pajamas and always fell asleep. Teens used the drive-in theater as the ultimate Lover's Lane. Two hours in a car with snacks and a movie playing, it's safe to say that a lot of couples did not watch the movie.

Within 25 years, there were close to 5,000 drive-in theaters in America. They were more than just a place to watch a movie. They became a classic archetypal "American" event, such as a Sock Hop, an Alcoholics Anonymous meeting, or a Sunday night with *The Ed Sullivan Show*. They also acquired a plethora of nicknames, including "auto havens," "fresh-air exhibitors," "ozoners," "open-air operators," "outdoorers," "ramp houses," "rampitoriums," and "under-the-stars emporiums." ("Honey, want to take the kids to the rampitorium tonight?")

Today, there are about 400 drive-in theaters in the United States. (My home state of Connecticut has only 3, from a high of 42.)

What is killing the drive-in? Multiplexes. When a Hoyt's or a Showcase Cinema opens up in the vicinity of a drive-in, the cost of acquiring a movie for that drive-in skyrockets. (Why? Because Hollywood says so.) And because one of the lures of the drive-in is the relatively low prices, a lot of drive-in operators can't afford to stay in business.

Today, there is a Drive-In Theater Preservation Society whose sole purpose is to keep the drive-in theater alive. Theirs is a tough row to hoe. When a family that owns a football-field-sized piece of land on which are nothing but hundreds of poles, a screen, and a concession stand is offered seven-figures by a developer who wants to put up a mall, it's tough to say no. Drive-in operators know they are unlikely to make a million dollars at "Adults $5, Children $3" admission fees. There is also the problem of showing R-rated movies on a screen that might be visible for miles, resulting in many drive-ins sticking with PG-13 or lower fare, which also limits audiences. (Some drive-ins do show R-rated horror on a regular basis; the weekend crowds for those shows are usually big.)

Is the American First the drive-in doomed?

Probably not. There is a drive-in revivalist movement in America, and the Internet has become a valuable resource for finding drive-ins. One Website, *www.driveintheater.com*, has a clickable U.S. map of all the open drive-ins, as well as other drive-in related info and history. Also, drive-ins are popular around the world. Currently, there are drive-ins thriving in Aruba, Belgium, Canada, Cayman Islands, China, Columbia, Cuba, Denmark, France, Germany, Haiti, India, Israel, Italy, Japan, Kuwait, Mexico, New Guinea, Nigeria, Panama, Puerto Rico, Russia, South Africa, Tahiti, and Zimbabwe.

Hollingshead became disenchanted with the drive-in theater business rather quickly. In 1935, he sold out most of his interest in Park-In Theaters, Inc. because he was discouraged by the poor sound and picture, the enormous expense to maintain such a large commercial space, and his misguided belief that drive-ins, while at the time a popular fad, were destined to fail. He was wrong, although it could be argued that he was right in the long run.

Randall Beach, a reporter for the *New Haven Register*, wrote an article about the demise of the Southington (Connecticut) Twin Drive-In. The article concluded with an incident at a liquor store across the street from the weed-strewn theater lot. A man who works at the store told him that the previous weekend, a van loaded with people from Manhattan had pulled up to the store and asked him what had happened to the drive-in. They were devastated when he told them it had closed. "One of the girls had just turned 18 and she'd never been to a drive-in before," the man recalled.[5]

Maybe that kind of excitement, especially among the younger generations, is what will be the ultimate salvation of the American drive-in theater.

(Special thanks to *www.driveintheater.com* and my friend Randall Beach for their help with this entry.)

# E

## Earplugs

Debut: 1962
Inventive Americans: Ray Benner and Cecilia Benner

It is a bit of a stretch to call earplugs an American First, simply because we know that since people first went into the water, they have been plugging up their ears to keep water out of them. A variety of materials have been used, especially wax, but Ray and Cecilia Benner were the first ones to create a moldable, reusable silicone earplug. Silicone earplugs are now available in a wide range of both water protection and noise reduction ratings, and, thanks to their ability to mold themselves to an individual's ear canal, they are extremely effective. Also available are foam earplugs, which were invented by American Ross Gardner in 1972.

## eBay®

Debut: September 1995
Inventive American: Pierre Omidyar

If there is *anything* that illustrates (and proves) the financial power of the Internet, it is eBay, the on-line auction site. With 50 million registered users and $16 billion in revenue (collected solely from taking a tiny piece of every auction in the form of a user's fee, along with a percentage of the final sales price), eBay is now a global behemoth with financial clout. Millions of items are auctioned on this site every day, and rules actually had to be written forbidding the sale of human body parts on the site.

Is there any truth to the eBay creation myth that Omidyar came up with idea of an Internet auction site to sell his girlfriend's Pez dispensers? No, but it was the perfect media bite for a new company, and many still repeat it as gospel.

On eBay, you can find just about anything, with the exception of the aforementioned human body parts, and guns, illegal drugs, and things that eBay pulls for many reasons. Within hours after the Columbia space shuttle disaster, purported shuttle debris began showing up on eBay. The auctions, some of which were pranks, were quickly pulled.

The strength of eBay is its community of users, many of whom have a fierce attachment to the site and demand input into any changes made, including such trivial concerns as the colors of seller stars.

eBay was the model for many other Internet auction sites, but it is still the biggest and most successful, the place where you can buy or sell anything from used underwear to the SUV Tony Soprano drove in the first two episodes of *The Sopranos*. (I believe it went for close to $90,000.)

eBay's "eclectic" inventory has even spawned a site called *whowouldbuythat.com* that exists solely to chronicle the bizarrest of the bizarre of eBay's auctions. There is no shortage of submissions.

# The 8-track Tape

Debut: 1965
Inventive American: William Lear

Prior to the introduction of the 8-track, the only prerecorded tapes on the market were reel-to-reel. Not very many people owned reel-to-reel tape decks and vinyl records clearly dominated. But then, in the 1960s, the era of the prerecorded tape began.

Did you know that before the 8-track tape, there was a 4-track tape? It held half the number of songs and, for a time, both tapes were available to consumers.

The 8-track tape gained widespread acceptance quickly when the Ford Motor Company began offering 8-track tape decks in its 1966 model cars. A year later, the home 8-track tape deck was introduced. By this time, the 4-track tape was doomed.

The 8-track tape had four programs of two tracks (songs) each. This provided a longer running time, and it also made any song on the album closer to every other song: Any single song on the tape was only three pushes of the track button away. For instance, if the listener was on program 1, song 2, and wanted to hear the first song in program 3, it was an easy move to that program.

Doubling the tracks for the 8-track often resulted in the song lineup on the tape not resembling in the least the lineup on the two sides of the vinyl album. The eight individual tracks required the manufacturers to rearrange the songs so that the whole record would fit on the eight tracks. For most albums, this was possible and, while unappealing to record purists, it did allow all the songs to fit on the tape. For some albums, though, the timing of the songs made this rearranging impossible. In these cases, the manufacturers actually did what would be considered a capital musical felony these days. They would split a song onto two tracks. When the track with the first part of the song ended, there would be a couple of seconds of silence, an obnoxious CLICK, and then the song would take up where it left off. Imagine trying to get away with something like that these days?

As the 8-track increased its dominance, converters were quickly produced to allow 4-track player owners to play 8-tracks in their deck. This did nothing to assist the 4-track's survival, regardless of its proponents (correct) insistence that the sound quality was better on only four tracks. In the beginning of the battle, this was true, but then technology allowed record companies to produce 8-tracks with sound quality equal to that of 4-tracks, and then that argument fell by the wayside.

Another nail in the coffin for 4-tracks was record companies' practice of simultaneously releasing vinyl and 8-track versions of new albums.

Eventually, 8-tracks took over and 4-tracks died. The 8-track would surpass reel-to-reel as well, and would end up being the ultimate choice for prerecorded tape buyers.

Until the cassette came along, that is.

The cassette was originally introduced in Europe and, after its debut in the U.S., was met with disdain by audiophiles. Cassettes were considered low-end, low-quality recordings and yet they boasted some truly appealing features for the average listener. They were smaller, the players were portable and battery-operated, they were cheaper, and they held more music than the 8-track. Once the quality improved, they were the dominant medium for prerecorded tapes.

Today, cassettes are still sold, although their future is grim. The CD is now king, and looks to be for quite some time to come.

# The Electric Chair

Debut: 1889
Inventive Americans: Alfred P. Southwick, Thomas Edison, Harold P. Brown, and others

It wasn't long after electricity was harnessed that thoughts turned to figuring out ways of using this new power to kill people. The intent, though, was noble: At the time, hangings were the reigning means of execution. Hanging was considered by many to be inhumane and a violation of the eighth amendment of the U.S. Constitution, which prohibits "cruel and unusual punishment." It was believed that a lethal jolt of electricity would be quicker, painless, and much more humane. (This was obviously before witnesses reported seeing flames shooting out of the head of the condemned, or blood running down their faces.)

It was a Buffalo, New York dentist named Alfred Southwick who first came up with the idea of using the newly harnessed power of electricity as a means of legal execution. A lobbyist for Thomas Edison, who himself supported the replacement of hanging with electrocution, built the first electric chair, and it was first used on August 6, 1890, when William Kemmler, a New York ax murderer, became the first person to be executed by electrocution. (Thomas Edison called it being "Westinghoused." They had to zap Kemmler twice because the current was too low the first time and the condemned man survived.)

Since 1890, a reported 4,300 people in 23 states have been executed in the electric chair—about one every 10 days for the past 113 years.

The electric chair is still officially in use in four states: Ohio, Florida, Virginia, and South Carolina. Lethal injection has replaced electrocution in the other 20 states that had once used the chair.

Most people do consider lethal injection to be a more humane means of execution, but, in some cases, it is the families of murder victims that have spoken out in favor of retaining electrocution.

Gerald Stano was one of this century's most vile mass murderers. He hated women and he ultimately raped, tortured, and killed 41 hapless victims. As Martin Gilman Wolcott writes in *The Evil 100* (Kensington, 2002):

> *Gerald Stano professed hatred for women—he was a textbook misogynist—and he coldly actualized his animosity and hostility, resulting in a horrible, deadly end for his forty-one* all female *victims. Stano admitted to killing forty-one women, ranging in age from pre-teen—one girl was twelve years old—to mid-thirties.*

The twin brother of one of Stano's victims attended the sadistic killer's electrocution:

> *"The power slammed into him and he jerked as much as he could and that was it," Raymond Neal told Robert Phillips of* www.thedeathhouse.com. *"I saw the life going out of his hands. Afterward, me and my brothers smoked cigars to celebrate. I'm so glad Florida has the guts to keep the electric chair. At least there was a split second of pain. With lethal*

*injection, you just go to sleep." (Florida has since switched to lethal injection.)*

As long as there is a death penalty, society must possess an efficient and humane method for executing the condemned. The electric chair, an American First that has *never* been exported outside our borders, may soon be abolished as one of those methods.

Considering the significance of this topic, I reproduced (thanks to Amnesty U.S.A.) this very interesting list of methods of execution around the world. You will see that the methods run the gamut from unspeakably barbaric—stoning and crucifixion—to the purportedly humane—lethal injection. The United States is the only country to use electrocution and lethal gas. Note that you do not find a single European country on this list. Thus, the United States is in some "interesting" company.

## Methods of Execution Worldwide
### (as of May 03, 1999)

| Method of Execution | Practiced In... |
|---|---|
| firing squad | 73 countries (sole method in 45 countries) |
| hanging | 58 countries (sole method in 33 countries) |
| stoning | 6 countries: Afghanistan, Iran, Pakistan, Saudi Arabia, Sudan, United Arab Emirates |
| lethal injection | 5 countries (sole method in Philippines): China, Guatemala, Philippines, Taiwan (Republic of China), United States |
| beheading | 3 countries: Congo (republic), Saudi Arabia, United Arab Emirates |
| electrocution | 1 country: United States |
| crucifixion | 1 country: Sudan |
| lethal gas | 1 country: United States |

Source: *www.amnestyusa.org*

# The Electric Razor

Debut: 1931
Inventive American: Jacob Schick

There are two types of shavers in the world: blade shavers and electric shavers. And when I say "shaver," I am talking about "those who shave." Blade shavers are those who started with foam and a blade and never switched. Usually, whatever the shaving-teaching parent uses is what the offspring uses. If the father shaves with a blade, he teaches his son how to shave with a blade. If the mother shaves her legs with an electric razor, she teaches her daughter how to shave with an electric razor.

What's the difference between the two? Ease of use and closeness of shave.

The blade razor is a pain in the butt to use, but it gives the closest shave. First, you have to wet your face, put on shaving cream, and then shave, being careful not to slice open your face. You have to repeatedly rinse the razor in water and, when you're finished, if you don't rinse your razor under running water but simply dunk it in a filled sink, the bowl of the sink is coated with shaving cream and hair. Lovely.

The electric razor is much more convenient and you only have to clean it after you're finished shaving. Also, it is very difficult to cut yourself with an electric razor, although it is possible to get a truly nasty razor burn that can become an especially annoying rash. Some men shave on a dry face with an electric razor, but their skin is used to it.

Jacob Schick did not have the option of choosing when he was in the U.S. Army in the early 20th century. All GIs in Uncle Sam's army were issued Gillette blade razors. As you know, blade razors require water and soap or shaving cream, two commodities sometimes difficult to come by in a foxhole. And shaving with a blade razor on a dry face often results in serious facial ravaging.

Schick came up with the idea of a small, portable electric razor that would not require soap or water to use. The first problem, however, was the fact that a motor small enough to work did not exist. So Schick built one, and patented it in 1923.

The next obstacle was public acceptance. Most men were so used to shaving with blade and soap that the idea of switching seemed unnecessary and a waste of money.

Schick was determined, however, and operated with the confidence of a visionary who knows, deep down, that his idea is right, and that it is important. (And might make him some money as well.) He borrowed lots of cash and began producing electric razors bearing his name in 1931 for the extraordinarily expensive price of $25.

Schick was resolute and began advertising on a regular basis. Within five years, he was selling two million electric razors a year, and electric razors from many manufacturers are now sold all over the world.

# E-mail

Debut: 1971
Inventive American: Ray Tomlinson

I will submit the manuscript of this book to my publisher by e-mail. I will attach a Microsoft Word document to an e-mail addressed to my editor, and within seconds, she will have the complete book on her computer as a Word document.

This process is now taken for granted. The notion of sending voluminous amounts of data—text, pictures, movies, music, spreadsheets, whatever—to someone else via cyberspace has become unimpressive; a mundane act; something almost as routine as making a phone call.

But e-mail (and all of the digital communication tool spin-offs such as text messaging, wireless Internet, etc.) is much more than that, and it exemplifies the paradigm of using great power for the most ordinary of purposes (and, when you factor in spam, the most annoying of purposes). Complex, highly sophisticated satellite technology, combined with amazingly powerful personal computers, are put to use so a 16-year-old girl in Dubuque can e-mail her best friend, "the nu pink cd sux!"

Some might lament this reality, grousing that such trivial exploitation of such advanced invention is a waste, a crime, a sin.

Nonsense. The use of technology has always spanned the realm of usefulness, from the trivial to the profound.

E-mail was not something that Ray Tomlinson set out to invent. In 1971, Tomlinson was working for a company called BBN (Bolt Beranek and Newman). BBN had been hired by the U.S. Defense Department to build ARPANET, a computer network that was the predecessor of today's Internet.

Thirty years ago, a simple text message storage program called SNDMSG allowed users of the same computer to leave each other messages in a "mailbox."

After experimenting with SNDMSG and augmenting it with other software, Tomlinson was able to send a message from one computer to another. The computers happened to be sitting right next to each other, but they were not physically connected in any way. Their only connection was over the ARPANET. Eureka.

Today, Tomlinson still works for BBN and admits not remembering the content of that first official e-mail message. When pressed, he'll suggest that he might have simply sent the top line of the keyboard—QWERTYUIOP—over the network. No "What God hath wrought" or "Watson, come here I need you."

After his success with sending that first message, Tomlinson came up with the signature e-mail element: the "@" sign. "The @ sign seemed to make sense," he told *PreText Magazine* in 1998. "I used the @ sign to indicate that the user was 'at' some other host rather than being local." (Personally, I have always wondered why computer and keyboard designers have never assigned a key to the "@" sign. It might be one of the most-typed symbols, and yet it is still a two-key step to type: Shift-2. Considering its ubiquity, the "@" symbol should perhaps switch places with the forward slash on the key next to the period, allowing a single-key addition of the symbol when typing an e-mail address. Just a suggestion.)

E-mail quickly became the most popular way to communicate among computer users who had access to the ARPANET. A couple of years after that initial message, it was estimated that 75 percent of the traffic on the ARPANET computers consisted of e-mail.

E-mail is now almost as important as the phone call for business and personal communication. Some might say it is equally, or more important, than the phone call, because e-mail is non-intrusive and fast; oftentimes, subjects that are difficult to discuss on the phone *can* be addressed in writing.

Around the world, more than 7 trillion e-mails were sent in 2002, and it is estimated that by 2005, 35 *billion* e-mails will be sent *every day*. (That's 13 trillion e-mails annually.)

What Ray hath wrought, eh?

# Enovid®

Debut: 1959
Inventive American: Frank Colton
(for the G.D. Searle pharmaceutical company)

Sex was never the same after the introduction of Enovid, the first birth control pill.

On October 29, 1959, two years after the FDA had granted the G.D. Searle company approval to market Enovid as a treatment for menstrual disorders, the company applied for approval to sell the drug as an oral contraceptive. (One of the "side effects" of using Enovid to treat menstrual troubles was guaranteed contraception.)

The FDA did not immediately approve the application.

Why? Because they were nervous.

Using Enovid as an oral contraceptive would be the first time a drug in America would be used *not* to treat a medical disorder, but rather for a discretionary lifestyle choice. Healthy women would be able to take a pill that would prevent them from becoming pregnant. The FDA's sanctioning of the drug as safe and effective could easily be interpreted by anti-contraception religious groups as a moral abomination, a government endorsement of birth control.

On May 11, 1960, after contentious meetings and stalling tactics, Enovid was finally approved for use as an oral contraceptive, the first of its kind. The FDA was not wholly supportive of the practice of *long-term* contraception, however. They limited the legal use of the pill to two years. Journalist and playwright Clare Boothe Luce commented, "Modern woman is at last free as a man is free to dispose of her own body." This was, for the most part, true, but the U.S. government determined that this modern woman could be "free" to dispose of her own body for only two years, and then, apparently, the FDA had no problem with re-scinding that "freedom."

Ultimately, birth control pills were approved for long-term use, and the decision as to how long to take them was left up to a woman and her doctor.

# The Escalator

Debut: 1891
Inventive American: Jesse Reno

An escalator is a moving stairway consisting of steps attached to a continuously circulating belt. When Jesse Reno designed and installed the first escalator in 1891, he called it the "inclined elevator." Today, escalators are found primarily in shopping malls, stadiums, and airports. Not surprisingly, one of the world's foremost manufacturers of top quality escalators is the Otis Elevator Company (see page 208).

Interestingly, there has been a history of some people having trouble stepping off an escalator. They can't seem to figure out when to take the step that will start them walking again. Sometimes people actually trip and fall at the bottom of the escalator.

Today's escalators are extremely safe, but some earlier models were designed so that there was a slight open space at the bottom where the stairs fed into the housing. Shoelaces, long dresses, and pants occasionally got caught, trapping and injuring people.

But as safe as they are, sometimes escalators do go crazy. The following story appeared on the news wire services on July 4, 2003:

> DENVER—*The Colorado Rockies shut down all their stadium escalators for last night's game, one day after a three-story escalator malfunctioned and tossed dozens of screaming base-ball fans into a heap.*
>
> *At least 32 people were injured, and nine remained hospital-ized last night with broken bones, cuts, and bruises.*
>
> *"It's like it had no brakes and everybody was just piling up at the end of it," said Cherri Brownfield, who was on the escalator Wednesday night (July 2, 2003) following a game and fireworks show.*

*The escalator was carrying people from the upper deck to street level about 10:20 p.m. when it suddenly sped up.*

*"I saw people's heads all hitting each other," said vendor Alex Frenierm.*

*"People were just sliding down like an avalanche," said witness Nick Nossinger.*

*Inspectors who looked at the escalator after the accident found nothing to explain what happened, Assistant Fire Chief Tom Trujillo said.*

*"The gears are intact. That's what's puzzling," he said.*

*The investigation has just gotten started," Keli McGreg, president of the Colorado Rockies baseball team, said last night. "Our No. 1 concern is for our guests that were injured last night."*

The fail-safe, computer-controlled models of today are designed to stop if any objects or body parts get caught between the escalator skirt panel and the steps.

# Express Delivery Service

Debut: 1970 (experimental, USPS);
1974 (FedEx); 1977 (USPS); 1985 (UPS)
Inventive Americans: United States Postal Service;
Federal Express

If you time-traveled someone from the 1950s to America in the 21st century, you can bet that one of their most profound cultural shocks would be the notion of overnight delivery.

"You mean that if I bring something to the Post Office before 5 p.m., someone in California can have it the following day?"

"Sure. In fact, FedEx and UPS also offer an earliest delivery service that gets it to someone by 8 a.m."

"Impossible. The package would have to be on a plane within hours, maybe minutes, of my dropping it off."

"Exactly."

"You're kidding."

"No, I'm not. Planes fly around the clock these days, and allow me to add even more astonishment to your worldview by telling you that when you ship something FedEx, you can drop it off until 7 p.m. the night before, even for 8 a.m. delivery, and—you'll love this—the package has to make a stop in Atlanta before going to California."

"Amazing."

"Exactly."

This theoretical exchange would not have been possible if it were not for the farsighted innovation and planning of the United States Postal Service, which began experimenting with overnight delivery in 1970. Express Mail Next Day Service became a standard postal service in 1977. FedEx began shipping overnight packages in 1974. UPS, the world's largest shipper, was late in coming to the table, not inaugurating overnight delivery until 1985, but now ships more than any other company, has its own fleet of planes, and is one of the 10 largest airlines in the world.

Overnight shipping almost anywhere in the world is now available from the U.S. Postal Service, FedEx, and UPS.

# F

## The Ferris Wheel

Debut: June 21, 1893
Inventive American: George Washington Ferris

I have never understood the appeal of the Ferris wheel. You sit in a swinging car and go around in a circle on a giant wheel. Ride over. Is it the height that people find appealing? Those few seconds when your car is at the top of the circle? Is it the gentle rotation of the wheel? I'm clueless.

George Washington Ferris built the very first Ferris wheelspecifically for the 1893 World's Fair in Chicago. It held 2,160 people in 36 enormous cars (each car held 60 people). The circumference of the wheel itself was 825 feet, and it was 250 feet tall. An astonishing 38,000 people a day rode George Ferris's wheel, at a cost of 50 cents each.

Ferris's wheel had been built in Detroit, Michigan and transported in pieces in 150 railroad cars to Chicago. The wheel's 45-foot axle weighed 45 tons and was the largest single piece of steel ever forged at that time. Two 140-foot steel towers supported the wheel, which was carefully assembled on the World's Fair grounds.

Ferris's gargantuan wheel was enormously profitable at the World's Fair, but the cost of disassembling, transporting, and reassembling it was $150,000 every time it was moved, so instead of bringing it to New York after the 10 weeks of the World's Fair, it was moved to North Clark Street in Chicago in 1895. Ferris did not do a fraction of the business in that location, though, but the wheel was used again for the 1904 St. Louis Exposition, after which it was torn down and scrapped.

Today, Ferris wheels are substantially smaller than the original 1893 version, although the London Eye by the Thames River in London is 500 feet tall and takes 30 minutes to make a complete rotation. "Standard" Ferris wheels are still very popular at carnivals and amusement parks.

George Ferris ultimately went bankrupt and sold his invention for $1,800.

# Fig Newtons®

Debut: 1891
Inventive Americans: Charles M. Roser, James Henry Mitchell

Charles Roser should be credited as the true inventor of the Fig Newton because he was the one who created the cookie's fig filling and sold it to the Kennedy Biscuit Works company in Massachusetts. But it was James Henry Mitchell who is responsible for the actual creation of the beloved fruit and cake cookie.

In 1891, Kennedy Biscuit Works employee Mitchell invented a mechanical device that was a simple yet brilliant advancement in cookie-making. Essentially, the device consisted of a funnel inside a funnel. The outside funnel pumped out cookie batter, while the inside funnel extruded a filling ingredient. The result was a continuous length of filled cookie dough that could then be cut into individual cookies and baked. Mitchell and Kennedy Biscuit Works plant manager James Hazen decided to use the new contraption to create a fig-filled cookie, using Roser's recipe. This new cookie was put on the market with the name "Newton." There has long been a rumor that the cookie was named after Sir Isaac Newton, but that is not true. The Kennedy Biscuit company had a long tradition of naming their cookies after towns and cities surrounding Boston, and the Newton was named for Newton, Massachusetts.

When the Kennedy Biscuit Works company changed hands in 1898, the new owner lengthened the name of the cookie to the Fig Newton, and, eventually, to the Fig Newton Cookie. The new company's name was the National Biscuit Company because America was still following the British custom of calling a cookie a "biscuit." Later, this convention was abandoned and, in the colonies, the term "biscuit" was then used only to mean a small, round bread item served as an accompaniment to a main meal. Today, the only dessert or snack items in the store called "biscuits" are cookies imported from England. When this transition occurred, the National Biscuit Company realized they had to do something about their name, and they did. They changed their name to Nabisco.

Fig Newtons are now Nabisco's third most popular cookie. (Oreos are first—no surprise there, eh?—followed by Chips Ahoy! in second place.)

Nabisco has expanded the Newton line and now offers in addition to the traditional Fig Newtons, Fat Free Newtons, Strawberry Newtons, Raspberry Newtons, Apple Newtons, Cherries'n Cheesecake Newtons, and Strawberry Shortcake Newtons.

## The Flashlight

Debut: 1898
Inventive Americans: David Misell,
Conrad Hubert, and Joshua Lionel Cowen

Misell was the first to come up with the notion of a portable, electric light. He designed and built a light that he intended to sell as a bicycle light, even though it would only burn for a few seconds at a time.

Misell gave the patent of his light to his boss, Conrad Hubert, the founder of the Eveready Battery Company. Hubert and

Joshua Cowen designed and built the first tubular flashlight, which they gave away to cops in New York City. Once the accolades started coming in from the policemen using the portable lights, they became available to the public, from both the Eveready Company and other manufacturers.

# FLOATING SOAP (IVORY®)

Debut: 1879
Inventive American: A careless
Procter & Gamble employee

The workers in Procter & Gamble's soap-making plant were supposed to turn off the soap-churning machines when they went to lunch. One day, an employee who is simply described now as "careless," left his soap-churning machine on during his lunch break. When Mr. Careless returned to work, he discovered that the batch of soap he had been working on was loaded with air bubbles and froth, far in excess of what was normal for Procter & Gamble's soaps.

A great deal of soap was seemingly ruined. But what was initially perceived as a problem for P&G, turned out to be a fortuitous windfall. The powers that be at P&G could not accept throwing away such a large quantity of soap, so they ordered the frothy batch be tested, and the results were good news: The bubbly soap batch was equal in properties to P&G's other soaps. They then decided to complete the manufacturing process and sell it anyway.

It turns out that the bubbly soap floated, and the consumers loved it. Further testing determined that the additional churning had also greatly purified the soap, making it milder and gentler and, in fact, there were only .56 percent of impurities in the soap. Thus, the slogan for the soap wrote itself: "99.44 percent pure."

But what to call it? Procter & Gamble initially marketed it as "P&G White Soap," but no one was pleased with such a bland, boring name. The answer came to Harley Procter one day in a place *many* people go for answers: a church. Procter was reading Psalm 45 when he came upon Verse 8: "All thy garments smell of myrrh, and aloes, and cassia, out of the ivory palaces, whereby they have made thee glad."

And thus, Ivory Soap was born.

On December 21, 1882, the first Ivory Soap ad depicting the "Ivory Lady" was published and, since then, P&G added Ivory Dishwashing Liquid and Ivory Flakes for laundry to the Ivory line.

Today, Procter & Gamble is a multinational company with sales in the many billions each year. Much of this success is due to a simple, floating soap that came about due to a lucky accident.

# Fluorescent Lighting

Debut: Late 1880s
Inventive American: Nikola Tesla

Dr. Marc Seifer is a friend and a colleague, and we share the same literary agent. Dr. Seifer is the author of the fascinating and authoritative biography of Nikola Tesla called *Wizard: The Life and Times of Nikola Tesla* (Kensington, 2001), the novel *Staretz Encounter*, and the two-volume set on consciousness called *The Space/Time/Mind Continuum*. He teaches psychology at Roger Williams University in Rhode Island, and I am honored that he graciously agreed to contribute the following essay from *Wizard: The Life and Times of Nikola Tesla* in which he talks about Tesla's invention of fluorescent lighting:

## Tesla's Fluorescent Lamp
### by Marc Seifer

*At the time, in the late 1880s, there was something called the Crookes tube, which was named after its inventor, Sir William Crookes. Crookes had experimented in wireless communication replicating the work of Hertz, from room to room. He probably was the first to use Morse code, but he didn't bother with publicity on this so he gets no credit. In any event, the use of Crookes tubes at this time was widespread, but it gave off a meager light.*

*The key to understanding Tesla's invention of fluorescent lighting is threefold. You needed high frequencies first. He had to understand the relationship between electromagnetic waves and light phenomena. He realized the real reason why lamps lit, and it had more to do with the vacuum than with the filament.*

*You couldn't have fluorescent lighting without producing high frequency AC currents. So, really, in some pure sense, you can't separate the two inventions. Tesla had invented the AC polyphase system, rotating magnetic field, etc. There were a number of key differences between the two. DC could only transmit about a mile and then only for lighting homes. You couldn't run a machine with DC if your home was, say, more than 300 feet from the power source. AC could travel hundreds of miles, and it was clean energy. It ran on waterfalls. DC ran on coal.*

*The other big thing was the size of the current. DC was dealing with a few hundred volts, AC with tens of thousands of volts. You have voltage and amperage, that is, frequency and power. So you could send, say 100,000 volts through your body, if you kept the amperage at a miniscule level, which is what Tesla did. This is also what he did when he created fluorescent lighting.*

*There are two types of fluorescent lights, those that use gases like neon, or fluorescent coating around the glass, so when the high frequency zaps it, these mediums give off light.*

*But Tesla wanted to out-do Edison. He was also very concerned about conservation. He knew that conventional Edison lamps wasted most of their electricity in the production of heat. About 90 percent of the energy goes into heat production. So Tesla wanted to produce pure light. Why waste it in heat?*

*He therefore took Edison's lamps and removed their filaments but kept the vacuum, created a high frequency in the room with his AC equipment, and by way of wireless, induced the vacuum in the lamp to convert its medium (ether) to produce pure light and essentially no heat.*

*"Dr. Hertz and Dr. Lodge had evolved the theory that the phenomena of light were related to the electromagnetic vibrations of ether or air, but it remained for Mr. Tesla to*

*demonstrate this fact and make the knowledge practically available."*[6]

*So Tesla realized that the vacuum was more important than the filament in Edison's lightbulb invention, but the reason that Edison or no one else could have invented the fluorescent light bulb was because 1) one needed to create extremely high frequencies (through Tesla's coil and AC invention) and 2) Tesla's realization that if one could resonate the medium in the vacuum at a particular frequency equivalent to light, illumination would result.*

*Tesla, of course, had studied Faraday and Maxwell's equations and therefore knew of the correspondence between EM waves and the production of light.*

*So, where the Edison lightbulb even today will last just a few months, a Tesla fluorescent light can last a decade. And where the Edison lamp wastes most of its energy in heat, the Tesla light is efficient as it only produces light and almost no heat.*

*For some peculiar reason, Tesla never got a patent for this invention, or the patent was well hidden. However, what he did get was a patent on was the concept of selective tuning. These lamps were lit by wireless communication, and he could construct different ones, (he created thousands of them) that would ignite (and in different colors) when different resonant frequencies were created.*

*So really, the invention of the fluorescent light was deeply embedded with the invention of the AC polyphase system, high frequency currents, wireless communication, the radio tube, and selective tuning, as well as fluorescent and neon lighting.*

*Morgan and the Westinghouse Corporation kept the secret of fluorescent lighting hidden for 50 years. Fluorescent lighting didn't really come into vogue until the early 1950s and only then because of the necessity to use it because the demand for power was so great. I did find letters suggesting that Tesla's lighting patents were obtained by Morgan in 1901, but I never found an actual patent for the design for just a simple fluorescent light. They had kept the patents hidden for all those years because they wanted electric bills to stay high and to continue to sell conventional Edison lamps that had built-in obsolescence.*

*Edison did mention that one of the key advantages his bulb had over fluorescent lighting is that the conventional lightbulb gives off a more pleasant light.*

# Fluoride Toothpaste

Debut: 1956
Inventive American: Procter & Gamble

What is fluoride, why is it good for us, and why do they put it in our water and our toothpaste?

There is and always has been a great deal of controversy about adding fluoride to toothpaste and water, but the development was an American First, so it is included here.

I do not believe there is a conspiracy to poison Americans through excessive fluoridation, but I do think that long-term studies may show that fluorosis (excessive buildup of fluoride in human blood and tissue) is real, and probably harmful.

We were first, though, and there is some concrete evidence that fluoride does help prevent cavities.

# The Flyswatter

Debut: 1905
Inventive Americans: Frank H. Rose; Dr. Samuel J. Crumbine

Why do flyswatters have holes in them? To get to the other side. (Sorry.)

If a mesh screen does a good job obliterating flies (and it most assuredly does), then wouldn't a *solid* piece of vinyl or plastic do an even better job?

In terms of total destruction of the insect, yes, it would. But if flyswatters were solid, you'd never get a chance to hit the fly.

Flies can easily sense the moving mass of air that swinging a flat solid piece of anything creates. And once they feel this tsunami of air approaching them, they will instantly fly out of its sphere of influence, leaving you standing there staring at the pristine underside of your swatter instead of trying to figure out how to get the strained remains of a dead fly off your weapon.

In 1905, almost two decades before the advent of home air-conditioning, windows were open and flies were everywhere. Today, the buzz of a fly in the house often provokes rabid hysteria and much jumping and swinging, usually by someone wielding a rolled-up magazine. Apparently, the denizens of 1905 were much less bothered by flies and, when you think about it, who could blame them? With flies everywhere, who had the time to attempt a genocidal extermination of an endlessly replenishing supply of the annoying pest?

Dr. Samuel Crumbine had a slightly different view of the fly problem. Crumbine was a member of the Kansas State Board of Health and he considered flies much more than a nuisance; he considered them a health hazard. While attending a softball game in Topeka one day, Crumbine heard the crowd chanting, "Swat the ball! Swat the ball!" and this gave him an idea.

Crumbine published the *Fly Bulletin*, which updated farmers, health officials, and the general public on the fly situation in Kansas. In the issue he published after the softball game, he used the headline "Swat the fly!" to encourage citizens to communally work to wipe out the buggers.

Frank Rose, a teacher, was inspired. He cut a piece of screen and attached it to the end of a yardstick. He called it a Fly Bat, and used it to execute as many flies as he could. (He must have been a sight in the classroom, eh? "Thomas Jefferson was president from 1801 to...excuse me..." SWAT!)

Crumbine liked Rose's idea and renamed it the Fly Swatter. The idea quickly caught on and people did, indeed, begin swatting flies and other flying annoyances in their homes. A contemporary ad of the time in *Ladies' Home Journal* quoted someone described as "a prominent lady" exclaiming, "It is the most prized article in my home."

# FM Radio

Debut: 1939
Inventive American: Edwin Howard Armstrong

FM stands for "frequency modulation" and was invented by Edwin Armstrong in response to AM radio's susceptibility to noise and static, and its lack of sound fidelity. It was a major improvement in radio broadcasting, but Armstrong had to fight for years to obtain an FM broadcasting license. Why? Because in the 1920s and 1930s, AM radio was king and there were a lot of people and groups that would stand to lose a lot of money if AM stations were deposed from their broadcasting throne.

Finally, in 1939, the FCC granted Armstrong a license to operate a 50 megahertz FM radio station in Alpine, New Jersey. FM radio was used during World War II by U.S. troops with great success, and after the war, the FM band was decreed to be 88 to 108 megahertz.

As the Steely Dan song goes, "FM....no static at all."

# The Fountain Pen

Debut: 1884
Inventive American: Lewis Waterman

When we type, we press a "button" (a key on a keyboard) and a letter instantly appears on a screen. Since all the keys on either a typewriter (quickly becoming obsolete) or a computer keyboard look and feel the same, the mental process of actually creating the letters we need to spell the words we want to use to communicate what we want to say is completely eliminated.

Writing by hand is unabashedly physical. This begs the question: Does creating words by drawing each individual letter change the writing process? Does the writer who works in longhand consciously or subconsciously edit his or her work to make the physical act of writing easier? Are pieces written by hand more economical in use of words?

These are important questions about the act of writing. Granted, there are many gigantic novels that were written by hand, but they were all written over long periods of time, and usually without a publishing contract.

That brings us to the fountain pen. Before Lewis Waterman developed a writing instrument that efficiently and securely stored its own ink, writing was mostly done with quills and inkwells.

The Magna Carta, the Constitution of the United States, and the Declaration of Independence were all written by repeatedly dipping a quill into a bottle or well of ink and scratching letters onto paper until the small amount of ink on the end of the quill was used up.

There did exist functional fountain pens before Waterman's 1884 patented fountain pen. Most were terrible, and were failed attempts to mimic and utilize the hollow tube running the length of birds' feathers. Feathers were commonly used as quill pens; nature suggested a means for storing ink in a writing instrument.

Waterman used some of these earlier pens in his work as an insurance salesman. He resolved to design a functional fountain pen after he ruined an important sales contract when the pen he was using leaked ink all over the paper.

Waterman's breakthrough was to add an air hole in the nib (the point of the pen) and three grooves in the feed mechanism. These improvements allowed a smooth, even flow. His 1884 patented pen was the state-of-the-art design that, in many variations and improved versions, still serves as the model for today's fountain pen.

Does anyone still write with fountain pens? Yes, but they are a miniscule segment of the writing instrument business. In the year 2000, 3.6 billion ballpoint pens were sold, compared to 16 million fountain pens—a share of the market of approximately one-half of 1 percent.[7]

# Free Public Schools

Debut: 1636
Inventive American: Reverend John Cotton

Educating young people can in no way be considered an American First (parents were teaching children the Scriptures and other sacred writings thousands of years ago), and yet 140 years before the signing of the Declaration of Independence, the first free public school was opened in Boston thanks to a bequest from Reverend John Cotton, who decreed that half his land should be used for a free school. Education at the time was either carried out in the home or in small private schools that only the wealthy could afford. Cotton saw that the underprivileged and children without parents were not being educated, and so established the first free public school.

Of course, nothing is really free, is it? The teachers in Cotton's school were paid by the parents of the children who attended. This is a paradigm of what goes on today: Taxes pay for the teachers at "free" public schools. Today, the word "free" simply means that parents do not pay tuition for their children to attend the school. But they do pay income tax, property tax, sales tax, estate tax, and other taxes that partly go towards paying the salaries of teachers.

But what makes the concept of a free public school an American First is the idea that the payment of taxes is not a prerequisite for attending a public school. Administrators do not ask parents to prove that they have paid enough taxes to cover their share of the burden of maintaining the public school system. In fact, the tax system in this country is expansive enough that even those who on the surface pay little or no tax, can send their children to public school. A single mother who does not work, doesn't own a car, lives with her parents, and doesn't spend any money would seem to be contributing nothing to the tax pool to pay for schools. Yet if she lives with her parents, they pay property tax on their home; if they feed her, they pay sales and excise taxes on the food and utensils, and sewer and water taxes; if they are within tax-paying age range, then they pay federal income tax. Ultimately, the cost of educating her child *is* paid for in some way by the people responsible for the child's mother.

Today, there is ongoing debate about the public vs. private school funding systems. Some taxpayers who willingly pay tuition to send their children to private schools contend that they should receive some kind of credit for the share of their taxes earmarked for public education. So far, the courts have ruled that their obligation to pay taxes that go toward education is not rescinded because they voluntarily choose not to avail themselves of the benefit of a free public education for their children.

I recently experienced a similar situation regarding municipal trash pickup. My condominium association pays to have two dumpsters on our premises. Why? Because the city of New Haven will not pick up trash in multi-dwelling developments with more than six units. So either we pay for our own trash removal or it doesn't get removed. Our options were, obviously, limited. And yet I and all my neighbors pay real estate taxes on our property that is used to pay for trash pickup. Are we entitled to a credit on our taxes? Nope. Yet, in our situation, we are not simply *refusing* an offered benefit; we are arbitrarily *denied* the benefit of trash pickup because our development has 21 units. Even with these compelling circumstances, we are not given respite from double payment for trash removal.

Flawed or not, the American system of free public education through high school is a model for a society that values learning and its role in the making and maintenance of a productive, progressive society.

# The Frisbee®

Debut: 1870s (Frisbie); 1948 (Morrison)
Inventive Americans: William Russell Frisbie;
Walter Frederick Morrison

No, Yale student Elihu Frisbie *did not* invent the Frisbee. This is one of those myths that simply will not die.

The story is told that the Frisbee came about one day in 1820 when Yale undergrad Elihu Frisbie (was there even an Elihu Frisbie at Yale in the early 1800s??) grabbed a round serving tray from a cafeteria cart and hurled it out a window. There are some at Yale who still lay claim to the honor of being the home of the Frisbee, and there is some truth to that assertion, but Yale's role in the invention of the toy/game did not come until much later.

In the 1870s, a Bridgeport baker named William Frisbie began embossing his name on the bottom of his metal pie tins. His pies were sold throughout the area (including New Haven, home of Yale University), and one of the pluses of buying a Frisbie pie was that the pie tin was reusable. Every housewife who bought a Frisbie pie was also getting a piece of cookware as part of the deal.

Mr. Frisbie's motives were not entirely altruistic in giving away a pie tin. Because his name was on the bottom of every tin, his hope was that the following thought would pop into the homemaker's mind when she saw his name: "Gee, it sure would be a lot easier to buy a Frisbie pie than to go through the trouble of making one." This type of grassroots advertising may have persuaded some to abandon their pie-making plans and buy a Frisbie pie, but as you have probably surmised by now, there was one problem with this ad strategy: the cost differential. Sure, it would be easier to buy a Frisbie pie than to make one from scratch, but the cost of ingredients for even the most luscious of pies was a fraction of buying one from a bakery.

The record is silent on the number of actual converts Frisbie's embossed name created, but the tins were everywhere and this is a part of the story as to how the Frisbee came about.

Fast forward to late 1948. Two businessmen in California, Walter Morrison and his partner, Warren Franscioni, designed and manufactured a plastic disc for tossing from person to person. They call it the Pluto Platter in an attempt to cash in on Americans' new interest in UFOs. The prior year, pilot Kenneth Arnold sighted nine UFOs flying in formation over Washington State and his sighting started the modern UFO craze. The media became obsessed with Arnold's experience and Morrison and Franscioni saw an opportunity. The following year, the Pluto Platter was born.

In 1955, Wham-O bought the rights to the Pluto Platter and Morrison went on a promotional tour of college campuses to increase sales. While in New Haven visiting Yale, Morrison saw Yale students flinging Frisbie pie tins around and he decided to change the name to "Frisbee."

Morrison became a millionaire and the Frisbie Baking Company went out of business.

# Frozen Food

Debut: 1923
Inventive American: Clarence Birdseye

Yes, there really was a Clarence Birdseye, and he was a taxidermist. Is this the same Clarence Birdseye who invented the process for freezing food?

Yes, it is. Clarence may have stuffed dead animals for a living, but he was really a frustrated chef who delighted in preparing food and cooking for his family.

Birdseye got the idea for freezing food from the Eskimos. During a visit to the Arctic, he saw the Eskimos place fish and meat in barrels of seawater, which would then quickly freeze in the near-zero temperatures. Upon further investigation, he learned that the meat and fish retained all their flavor and did not spoil when they were thawed out months later.

When he returned home, he tried an experiment. He spent seven dollars on an electric fan, a few buckets of brine, and several blocks of ice. He tried fast-freezing some food, and it worked. He later developed a wax-lined cardboard box in which vegetables and other foodstuffs could be frozen, and the block of frozen spinach was born. The first frozen food was sold in Springfield, Massachusetts with the brand name Birds Eye Frosted Foods®.

Today, just about *everything* is available frozen, and the frozen food business is a multibillion dollar, worldwide industry.

# G

## The Gas Mask

Debut: 1914
Inventive American: Garrett Augustus Morgan

Garrett Morgan, one of America's most gifted and prolific African-American inventors, had to pretend he was an Indian chief to demonstrate his gas mask invention.

Racism was rampant in 1914. Morgan's parents were freed slaves and, in the year he debuted his gas mask, he was in his 30s and blacks were still feeling the societal prejudice from having been an enslaved race.

The "all men are created equal" credo was part of America's legacy, and was its defining mission statement, but with the Civil War still a relatively fresh memory, blacks had to constantly fight against the discrimination many whites heaped upon them— Emancipation Proclamation or not. The misanthropic mistreatment of blacks brought over from Africa as slaves had become engrained as justifiable in many sectors of society, particularly in the South. There were many whites who had become so used to treating blacks like animals and property that there was no way they could simply turn off their prejudiced perceptions of the entire black race. Blacks wanting to educate themselves and move up in the world were considered "uppity." Southern whites may have been forced to accept blacks as free and equal American citizens, but racism runs deep and society would need a few more generations of "reprogramming" before racism was widely accepted as a societal wrong.

In the early 20th century, Indians (they were decades away from being referred to as Native Americans) were somewhat more accepted than blacks. Thus, it was "Big Chief Mason" who put on a dramatic advertising demonstration showing the effectiveness of Garrett Morgan's safety hood. A substance was burned (oil, tar, or rubber perhaps?) to generate a thick black smoke, and Mason sat in the midst of it for 20 minutes wearing the new Morgan safety hood. At the end of the demonstration, he was unharmed. People were amazed, the demonstration was a success, and sales of Morgan's hood took off.

Two years later, a mine explosion under Lake Erie on the shore of Garrett's hometown of Cleveland trapped many workers, and Morgan was called upon to don his safety hood and help rescue the trapped miners. The mine was filled with noxious gases, and yet Morgan and volunteers willing to place their safety in Morgan's hands, donned his masks and ran in and out of the shaft, bringing 32 workers to safety. It was then that the true identity of the gas hood's inventor was revealed and, instead of people praising Morgan and his sales increasing, his business actually suffered because some whites simply refused to buy anything invented by the son of former slaves.

One "group" that did not care one whit about the race of the inventor was the United States Army. After Morgan's heroic rescue of the miners, the Army ordered gas masks from Morgan, and they were modified and used successfully during World War I. Fire departments around the country were also colorblind and likewise ordered many of Morgan's protective gas hoods for firefighters.

Today, gas masks are smaller and more effective. After September 11, 2001, and the threat of biological or chemical weapons being used against Americans became a real threat, sales of gas masks skyrocketed. The 2003 SARS epidemic contributed to the boom.

Garrett Morgan also invented the traffic signal, a curved-tooth comb, a hair-straightening cream, a zigzag stitching attachment for sewing machines, and he was the founder of his own newspaper, the *Cleveland Call*. He was a successful, creative, and hard-working businessman throughout his life.

Morgan died in 1963, the year of the 100th anniversary of the Emancipation Proclamation.

# Geodesic Dome

Debut: 1954
Inventive American: Buckminster Fuller

The geodesic dome is a domed or vaulted structure of light-weight straight elements that form interlocking polygons (there's one at Epcot). The American Institute of Architects has described it as the "strongest, lightest, and most efficient means of enclosing space yet devised by man."

The geodesic dome is all of that, and more, and is used today for houses, greenhouses, and commercial and government buildings all over the world.

# The Golf Tee

Debut: 1898
Inventive American: George Franklin Grant

George Grant was one of the first two black graduates of the Harvard Dental School and he did not like to get his hands dirty. (This would likely prove to be a great comfort to his future patients, eh?)

Grant loved golf, but he hated the way golfers had to mix together water and dirt to make a small mound from which to tee off.

He specifically invented the golf tee so that he would not have to indulge in such a repugnant practice.

Golfers everywhere probably thank him on a daily basis—except when they slice, of course.

American golfers use approximately 2 million tees a year. The latest fad is taller tees, to compensate for larger drivers.

The *Farmer's Almanac* once proclaimed that the golf tee was one of the 10 inventions that changed sports for all time.

# The Graham Cracker

Debut: 1829
Inventive American: Sylvester Graham

One of the world's all-time most popular cracker was invented by a man who, to put it kindly, was about two beers short of a six-pack. One 19th century newspaper described him as "an eccentric and wayward genius." Another called him a "disgusting writer."

Sylvester Graham was a cleric and a social reformer with some very unusual beliefs. Some of his most notorious were that ketchup would destroy the human brain, that sex irritated and damaged the body and caused disease, and that drinking wine and gin was beneficial for nursing mothers. He suffered a nervous breakdown when he was 36 and, after he recovered, he devoted his life to "cleaning up" America.

Graham was a social firebrand, and his lectures were attended by thousands of his followers, known as Grahamites. He was a staunch advocate of vegetarianism, and he believed that eating meat poisoned the human body. He came to this conclusion after determining that man was closest physically to the orangutan, and that because the ape was a vegetarian, man only ate meat because he had learned how to overpower and kill animals—because it was convenient. Evolutionarily, Graham believed we were meant to be vegetarians. (His point is somewhat supported by what has happened to the increasingly superfluous human appendix, an organ originally evolutionarily designed to digest grasses, but which quickly became unnecessary after hominids began killing and eating flesh. The appendix in the cow, on the other hand, is still fully functional and an important organ. Today, the human appendix is good for nothing except causing appendicitis.)

At his lectures, Graham instructed people on how to live a healthy life. He preached that they needed to abolish any and all "stimulants" from their diet. Liquor, wine, cider, tea, coffee, and tobacco topped his list of substances to avoid—unless, of course, you were a nursing mother. (Yes, old Sly was a tad inconsistent.) As you might imagine, the tobacconists, tea and coffee merchants, spirit purveyors, and butchers all hated Graham.

Graham also expounded graphically on healthy and unhealthy sex practices. Apparently women were quite fragile back then, for many of the ladies in his audiences passed out upon hearing such things. (He later toned down the sex talk and concentrated on touting the benefits of vegetarianism and eating healthy.)

Graham created the graham cracker as a healthy alternative to breads made from refined flour that, he claimed, had all of its nutrients removed. It became immediately popular and is still one of the best-selling crackers all over the world.

All of his eccentricities and weird beliefs aside, many of Graham's recommendations are accepted today as healthy practices. Many believe that eating meat does cause long-term damage and that vegetarianism is a much healthier way to eat.

There is a scene in *Beverly Hills Cop* in which Judge Reinhold tells his partner that he read in *TIME* magazine that by the time the average American is 50, he or she has five pounds of undigested red meat in his or her bowel. Apparently, this happens to be true. Having all that animal flesh fermenting in your intestines certainly cannot be good for you, and it might explain the increase in gastrointestinal cancers and ailments over the past century.

Maybe Graham was onto something, although he was certainly way off base about sex.

Graham cracker, anyone?

# The Grocery Bag

Debut: 1868
Inventive American: Margaret Knight

Margaret Knight was the American inventor who designed a machine to make the ubiquitous flat-bottomed paper grocery sack. Prior to Margaret's insightful realization that the bags of the time were somewhat lacking, bags were completely flat.

Imagine trying to squeeze a dozen eggs, a loaf of bread, a bottle of milk, and a few apples into one of those flat bags that are now only used for magazines and greeting cards. No wonder Margaret saw a need and decided to fill it.

Margaret had started working in a mill when she was barely in her teens. Child labor was commonplace in her time, and Margaret was eager to work. She was not interested in the usual "little girl" things like dolls and tea parties, but instead liked working with machines and coming up with ideas to make her factory work easier.

When Margaret was 30, she invented a part for a standard bag-making machine that would enable four flaps to be cut in the paper stock then folded into a square bottom. Her initial goal was to make a bag that would stand up on its own. This is so taken for granted these days that it truly speaks to her creativity that she was able to foresee such a product during a time when nothing like it existed.

At first, as we can easily imagine, the male workers at the mill refused to even consider trying Margaret's invention. What could a young woman possibly know about machines and manufacturing? Margaret was adamant, though, and after her design improvement was installed, it actually worked, and the market snapped up the new product, Margaret was vindicated.

Two years later, at the age of 32, Margaret Knight formed her own company—the Eastern Paper Bag Company, which is still in existence today, and which still makes flat-bottomed grocery bags using the machinery Margaret Knight designed.

Interestingly, many in the grocery industry believed that the introduction of the thin one-piece plastic grocery bag with handles would be the death knell for the paper grocery bag. Shoppers would no longer have to cradle loaded paper grocery bags in their arms after checking out. Some industry execs also thought that the plastic-handled bag would increase grocery store sales because shoppers could carry several plastic bags with handles instead of the one or two paper bags they could carry previously.

# H

## The Hacky Sack®

Debut: 1972
Inventive Americans: John Stalberger and Mike Marshall

The Hacky Sack is a beanbag that is used in a game called Hacky Sack, also known as Footbag. The idea is to keep the bag in the air using only your feet.

In the early 1970s, Mike Marshall of Oregon City, Oregon, made a beanbag that he tossed and kicked around as a diversion. In 1972, his friend John Stalberger started using the bag to exercise his knees following knee surgery, and Hacky Sack was born.

Today, Hacky Sack is a popular sport, and there is even a National Hacky Sack Association.

BENJAMIN FRANKLIN ON PROGRESS AND THE FUTURE

On May 31, 1788, Benjamin Franklin, then 83 years old and in pain from age-related maladies, wrote a letter to Reverend John Lathrop of Boston, in which he talked about what was to come. Not surprisingly, he was remarkably prescient.

*I have long been impressed with the same sentiments you so well express, of the growing felicity of mankind, from the improvement in philosophy, morals, politics, and even the conveniences of common living, and the invention of new and useful utensils and instruments; so that I have sometimes wished it had been my destiny to be born two or three centuries hence. For invention and improvement are prolific, and beget more of their kind. The present progress is rapid. Many of great importance, now unthought of, will, before that period, be produced.*

# "Happy Birthday to You"

Debut: 1893
Inventive Americans: Patty Hill and Mildred Hill

Yes, it's true that the Hill estate receives a royalty every time the "Happy Birthday" song is sung in a movie.

This simple ditty, which has been sung in almost every language and in every country around the world, was originally written as a song to greet students every morning. Patty Hill was the principal of Louisville Experimental Kindergarten, and her sister Mildred, also a church organist, taught there. The two teamed up in 1893 to write "Good Morning to All," which they sang every morning to their students.

Mildred Hill died at the age of 57, and her sister Patty went on to teach at Columbia University Teachers College.

Thirty-one years after "Good Morning to All" was copyrighted by the Hill sisters, the song appeared in a book of sheet music edited by Robert Coleman. Coleman had reproduced the first verse as it had been written by the sisters, but he had rewritten the second verse as, you guessed it, "Happy Birthday to You."

This second verse quickly overshadowed the first and, within a short time of the book's publication, the song was known to all as "Happy Birthday to You."

Patty seemed not to mind the changes, but then, in 1934, Irving Berlin used the song in the musical *As Thousands Cheer*—apparently without the Hill family's permission, and a third sister, Jessica, decided to act. She sued for royalties, won, and now every time "Happy Birthday to You" is sung publicly, the Hills get paid.

Did you pay *your* royalty when you sang it at your niece's birthday party at Chuck E. Cheese's last summer?

# I

## Instant Replay

Debut: 1964
Inventive American: Jim Wheeler

Instant replay is either the greatest boon to televised sports or the worst thing that has ever happened to it. Why? Because it allows valid challenges to an umpire or referee's call. Instant replay puts the human element in sports "on trial," so to speak, and the referee's call—while still the final word—is no longer accepted as always being the *correct* call. It may be accepted as the final word on the play or the game, but that no longer means it was the *right* word—and fans argue ceaselessly about how the outcome of games would have changed if the instant replay review had been used for the ref's decision instead of the eyewitnessing of the play.

As with many instantly popular inventions, instant replay was discovered or developed by accident. Its inventor, Jim Wheeler, recounts how it all happened in this Guest Essay that follows. He provides insider info, including how instant replay revolutionized the taping of professional sports.

Jim Wheeler is an engineer with 32 years experience as a tape engineer and tape recorder design engineer at Ampex Corporation, the company that developed both the audiotape recorder and the videotape recorder. He currently serves as an expert witness for

tape problems, does forensic analysis of tapes, and assesses audio-
and videotape collections. He is considered a world authority on
tape problems and restoration and has been a legal consultant on
many cases, including murder trials and civil cases. He was a tech-
nical advisor for the Watergate tape project, and is now a consultant for NASA, the FBI, the Library of Congress, the U.S. National
Archives, and the National Transportation Board. In addition to
inventing instant reply (and winning an Emmy for it), he was also
a member of the team that developed the first home videotape
recorder. Jim also invented in-flight video, which is now common
on all commercial flights.

## INSTANT REPLAY, SLO-MO, & STOP ACTION
### by Jim Wheeler

*In Nov. 1963, I was responsible for developing a tape tension
control for a small TV broadcast videotape recorder (VTR).
Its code name was "Junior" because the Ampex Quad VTR
was the videotape machine in those days and it weighed hundreds of pounds. "Junior" became known as the VR-660. The
660 used two-inch-wide magnetic tape because that was what
was available in TV studios.*

*I used various tapes to be sure that the tension servo [a
servomotor, used in the automatic control of a mechanical
device] would work with all types of tapes. 3M sent me ten
reels of a new tape to try. While testing one of these reels, the
lab telephone rang. After about ten minutes on the phone, I
returned to the machine. By mistake, I had left the scanner
running with the tape threaded. This was a no-no for rotary
head machines because the video heads would load up and
slice the tape into two pieces. Also, if you stopped the tape on
a Quad machine, a small portion of the video was repeated
16 times. The 660 was a helical machine and one head would
play one full video frame—a new ballgame (which we did not
appreciate at that time).*

*I was amazed to see that the video heads had not clogged
and were playing the same video frame over and over. I
grabbed the two reels and was able to make the tape move
forward and reverse. I had recorded a scene of a guy diving*

*off a diving board so I could make him go from the water back to the board. Another engineer on the 660 saw what I was doing and liked it. We found a small 12 volt motor and mounted it so that it would make the capstan move forward or reverse. I still have this motor.*

*The Project Manager, John Streets, liked it and had it added as a feature of the 660. We could use a simple control to make the tape move forward, reverse, or stop at any speed up to play speed. We called it "Stop Action" and "Slo-Mo." Later, the term "Instant Replay" was used by the TV networks. CBS had coined the name for a method they used to erase a piece of audio if someone said a bad word on the air. It consisted of two Quad machines with a long 2x4 bolted in between them. The tape was recorded on the left machine [and then] guided to the right machine where it was played. There were a few seconds of time delay so the viewing audience [thought] it was live.*

*We didn't know what to do with this feature. We rented a Studebaker station wagon which had a sliding roof in the rear. We mounted a 110 volt AC generator on the engine. One person drove and the other used a video camera with a tripod. I was the cameraman. We drove around town and out on the freeway. We stopped at the local high school and taped players practicing bating. The coach liked it because the kids could see what they were doing. We drove over to the Stanford Stadium and taped football practice. Again, the coach liked it for training.*

*The first practical use came when the NAVY wanted to use it to play tapes of planes crashing during landing on a carrier. Ampex had sold the NAVY several Quad machines to play movies as well as for PLAT—Pilot Landing and Takeoff.*

*The few Quad tapes with crash scenes were dubbed to a 660 and played back in slo-mo. ABC bought six 660s for sports. Ampex agreed that the Slo-Mo machines would not be sold to anyone else for two (or three) years. The President of ABC Engineering, Frank Marx, saw the potential of this machine for sports TV. ABC tried it during the winter*

*Olympics in 1994 but the 150 pound machine was too cumbersome to lug around on the ski slopes. ABC (probably Roone Alredge), decided to give the 660s a trial on the Atlantic City boardwalk during the 1964 Democratic Convention. The machine worked but the union VTR operators refused to use it. It was too easy to operate so they were afraid they would be replaced by lower pay people.*

*We had a major problem and that was that tape will cling to the scanner when wet and the humidity was near 100 percent. I told Frank that these machines cannot work with salt spray and the high humidity. Frank put his hand on my shoulder and said "Can't is not in my vocabulary." He had his gopher go out and buy six electric blankets to be used when the machines were in standby. It worked! There are a lot of "Frank Marx stories" in ABC engineering—even today.*

*The six 660s finally debuted on ABCs "Wide World of Sports" during the 1964 football season. During the Democratic Convention, Frank told me that ABC had only 4 percent of the viewing market and that ABC was gambling on Instant Replay to save ABC.*

*I did not see the significance of Instant Replay until I saw it being used for football. The reason is that I had an 8mm projector that would slow the film, stop it, or reverse it. Doing this with tape was just another technique.*

*Coaches could use film for training—it just took a couple of days to get the film back. I'm not a sports fan. I'm just an engineer who stumbled on something.*

## Regarding the Future

*In 1976, three of us were involved in patenting a special device that would keep the video head on track. Initially, we did this so that poorly recorded tapes could be played. After we developed a working model, we made some changes that made Instant Replay possible. Ampex had good sales for the Instant Replay disk [and because of this], Marketing didn't like the potential competition. Once Marketing saw that the* tape version of Instant Replay did not have the time limit the disk had, they were sold.

In 1979, I was at a trade show. The Ampex Marketing Manager for Instant Replay introduced me to an ABC engineer. He told me that my AST invention had cut the costs of producing soaps in half! Also, I noticed at the trade show and on TV that the AST was being used for special effects. Since 1979, digital has replaced the AST for special effects. New ballgame.

I spent a week very close to Frank Marx and learned a couple of major things. One is that "can't" is not a good answer and the other is that engineers can develop new things but it takes a visionary to see how to use it.

## Instant Replay: My Opinion

Engineers don't always have a purpose in mind when creating a new invention. Many times, it is someone else who adapts the invention for a use that the engineer never considered. Instant Replay is such an invention. I saw it as a tool for training and for fun. It was someone else who adapted it to sports.

How Instant Replay is used by referees to make a call on a play depends on the angle and the composition by the cameraman—not the technician operating the Instant Replay. Instant Replay is only a tool in this case. I believe that it is a great tool and that it has added a new dimension to how sports are viewed.

I now believe that Instant Replay revolutionized sports by making it possible for viewers to see clasps of how a play was made. I didn't realize this until I was made aware of it by friends.

# J

## The Jacuzzi®

Debut: 1968
Inventive American: Roy Jacuzzi

The whirlpool bath existed prior to Roy Jacuzzi's invention of the Jacuzzi, but Roy was the first to design and build tubs with the whirlpool jets built into the side of the tub. Today, "Jacuzzi" is a patented trademark, but it has also come to be used as a generic term for any whirlpool bath (much to the presumed annoyance of the Jacuzzi company).

Roy Jacuzzi was an Italian immigrant who, with his brother, also invented the monoplane used by the U.S. Postal Service, and developed advanced agricultural pumps. Their most famous invention, however, remains the Jacuzzi Whirlpool Bath.

## Jazz

Debut: early 20th Century
Inventive Americans: Too many to name

There is a hilarious scene in the movie *Jerry Maguire* in which Renee Zellweger's male nanny ("I prefer 'child technician,'" he pompously proclaims) gives Tom Cruise a cassette of Miles Davis and John Coltrane performing live and then opines to them of jazz as something almost akin to a supernatural art form. During a romantic bedroom interlude later, Cruise and Zellweger do listen to the tape but, after a few minutes, Cruise blurts out, "What *is* this music!?"

This is the problem with jazz, a uniquely American musical art form—you either love it, hate it, or you simply don't get it. I actually fall into all three categories. Some of it—like Dave Brubeck and the big band stuff officially considered jazz—I love. The noisy, free-form, dissonant musical wanderings, I hate. And the weird, abstract, yet relatively melodic stuff, I just don't get. Or at least I don't understand it as music as I have come to know and play and listen to. (A perfect example of "I don't get this" music is Anton Webern's "Variations Op. 27," which would probably be considered classical, but it'll do as an example. It seems to consist of nothing but random high notes hit at will, with no sense of melody, rhythm, or form. Like I say, I just don't get it.)

Jazz is the abstract art of music. Oftentimes free-form and meandering, it requires complete immersion in the music and attention to the sounds of the individual instruments to fully appreciate it. The spare structure of some pieces of pure jazz can be difficult for many people to enjoy, especially those raised on music with a deliberate organization.

Jazz is a musical feast, and its recipe includes African-American gospel spirituals, blues, ragtime, and other musical forms popularized and remade by American musicians. The earliest pioneers of jazz were the New Orleans Dixieland musicians who taught themselves to play, but who could not read or write music. They would turn beloved old favorites like "When the Saints Come Marching In" and "The Battle Hymn of the Republic" into rollicking, free-form musical epics.

From there, the musical form evolved in the hands of innovators like Louis Armstrong, Benny Goodman, Paul Whiteman, Bix Beiderbecke, Count Basie, and Duke Ellington, and soon was assimilated into other forms, including bop, hard bop, swing, boogie-woogie, and experimental. Jazz also influenced the development of rock, and was yet again modified, as in the jazz-rock songs of Steely Dan and the big-band influenced works of horn groups like Chicago.

Love it or hate it, jazz is eternal, and an authentic American First.

# Jell-O®

Debut: 1845 (Cooper); 1897 (Wait)
Inventive Americans: Peter Cooper; Pearl and May Wait

The FDA does not classify Jell-O as a meat product, yet some strict vegetarians will not eat it.

Why? Because Jell-O is flavored gelatin, which is made from the processed hides, bones, and skins of animals. The "renderings," as they are called, are boiled and filtered, then boiled and filtered again, and then purified and reduced yet again, until it becomes a substance called collagen, which is then used to produce Jell-O by adding flavorings, sugar, etc.

Gelatin was first produced in 1845 by Peter Cooper (the inventor of the Tom Thumb engine), who figured out how to extract the collagen from animal parts. He then obtained a patent for the process and for the first gelatin dessert. Sales were less than spectacular. Fifty years later, Pearl Wait, a cough syrup manufacturer and carpenter from LeRoy, New York, developed a fruit-flavored version of Cooper's gelatin dessert, and his wife May christened it Jell-O. The four original Jell-O flavors were strawberry, orange, lemon, and raspberry.

A few years later, Wait sold his Jell-O business to his neighbor Frank Woodward for $450. Woodward began advertising the product, boosted production and distribution, and now 300 million boxes of Jell-O are sold in the United States every year.

Little-known Jell-O Facts:

✪ The first Jell-O print ad appeared in 1902 in *Ladies' Home Journal*. This was the first time Jell-O was pitched as "America's Most Famous Dessert."

✪ Immigrants to America were given Jell-O as soon as they stepped off the boat at Ellis Island as a "Welcome to America" gift.

✪ In 1942, cola-flavored Jell-O was introduced. It lasted a year. (Cola Jell-O sounds good...wonder why it tanked. I'll bet Coca-Cola Jell-O would be successful today.)

✪ In the 1950s, Jell-O introduced several new flavors, including apple, grape, black cherry, and black raspberry.

(Today's flavors include watermelon, berry blue, grape, berry black, cranberry, cranberry-raspberry, and cran-berry-strawberry.)

✪ In 1991, the Smithsonian Institute held a conference on Jell-O history, featuring topics such as "The Dialectics of Jell-O in Peasant Culture," "The Semiotics of Jell-O," and "Jell-O Salad or Just Desserts: The Poetics of an American Food."

✪ In 1996, Jell-O was eaten on Russia's Mir Space Station.

✪ There is a Jell-O museum in LeRoy, New York.

✪ Jell-O is the official state snack of Utah.

# The Jukebox

Debut: 1889 (as the Nickel-in-the-Slot machine)
Inventive Americans: Louis Glass and William S. Arnold

The jukebox is an American First that has an interesting history, much of which revolves around money.

The first jukebox was invented by Louis Glass in 1889. He placed a machine in a saloon in San Francisco that played one song, and one song only, for a nickel. Glass changed the selection on almost a daily basis and profited quite nicely (and repeatedly) from a single recording.

In the 1930s, the multi-selection jukebox came into play, but they were known as Coin-Operated Phonographs. No one is completely certain who first coined the term "jukebox," but it is known that it was derived from the slang term "jook house," which black field-workers of the time called the house where they would all gather to dance and drink. There is also historical evidence that brothels of the time were similarly known as "jook houses."

One of the largest manufacturers of early jukeboxes was the Wurlitzer Company, which had been founded by Farney Wurlitzer.

Farney banned the use of the term "jukebox" because he felt it was racist and insulting. For four decades, Wurlitzer referred to their machines as "automatic phonographs." In 1972, the word "jukebox" was used for the first time in a Wurlitzer advertisement. Why the change? Farney died.

Early jukeboxes played 78s and 45s; the newer ones (from 1987 on) play CDs. Collectors estimate that approximately two million jukeboxes were manufactured during their heyday and there is a thriving culture of jukebox collectors. Prices for used jukeboxes range from $100 to $30,000.

You may be wondering if those little jukeboxes on the wall of booths in diners are considered actual jukeboxes. The answer is no, they are not. Those machines are nothing more than selection machines that are hooked to the main jukebox. They are called "wallboxes" or "remote selectors." Interestingly, they are one of the most profitable of the music selection machines in the jukebox family. Why? Because the jukebox can only play one selection at a time, therefore, it is quite possible that 10 different customers can pay for the same song, a song that is then only played once. (The machine ignores multiple selections of a song, but the customers still pay for "their" selection.) The most cunning aspect of the wallbox system is that as soon as the song is played, everyone who paid for it thinks it is their selection. So the jukebox collects 10 times for one play. Brilliant, eh?

Maybe some people have figured this out and that's why so many are carrying portable CD players and wearing headphones in restaurants and elsewhere these days.

# Junior High School

Debut: 1909
Inventive Americans: The Indianola, Ohio
Board of Education

America was the first country to split the pre-college education system into three parts: grammar school, which is grades kindergarten through sixth; junior high school, which is grades seventh and eighth; and high school, which is grades ninth through 12th.

This system was structured so as to put a two- or three-grade learning zone between the elemental subjects studied in grammar school and the more advanced pre-college subjects studied in high school. (Not all school systems adhere to this system and, in many jurisdictions, grammar schools run through the eighth grade, followed immediately by admission to a four-grade high school.)

The first junior high in America was the Indianola Junior High School in Indianola, Ohio, which opened in 1909.

# K

## Kevlar®

Debut: 1965
Inventive American: Stephanie Kwolek (for DuPont)

The American Firsts detailed in this book are listed alphabetically, yet if they were listed in order of importance and value to society, it is likely that Kevlar would be very close to the top of the ranking.

Kevlar stops bullets.

Kevlar is an aramid polymer fiber that is five times stronger than steel, and it is used in many items other than bulletproof vests, including trampolines, tennis rackets, gloves, hoses, tires, and helmets. Chemist Stephanie Kwolek discovered it accidentally one day in 1965 when she was mixing polymers in a DuPont lab, looking for new synthetic polymers.

A Kevlar vest, first sold in 1975, weighs only 2.5 pounds, but can stop a .38 caliber bullet fired point-blank from ten feet away. Kevlar vests are standard issue for law enforcement personnel and people in high-risk professions and situations. Hillary Clinton wrote in her 2003 book, *Living History,* that she only fully realized that she was a target when the Secret Service one day insisted she put on a bulletproof vest for a public appearance. Thankfully, she did not need it. But thanks to Stephanie Kwolek, it was there if she did.

# Kitty Litter®

Debut: 1947
Inventive American: Edward Lowe

I have had cats in my world my entire life and, except for a few years when I was a kid and we had a couple of outdoor kitties, they have all been indoor cats.

This means that I have an intimate relationship with cat litter and I must thank Edward Lowe for making that possible.

What did people use before the introduction of absorbent, clay cat litter? Sand, ashes, and newspaper.

Lowe went to work for his father's company after retiring from the Navy in 1945. The company sold industrial absorbents and one of the products they carried was a clay called Fuller's Earth. When one of his neighbors asked for some sand for her cat's litter box (she was one of those using ashes and she simply could not take sooty paw prints all over the house anymore), Lowe gave her a bag of Fuller's Earth clay pellets instead.

She loved it, the lightbulb over Lowe's head went off, and Kitty Litter was born. Lowe experienced resistance from merchants, however, because sand was free and Kitty Litter was 65 cents per bag. Once people tried it, though, the demand quickly quieted the faultfinders. Now, Edward Lowe's company sells more than $200 million of Kitty Litter a year. We cat lovers thank Mr. Lowe every time we change the litter box. (Ashes?!)

# Kool-Aid®

Debut: 1927
Inventive American: Edwin Perkins

General Foods, the owners and manufacturers of Kool-Aid, want you to know that Jim Jones's People's Temple followers did not commit suicide by drinking cyanide-laced grape-flavored Kool-Aid. From the Kool-Aid FAQ: "It is a popular misconception that 900 followers of cult leader Jim Jones committed suicide by drinking Grape Kool-Aid laced with cyanide at their commune in Jonestown,

Guyana in the late 1970s. The followers of Jones actually drank cyanide-laced Flavor-Aid, a cheap imitation of Kool-Aid."

It's easy to understand their defensiveness: The last thing a company needs is to have their non-carbonated flavored drink associated in the minds of the public with mass suicide.

In the beginning, Kool-Aid was not a powdered drink. It was originally a liquid beverage sold in four-ounce bottles under the name "Fruit Smack." Later, it was renamed "Kool-Ade," then "Kool-Aid," and reformulated as a powdered drink that the consumer mixed with water. Interestingly, the original name, "Kool-Ade," is closer to what the actual product is—a sweetened beverage (the "ade" part)—than "Kool-Aid," which suggests that drinking it will help the drinker...be "kool," I guess?

The seven original Kool-Aid flavors were: cherry, grape, lemon-lime, orange, raspberry, root beer, and strawberry.

# L

## The Lever Voting Machine

Debut: 1892
Inventive American: Jacob Myers

Jacob Myers was a maker of safes in New York who one day realized that counting paper ballots simply took too long for an efficient democracy.

Myers invented the lever voting machine, which assigned a single lever to each candidate or ballot choice. In 1896, he started the United States Voting Machine Company in Jamestown, New York. By 1930, lever voting machines had been installed in almost every major city in America and, by 1960, approximately half of all Americans voted using lever machines.

These machines, which were no longer manufactured after 1982, were a vast improvement over paper ballots, but they too had their drawbacks. One of the biggest problems with the lever voting machine is the fact that there is no paper trail of votes in case there is the need for a recount.

When you enter the lever voting machine booth and the poll tender pulls the curtain shut behind you, the machine's levers are all set to the horizontal "ready" position. The voter pulls down the lever above the candidate or issue he or she is voting for, and each voter is only allowed a single vote for a row. Mechanical interlocks prevent the voter from multiple votes.

Once the voter is finished, he or she pulls the large red lever below the ballot rows and the vote is officially registered in the machine and the curtain opens. (Then the nice lady with the red, white, and blue scarf slaps an "I Voted Today!" sticker on you before you leave the firehouse or grammar school.)

Today, almost 20 percent of American voters still use lever voting machines, although as the old lever machines break down, they are often replaced by computer voting systems, touch-screen, or optical scanner systems because new machines are no longer being manufactured.

We should mention one of the other voting systems still in use today—the punch-card. With this system, the voter is handed a cardboard card which he or she then punches holes in with a stylus for the candidate or issue. The little piece of cardboard that pops out of the hole is called a "chad."

This system holds the greatest potential for human error, as the 2000 presidential election debacle proved. That election introduced the term "hanging chad" into the American idiom, a phrase describing the problem of a chad not being completely separated from the card. That's how human error became part of the equation: People did not punch the card hard enough with their stylus and the chad did not fully detach. The sight of rows of vote counters laboriously holding ballot cards up to the light to see if the chads were completely detached after the 2000 election made America a laughingstock in the eyes of the world. As you know, the Supreme Court had to step in and declare George W. Bush the winner. Many Democrats and Gore partisans still do not believe that Bush was lawfully elected, but because a Supreme Court ruling becomes de facto (the law), their argument is moot.

With computer technology so inexpensive and so prevalent, it is my opinion (and the opinion of many others) that a fail-safe, secure touchscreen voting system should be installed in every polling place in America. (As well as on the Internet.)

# Life Savers®

Debut: 1912
Inventive American: Clarence Crane

The first Life Savers flavor was peppermint, although Clarence Crane went with the "Pep-O-Mint" spelling that is now a trademark and is still used today.

Crane was a chocolatier and he always had a problem during the summer months. Everything melted. Air-conditioning had been invented (See page 20), but it was still used mainly in department stores and movie theaters.

So Crane came up with the idea of a sugar-based solid candy that did not use chocolate, and the Life Saver was born. None of his equipment was useable for the idea of a round peppermint candy, though, so he bought a pill-making machine and used it for his combination of sugar and flavorings. He punched a small hole in the middle of each candy and came up with the name "Life Savers" because...well, because they looked like nautical life savers.

Crane sold his Life Savers patent to Edward Noble in 1913 for $2,900.

Today, Life Savers are available in 24 flavors, as well as "specialty" flavors like Fusions, Creme Savers, and Kickerz. My favorites are Wint-O-Green and Wild Cherry, but I loathe Butter Rum.

Life Savers facts:

- There are 14 Life Savers in every roll.
- The original Five Flavor roll consists of orange, pineapple, cherry, lemon, and lime, but this is soon to be changed. An Internet vote was held, and the new Five Flavor assortment will reflect the wishes of the consumer.
- The Tropical Fruits Five Flavor roll consists of fruit punch, pina colada, mango melon, tangerine, and banana.
- The top-selling Life Savers flavors in order of preference are Five Flavor, Wint-O-Green, Pep-O-Mint, and Butter Rum.

- ✪ Three million rolls of Life Savers, using 250,000 pounds of sugar, are made every day.
- ✪ Every Halloween, 88 million "mini" rolls of Life Savers are given out to trick-or-treaters.
- ✪ The shortest runs for a single flavor roll were the Pineapple roll (1936–1939) and the Watermelon roll (1992–1995). The longest run is the Wild Cherry roll, which debuted in 1934.

# Liquid Paper®

Debut: 1951
Inventive American: Bette Nesmith Graham

Most people would probably assume that word processors have taken a big bite out of the Liquid Paper business. When typewriters ruled the world, a bottle of the white correction paint was on every desk. Today, though, with instant onscreen corrections and spellchecking in all word processing applications, by the time a page is printed, it's perfect, right? Wrong.

The Liquid Paper business is as healthy as ever and constantly growing.

But what about computers? Why do we need Liquid Paper when we can fix everything before it's printed?

Because we *don't* fix everything before it's printed.

Here's a typical workday scenario: You're printing out a 50-page report at work and you notice that a sentence on page 35 has two periods. For some reason the spellchecker didn't pick this up. What do you do? You can correct it in the original document and then print out a new page 35, but the printer station is at the opposite end of the floor from where your office is located. It also happens to be 4:45 and you have to pick up your kid across town at day care at 5:30, and the report has to be on your boss's desk before you leave for the day.

Well, what about Liquid Paper? You can dab a drop of white on the period and, voilà, the offending punctuation mark is gone. But you hesitate. This solution means that page 35 will have a glob of white at the end of a sentence, and it will stick out like a sore thumb. You just know your boss will frown and you want the pages to be perfect.

The solution to the problem *does* use Liquid Paper, but office workers have come up with a two-part solution: first, white-out the mistake with Liquid Paper, and then *photocopy the page*. The Liquid Paper will show up as plain, flat white on the photocopy and no one will be the wiser. And you won't have to pay extra because you're late picking up Susie at day care.

This scenario is why Liquid Paper still sells.

In 1951, Bette Nesmith Graham was an executive secretary when she first developed a white paint-based liquid for correcting typed mistakes. Her coworkers began clamoring for it, and she started selling bottles of the fluid under the name Mistake Out. For many years she manufactured the product in her kitchen, ably assisted by her son Michael, who would later become famous as a member of The Monkees. In 1968, Bette changed the name of her company to Liquid Paper and moved into an 11,000-square-foot production facility.

By 1975, Bette's company was selling 25 million bottles a year and exporting the product to 31 countries.

Gillette bought the company in 1979 and now produces the entire Liquid Paper line in St. Paul, Minnesota.

Today, Liquid Paper is available in three popular forms: bottle and brush, correction film, and correction pen, and is the number one correction product.

# Liquid Soap

Debut: August 22, 1865 (Shepphard); 1980 (Minnetonka)
Inventive Americans: William Shepphard; Minnetonka Corp.

Today, many manufacturers offer liquid soap, and it comes in a wide variety of scents and formulas. There are herbal liquid soaps and aloe-laced liquid soaps. Strawberry and apple, too.

The first liquid soap was patented in 1865 by William Sheppard, but it was the Minnetonka Corporation that introduced the modern version of liquid soap to the world in 1980. And they immediately created a monopoly, too.

How?

Liquid soap comes in a jar with a hand pump. Without the pump, you really cannot use the soap, unless you pour some out, which is guaranteed to create a bigger mess than might be imagined. Many people would be tempted to live with their dirty hands.

In 1980, Minnetonka cornered the market by buying up every single plastic pump available. By the time other manufacturers tried to get into the game, Minnetonka's brand owned the field. Seven years later, Minnetonka sold their liquid soap business to the Colgate-Palmolive Company and they renamed it Softsoap, which is still sold today, although now, it has some competition.

# The Long-Lasting Incandescent Lightbulb

Debut: 1879
Inventive American: Thomas Edison

Comedian Chris Rock does a hilarious routine about American children's lack of appreciation for their daddies. He notes that kids are always taught to thank their mommas for everything, but that no one ever thanks daddy for "knocking out the rent" and for the other creature comforts that make their lives better. No one ever says, he raves, "sure is easy to read with all this light!"

Well, the person all Americans should *actually* thank for their lights is the seminal American inventor Thomas Edison.

A word of clarification is necessary here, though. Thomas Edison did not actually invent the lightbulb. A Canadian named Henry Woodward first patented a lightbulb in 1875. At the time, Edison was working on an identical invention, and because Woodward and his colleagues could not raise the money to commercially market their idea, Edison bought their patent and then set to work modifying it and creating the world's first long-lasting incandescent light bulb. In his design, he used an electrical current to heat a filament inside a glass bulb to incandescence. He successfully demonstrated it in 1879, and it immediately became an integral part of modern society. The bulb was born, and since then, enormous improvements and variations have been made to the simple glass globe, resulting in a wide array of brightnesses (watts), hours, and styles. Colored incandescent bulbs are now available, too, which makes decorating for Christmas a little easier.

# M

## The Mailbox

Debut: October 27, 1891
Inventive American: Philip B. Downing

Many inventions have come into being as a response to man's oftentimes larcenous behavior. The street mailbox is one of them.

African-American inventor Philip Downing's invention debuted in the late 19th century and was developed to protect the mail and to make the mailman's job easier.

The mail was critically important in the 1890s. There were no other means of reliable communication available to people and businesses other than the mail and personal contact. People sent everything through the mail, including legal documents, money, and other valuables. The first mailboxes, however, were (incredibly) open to the public. Once someone dropped in a letter or a parcel, anyone could walk up to the box and remove it. Also, rain and snow could get into the boxes, so the mail that wasn't stolen was often soaked by the elements.

Downing came up with a public dropbox that had two doors, an exterior door accessible to the public, and an interior safety door that could not be opened until the exterior door was closed. People pulled the outside door up and placed a letter on a platform inside. As soon as the door was closed, the interior safety door would swing open, dropping the letter into the body of the mailbox. There was no way of getting at the mail once it fell into the box. The mailman was the only one who could open the bottom of the box and retrieve the mail.

The design of today's street mailboxes is very similar to Downing's original invention, and it is impossible to reach inside the box. The mail is safe and it stays dry thanks to the innovative creativity of one American inventor.

# The Microprocessor

Debut: 1969 or 1971?
Inventive Americans: Marcian "Ted" Hoff,
Federico Faggin, and Stan Mazor? Or Raymond Holt?

Did three engineers working together at Intel develop the first microprocessor? According to Intel, the answer to that question is an unequivocal yes.

According to Intel, in 1971, Marcian "Ted" Hoff, Federico Faggin, and Stan Mazor put the elements of a refrigerator-sized computer onto a single silicon chip, thereby ushering in the beginning of the digital revolution. Again, the year was 1971.

But Raymond Holt begs to differ.

Holt claims that he (and a team of 25 engineers) developed the microprocessor in 1969 as part of a classified project for the United States Navy. The chip was used in the F-14A Tomcat fighter jet; thus, its development was kept secret for national security.

Intel never patented their microprocessor chip because they did not consider it an actual invention. Hoff, Faggin, and Mazor's work drew from the transistor and the silicon chip. Intel believed that the microprocessor was a collaborative, logical, inevitable, "next step" development in technology, not only a result of the three men's work, but also as a collaboration of existing technologies and new thinking.

Intel and Holt can argue until doomsday about this, and each side has points that can be made in their favor, but none of it really matters in the big picture of technological advancement.

The microprocessor *was* created, it *did* change the world, and it is now used in everything from hearing aids and toasters to computers and automobiles. Most importantly, for purposes of this book, it was, unquestionably, an American First.

Whomever history ultimately deems as the creator of the microprocessor, we must simply delight in the fact that it was created and the world is a much better place because of it.

# The Microwave Oven

Debut: 1946
Inventive American: Dr. Percy LeBaron Spencer
(for the Raytheon Corporation)

How did we survive without microwave ovens? This most useful of kitchen appliances had its genesis as a spin-off of World War II research on radar.

Dr. Spencer, who was working with magnetrons while performing his radar research for Raytheon, noticed that a candy bar he had been carrying in his pocket had melted.

Spencer eventually figured out that he had been blasted with microwaves while performing his experiments, and that those microwaves had "cooked" the candy bar.

This led to experiments using microwaves on food substances and in 1954, Raytheon released the first microwave oven for consumer use, the 1161 RadarRange.

Today, microwaves are as ubiquitous in the modern kitchen as the standard electric or gas stove.

# Monopoly®

Debut: 1936
Inventive American: Charles Darrow

Rituals have arisen surrounding the game of Monopoly. Some people will only play if they are the thimble, or the top hat. Some will only target certain properties to purchase. Some will take a drink every time they pay rent. And then there's naked Monopoly...but we won't go there.

Monopoly is the world's best-selling board game. Yes, in this age of computer and video games and astonishingly high-tech handheld games, the defiantly low-tech Monopoly is still the king.

Who invented the game of Monopoly? History accepts Charles Darrow as the inventor because he was the one who went to Parker Brothers with the idea, he was the one from whom they bought the rights, and he was the one who became a millionaire from Monopoly royalties.

However, there is compelling evidence that Darrow was taught the game by a woman who had been playing something she had invented, called The Landlord's Game, for years. The Landlord's Game was very similar to today's Monopoly except that the goal was not to acquire property, but rather to denigrate property ownership and landlords.

The story told by those in the Darrow camp is that Darrow came up with the idea for Monopoly when he was unemployed during the Great Depression. He nostalgically sketched out the streets of his childhood hometown of Atlantic City, New Jersey, and eventually developed the idea of buying and selling property as the "play" of the game. Supposedly, his friends and neighbors loved the game and would spend evenings playing it at the Darrow home. Darrow began making copies of the game board and rules and selling them for four dollars apiece. He also began offering it to stores in Philadelphia.

The game's burgeoning popularity spurred Darrow to offer it to Parker Brothers, who turned it down because it took too long to play and because they said it was too complicated. Darrow was not discouraged, though, and continued to market the game on his own.

How did it eventually end up a Parker Brothers game after Parker Brothers rejected it? A friend of one of George Parker's daughters bought one of Darrow's games and recommended it to Parker's daughter Sally. This time, Parker Brothers sought out Darrow and bought the rights to the game.

This story is the "official" version. There have been several lawsuits, however, regarding the true genesis of the game, and Parker Brothers has paid out cash settlements to people who have shown that Darrow likely did not create Monopoly on his own.

All this aside, though, the world's most popular board game is still unquestionably an American First. Do not pass Go.

# The MoonPie®

Debut: 1917
Inventive American: Earl Mitchell, Sr.

The MoonPie was originally invented to feed coal miners.

The story of its genesis was told by Earl Mitchell, Jr., the son of the original creator, to Ronald Dickinson, author of *The Great American MoonPie Handbook*.

Earl Mitchell, Sr. was a salesman for the Chattanooga Bakery, a subsidiary of the Mountain City Flour Mill in Chattanooga, Tennessee. The Chattanooga Bakery sold over 200 baked items to stores in Kentucky, West Virginia, and Tennessee. One day, while Earl Sr. was visiting a coal mine's company store in one of the states he serviced, he got to talking to some of the miners and asked them what they would enjoy as a tasty snack. The miners told him that they would like something sweet for their lunch pails, and that it had to be filling. One of the miners told Earl that it should be as big as the full moon that was rising above the mines.

Back at the bakery, Earl had a brainstorm. He knew that the workers in the plant liked to cover graham crackers with marshmallow spread and allow the topping to harden. Earl put another graham cracker on top of the marshmallows, covered the whole thing in chocolate, and the MoonPie was born.

It was instantly popular and, by the 1950s, the Chattanooga Bakery abandoned making anything but MoonPies, such was the demand.

# Morse Code

Debut: 1838
Inventive American: Samuel Finley Breese Morse

Early models of the telegraph used a burdensome number of wires to transmit signals. Samuel Morse designed and built a single-wire telegraph that was introduced in 1837, and then worked (with his assistant Arthur Vail) on a system of dots and dashes, with each pattern representing a number of the alphabet and the 10 numeric digits. Morse code was officially unveiled in 1838 at an exhibition in New York where Morse sent 10  words a minute over his improved telegraph using his new code.

Five years later, in 1843, Morse finally (he had applied for the money in 1837) finagled $30,000 out of Congress to run a telegraph wire from Baltimore to Washington, D.C. On May 11, 1844, Morse sent the first Morse code message between two cities. He sent the message *What hath God wrought?* from Washington to a train depot in Baltimore. (*What hath god wrought?* in Morse code is: — .... .—/ .... .—.... / —. — -.. / .-- .-. — ..- —. ....—..—.. The message had been decided on by the daughter of Morse's friend, the Commissioner of Patents. She was granted this honor because she was the one who told him he had been awarded the money.)

Soon after, Morse was asked to move his contraption to the Supreme Court room of the Capitol so congressmen and other government officials could watch him talk over a wire.

This was part of the exchange between Morse in Washington and his assistant Vail in Baltimore:

MORSE: Have you any news?
VAIL: No.
MORSE: Mr. Seaton's respects to you.
VAIL: My respects to him.
MORSE: What is your time?

VAIL: Nine o'clock, twenty-eight minutes.

MORSE: What weather have you?

VAIL: Cloudy.

MORSE: Separate your words more.

VAIL: Buchanan stock said to be rising.

MORSE: I have a great crowd here.

VAIL: Van Buren cannon in front, with foxtail on it.

People were convinced.

Within 10 years of Morse's public demonstration in the Supreme Court, 23,000 miles of wire crisscrossed America, often following train routes.

In 1851, as America was becoming increasingly "wired," as is the American way, a company sprang up to effectively use (and profit from, of course) this new mode of communication. The company was Western Union.

By 1868, transatlantic messages were being sent using the telegraph and Morse code.

Four years later, Samuel Morse died of complications from pneumonia at the age of 81. Although he is best known for his contributions to communications technology, many are not aware that he was also a highly regarded portrait painter who painted subjects like Lafayette and other icons of his times, as well as the House of Representatives in Washington (which he couldn't sell) and an elaborate study of the Louvre, with copies of many of the art museum's most famous works.

(By the way, Samuel Morse's father was an acclaimed geographer who, in 1796, published *The American Gazetteer*, the first comprehensive geography of North America. It boasted seven large foldout maps and seven thousand articles. Perhaps this helps us understand young Samuel's fascination in communicating with "other places.")

# The Motion Picture

Debut: 1891
Inventive American: Thomas Edison

America not only invented the motion picture, America also invented Hollywood. Hollywood is more than a place. Like New York, Hollywood is also a state of mind, a place of dollars and dreams, contracts and craftsmanship, brilliance and bombs, and artifice and art.

If it were not for this American invention and perfection of the motion picture, we would never have experienced any of the following[8]:

- Joe Pesci's "I amuse you?" scene (much of which was supposedly improvised) in *GoodFellas*.
- Robert De Niro's "You talkin' to me?" scene in *Taxi Driver*.
- Shirley MacLaine's "Give my daughter the shot!" scene in *Terms of Endearment*.
- The "I Should Have Known Better" sequence in *A Hard Day's Night*.
- The "I'm walkin' here!" scene in *Midnight Cowboy*.
- The airport scene in *Casablanca*.
- The eerie opening montage of *Citizen Kane*.
- The resurrection scene in *E.T. The Extra-Terrestrial*.
- The "Twist and Shout" scene in *Ferris Bueller's Day Off*.
- The opening half hour of *Saving Private Ryan*.

In 1891, Thomas Edison successfully demonstrated the kinetoscope, the earliest movie system, and in 1893, he opened a studio to create short films using his invention.

The subsequent growth of both the movie technology and the movie industry was explosive, and, today, the movie business is a multi-billion dollar, worldwide endeavor led (by a very long lead) by the United States.

# The MRI
# (Magnetic Resonance Imaging)

Debut: 1970
Inventive American: Raymond Damadian

Have you ever had an MRI? I've had two: one for my back and one for my neck. When they slid me out after the first one, the technician asked me if I was all right. "I'm fine," I replied. "I'm just deaf."

You show up for your appointment, you sit down, and while you're waiting, you flip through *People* and *TIME*, and half-watch CNN on the TV up in the corner of the waiting room.

When you're called in, a nurse tells you to get undressed and put on paper pants, a paper top, and paper slippers. You place everything in a locker (yes, your wallet and valuables remain in the locker), close and lock the door, and take the key. Inside the MRI room, they place the key on a hook or a chair where you can see it.

The MRI tech then tells you what's going to happen and asks if you have any questions. For my second MRI, I was told that two-thirds of the way through I would have to receive a contrast dye injection for clearer images of the disks in my neck. I was told that the possible side effects of the dye were a blinding headache and nausea, neither of which I had scheduled into my day when I got up that morning.

So I asked him when would I know if I would have a negative reaction to the dye. "Oh, within seconds," he replied. "So if I sit there a minute and I'm all right, I won't get the headache or nausea?" I clarified. "You got it. If we end up sliding you back in, you've passed the 'side effect' hurdle," he said.

Thankfully, I did not get sick. The first time I had an MRI, I was not offered earplugs or headphones. How loud was it? Imagine a jackhammer being used a foot from your head. That's how loud it was. The second time I was given earplugs and it made a slight difference. My ears were still ringing as I walked to the parking lot.

Some people never make it all the way through the 30- to 45-minute MRI test. I know one man who began shouting "Stop! Stop! Get me out!" the moment his head entered the tube. Claustrophobes have a real problem with MRIs, and this led to the invention of the open MRI, which does not require being slid into a tube smaller than a coffin, where the ceiling is three inches from your face.

Its scary unpleasantness aside, though, the development of the MRI was a major medical breakthrough. The MRI is a non-invasive, painless test that produces detailed electronic images of human tissue, organs, and cells using a nuclear magnetic resonance spectrometer.

The principles behind MRI scanning were discovered in 1970 by Dr. Raymond Damadian, who now heads Fonar, a company that specializes in the design and manufacturing of advanced MRI equipment. Their latest breakthrough is the "Open Sky" MRI which is, essentially, an entire MRI room, with the magnets above and below the patient. The patient is never confined, and the walls of the room can have tranquil murals designed to calm the anxious.

MRIs are more expensive than traditional x-rays and other diagnostic tests, but their benefits far outweigh the costs, which is why they are so widely used today.

# N

## The National Parks System

Debut: 1832
Inventive American: George Catlin

The National Parks Service is consistently rated as one of the most popular U.S. federal agencies. We Americans love our National Parks—we visit them in droves, and we are passionate about maintaining them as natural sanctuaries.

In 1832, artist George Catlin, while traveling through the Dakotas, started thinking about the impact of America's relentless westward expansion and came up with the idea of a program designed to protect wildlife and natural "scenery of supreme and distinctive quality or some natural feature so extraordinary or unique as to be of national interest and importance."[9]

In 1864, Congress donated Yosemite Valley to California for preservation as a state park. In 1872, Congress decreed the Yellowstone area in northwest Wyoming and southeastern Montana to be the first official National Park.

By 1999, the National Parks System was comprised of 379 areas in every state and U.S possession, including—in addition to wildlife areas—official historic sites such as battlefields, forts, and war memorials.

America led by example when we created the world's first national parks system, and now they exist in many countries all around the world.

# Norplant® Implantable Contraceptive

Debut: 1991
Inventive Americans: Wyeth-Ayerst

The implantable contraceptive was as important a development in birth control as was the birth control pill.

For the first time, a woman could decide to be infertile for a specific period of time—five full years—and she did not have to worry about tending to a daily pill-taking regimen. The birth control pill gave women the ultimate decision regarding being pregnant—or not. The implantable contraceptive not only continued to allow them that power, it removed the the need to make that decision on a daily basis.

Norplant implants are six plastic capsules, each about the size of a matchstick, that are inserted beneath the skin of a woman's arm and left there for up to five years. The implants trickle a very small amount of the hormone progestin into the bloodstream and can prevent pregnancy for 60 monthly cycles. They can be removed at any time.

Approximately 1 in 1,000 women will experience an accidental pregnancy while using the Norplant contraceptive implants.

Insertion is done under local anesthetic and takes 10 to 15 minutes. A small incision is made in the upper arm. Removal is likewise done under local anesthetic, but can take up to 45 minutes or longer and may require two visits. Removals are more difficult when the rods have become deeply embedded over time.

Immediately after removal, a fresh set of implants can be inserted, providing another five years of contraception.

The side effects of Norplant include irregular periods, depression, nervousness or anxiety, nausea and vomiting, dizziness, hair loss or excessive hair growth, weight gain, acne, breast sensitivity, and high blood pressure. Many side effects cease after six months of use.

Norplant implants are now being administered to women in Third World countries where the birth rate needs to be reduced on a consistent basis.

# Novocaine®

Debut: 1905, 1907 (USA)
Inventive American: Alfred Einhorn

We are bending the rules here a little and including Novocaine, which was originally synthesized by German chemist Alfred Einhorn in 1905 (as a replacement for cocaine, which was then widely used for anesthesia), but only became the world's most popular dental anesthetic after it was introduced in the U.S. in 1907. The monumental impact Novocaine had on the world's dental patients came about *after* it became the standard dental anesthetic in America.

That said, here is a scene from the world's pre-Novocaine days:

You are a clothing merchant living in England in the 17th century. As we learned in the section on deodorant, it is an unavoidable fact that you stink. But everyone does, so it doesn't really matter. But in addition to your body being vile, you also have a repulsive, rancid mouth, with a dozen, maybe eighteen or so remaining teeth in varying stages of decay. Since adulthood, your routine has been the same. You eat and drink, and you never brush your teeth or clean your mouth—with the occasional exception of rinsing your mouth out with a little salt water, more or less just for the hell of it, and perhaps for the short-lived tingly clean sensation the water provides. But for some reason, it never occurs to you (or anyone else of the time, for that matter) to do this on a regular basis.

Every year or so (sometimes longer if you're lucky), one of your teeth begins to hurt. You put up with the pain and the sensitivity to hot and cold for as long as you can, but then one day you bite down on a piece of apple, or a walnut, or a hard crust of bread, and the excruciating pain literally makes your eyes water. When this happens, you know it is time to see Eric, the barber/surgeon. Eric performs bloodletting (usually with leeches), wound surgery, boil lancing, and tooth extraction. You have often seen him hanging bloody bandages on the pole outside his shop. Sometimes, the wind wraps them around the pole, creating a red and white striped effect. (You don't know it now, but those bandages would ultimately inspire the red and white barber poles of later centuries.)

You always put off seeing Eric because you know that all he will be able to do is grab the black iron pliers that hang on a hook above his barber chair and, after you reluctantly sit down and open your mouth, reach in and yank the rotten tooth out of your jaw.

You have seen men faint from the pain of having a tooth ripped out in this manner, and you can understand why some are willing to put up with a constant toothache, rather than undergo "treatment" by Eric the barber. Women seem to handle the pain better than men, you have come to know over the years. This is not all that surprising when you consider the pain they must endure bringing a child into the world. After suffering through labor, the relatively quick pain of a tooth pull is apparently not all that vexing to the fairer sex.

At your clothing store the following morning, you look across the street into the front window of Eric's barber shop and you see that there is no one sitting in Eric's barber chair. You grab your scarf and coat, tell your clerk you will be back shortly, and you step out onto the sidewalk, your tongue spontaneously moving to the bad tooth. Steeling yourself, you cross the street (being sure to avoid stepping in the mounds of horse dung piled everywhere), and walk to Eric's shop.

As soon as you enter the shop, the rusted bell above the door making a sound that cannot even generously be described as a toll, your face gives away your pain.

As you remove your coat, Eric reaches for his pliers, and you are comforted to see him wipe it off with his apron. Granted, the apron is filthy and also covered in blood—but you are grateful for the gesture nonetheless.

Eric nods toward the chair, and you sit.

You lean your head back against the leather headrest and close your eyes.

"Brandy?" Eric asks.

You shake your head and you hear the sound of Eric dunking the pliers in a barrel of water and swishing it around. When he pulls it out, you hear the water dripping onto the floor. You open your eyes and you see him again wipe it on his bloody apron. You immediately close them again.

"Open up."

You open your mouth as wide as you can, and you can feel Eric's breath as he leans forward to peer inside.

"Your right, my left?"

You nod tightly and inhale deeply.

"All right, then."

Eric opens the jaws of the pliers and gently places it inside your mouth. Blazes of pain shoot through your head as the heavy metal pliers touch your bad tooth. It seems like it takes an eternity for Eric to get a solid grip on the tooth, but then, suddenly, he freezes. You can feel the pliers clamped onto the tooth, and you hold your breath.

"Got it. You ready?"

You grunt assent and then Eric squeezes the pliers, slightly rotates its jaws (you can feel the tooth moving in its socket, causing pain you did not know you were capable of feeling), and then with a grunt, he yanks with all his might.

You feel the roots of the tooth rip from the flesh of your jaw; you feel the nerves being savagely ravaged; you feel waves of pain rushing through your body, enough to make you nauseous. You gasp in agony as your heart races and the sweat pours off you in torrents. You open your eyes and see Eric standing above you, proudly examining the bloody rotten tooth still held in the tongs of the pliers, turning it this way and that.

"What a mess, sir. 'Tis no wonder you wished to be rid of it."

You catch your breath and move your tongue cautiously to the spot where your tooth had been. Each stab of the tip of your tongue brings a fresh wave of pain, but it is not the type of pain the decayed tooth had delivered. It was a soreness that you knew would fade.

"Brass."

"Yes, sir!" Eric responds as he puts the pliers and tooth down and bends to pick up a spittoon from beside the door. He carries it to you and holds it beneath your mouth. You spit, and the fresh blood mixes with the black tobacco juice, almost completely erasing the red.

"Port."

"Right away, sir!" Eric grabs a clay jug out of a small cabinet and hands it to you.

You take a swig, carefully slosh it around in your mouth, and again spit into the spittoon.

You take a second swig, but this one you swallow.

The pain is beginning to ease somewhat, and you relax into the chair as you take a second swallow.

After a minute or so, you feel well enough to leave, and you hand the jug back to Eric. You stand and reach into your pocket.

"How much?"

Eric places the jug back into the cabinet and shakes his head. "This one is gratis, sir." At your quizzical look, Eric says, "Ye sewed me pants a fortnight ago, sir, and ye didn't even charge me a farthing. Ye has me gratitude, and I am happy to be able to pay ye back, in this small way."

You nod in understanding, but reach further down into your pants pocket and pull out a pence anyway. You flip it to Eric, who catches it. Before he can protest, you say, "Buy the lad a bag of chestnuts."

Eric smiles and nods, and pockets the pence. You leave his shop and cross back over to your store. Upon your entrance, your clerk Bob looks expectantly at you, wondering if he should ask how you are.

"I'm fine, Bob. Shall we work on the display for the window, then?"

Bob smiles and nods and you both begin arranging clothes in the front window for passersby to gaze at. As you work, a headache forms from the ordeal you just underwent. It will be three days before it passes.

Novocaine (which is the trade name of the powder form of procaine) has never lost its popularity among both patients and doctors. New anesthetics have been introduced in the past few decades, but, tellingly, the majority of them have been compounded using procaine as their main ingredient.

# The Nuclear Power Plant

Debut: 1957
Inventive Americans: The Sodium Reactor Experiment in Santa Susana, California (a civilian unit); Shippingport, Pennsylvania—the first full-scale plant

Since the Three Mile Island accident in 1979, there has not been a single new nuclear power plant ordered for construction in the United States.[10]

Is this a good thing? Or is this a bad thing?

As with most controversial and complex questions, the answers depend on who you ask.

According to the Nuclear Energy Institute, America's appetite for computers and its increasing reliance on a digital economy is expected to increase demand for electricity up to 35 percent by 2010. Today, computers and peripherals account for 13 percent of all electricity use. This will rise to 25 percent by 2020.[11]

Electricity production costs vary widely depending on the source. Natural gas is the most expensive, at $.0352 per kilowatt hour, followed by oil at $.0324, then coal at $.0207, and, finally, nuclear at $.0183.

Nuclear power costs almost half what natural gas costs.

Yet, we are no longer building them because of fears of a meltdown. The September 11, 2001 terror attacks added to the reluctance to dot the landscape with more nuclear power plants after it was learned that there was evidence that terrorists had targeted America's nuclear plants for attack. The biggest fear is that terrorists will hijack a plane and crash it into a nuclear plant's containment dome, releasing deadly amounts of radiation into the atmosphere.

Nuclear power is neither feared nor avoided elsewhere in the world. Many countries, especially France and Japan, generate an enormous percentage of their domestic electricity by nuclear power.

In the early years of the 21st century, we are faced, then, with the irony of a monumentally important and influential American First—the nuclear power plant—no longer being embraced by U.S. power generators, as the rest of the world builds them as fast as their budgets allow.

# Nylon Stockings

Debut: 1939
Inventive Americans: DuPont (utilizing Dr. Wallace Carother's invention of the synthetic polymer, nylon)

Nylon stockings not only replaced silk stockings as the preferred woman's hosiery garment, the filmy legwear also created an enormous and ardent fetish subculture. For many men, nylons and garter belts are the ultimate turn-on. (Personally, I prefer women utility workers' tool belts. That's a joke. Maybe.)

Nylons are manufactured on sophisticated machines that are able to produce both seamed and seamless stockings. After their introduction in 1939, it took some time for the new garment to become widely accepted. Part of the reason was World War II. Nylon, like rubber, tin, gasoline, sugar, and other "war-useful" commodities became almost impossible to acquire, and what was available was strictly rationed. Thus, it took some time, but eventually nylon stockings became the less expensive alternative to silk.

As nylons became increasingly accepted and popular, a new social etiquette developed for women: It was soon considered a faux pas to have crooked seams. The seamless nylon eliminated that problem, but they did not have the classic look of an old-fashioned seamed stocking. (The seamed look has remained consistently popular; today, even one-piece panty hose is offered in "seamed" versions.)

In these days of inexpensive panty hose, do women still wear nylon stockings? Hell, yeah. In fact, nylons and garter belts are as popular as ever. (Many sites on the Internet offer a wide selection of garter belts in all styles and colors, which they say can be worn with or without panties.) There are also stockings available that stay up on the leg without a garter belt, thanks to an elasticized band at the top of each stocking.

Another fact worth noting: If it weren't for nylons and garter belts, Bettie Page probably would have never had a career.

# P

## The Package Saver Pedestal

Debut: 1983
Inventive American: Carmela Vitale

You drove carefully all the way home. You placed the pizza box flat on the floor of the passenger side and made slow turns. No quick stops, either. Nevertheless, when you get home, slit the paper tape holding the box closed, and flip open the top, half the mozzarella is stuck to the underside of the cover. You scrape it off and try to evenly distribute it onto the defiled slices, but it's not the same. Someone should do something about this, you think.

In 1983, someone finally did.

Thanks to Carmela Vitale, the mozzarella no longer sticks to the cardboard box cover. Pre-Carmela, pizza lovers would often have to scrape the mutz off the cover when they opened their pizza box. Why did this happen? Because it did not take much pressure for the flimsy cardboard to cave in into the cheese and stick to it. Carmela's invention—that little plastic pedestal that keeps the cover off the cheese—was her response to this frustrating pizza problem—and pizza lovers all over the world thank her.

# Panty Hose

Debut: 1959
Inventive American: Allen Gant, Sr. (for Glen Raven Mills)

In the 1940s and 1950s, women wore nylon stockings held up by garter belts. In the days of longer skirts, this worked out fine, except for the nuisance of actually having to wear a garter belt, of course.

But then, in the late 1950s, Mary Quant came up with the idea of the miniskirt, and, suddenly, women who wanted to wear the revealing "mod" garment had a problem: the new skirts were too short to hide a garter belt.

Allen Gant came to the rescue.

Gant invented panty hose—a one-piece undergarment consisting of a panty and attached stockings.

Panty hose are now a worldwide, billion-dollar business.

# Paper Money With Images

Debut: 1861
Inventive American: The United States Treasury

Prior to 1861, American money did not have pictures on it. From 1861 to 1864, Secretary of the Treasury Samuel Chase was on the $1 bills. He was deposed by George Washington, who has held the hallowed position ever since.

Later, in 1925, the decision was made *not* to require that *only* presidents be on the bills, allowing American notables such as Alexander Hamilton and Benjamin Franklin to be depicted on U.S. currency. In 1962, the Department of the Treasury was given the legal responsibility of deciding whose portraits adorned American currency. (At one point, even Martha Washington was on an American bill.)

Paper money with pictures is now commonplace around the world. (Following the Iraqi War, the United States authorized re-printing more Iraqi money in an attempt to stabilize their economy, even though the bills still had a portrait of Saddam Hussein on them. Also, did you know that since 1874, our U.S. Mints have been producing currency for many foreign governments? There have been periods where the combined orders for foreign currency have exceeded the volume of domestic U.S. currency production.)

Currently, these are the images on the front of U.S. currency:

- ❂ The $1 bill—George Washington, first President of the United States (the Great Seal of the United States on the back).

- ❂ The $5 bill—Abraham Lincoln, 16th President of the United States (the Lincoln Memorial on the back).

- ❂ The $10 bill—Alexander Hamilton, first Secretary of the Treasury (the Treasury Building on the back).

- ❂ The $20 bill—Andrew Jackson, seventh President of the United States (the White House on the back).

- ❂ The $50 bill—Ulysses S. Grant, 18th President of the United States (the U.S. Capitol on the back).

- ❂ The $100 bill—Benjamin Franklin, Founding Father (Independence Hall on the back).

- ❂ The $500 bill—William McKinley, 25th President of the United States (the numeral 500 and the ornamental phrase "Five Hundred Dollars" on the back).

- ❂ The $1,000 bill—Grover Cleveland, 22nd and 24th President of the United States (the numeral 1,000 and the ornamental phrase "One Thousand Dollars" on the back).

- ❂ The $5,000 bill—James Madison, fourth President of the United States (the numeral 5,000 and the ornamental phrase "Five Thousand Dollars" on the back).

- ❂ The $10,000 bill—Salmon Chase, Secretary of the Treasury under President Lincoln (the numeral 10,000 and the ornamental phrase "Ten Thousand Dollars" on the back).

- ❂ The $100,000 bill—Woodrow Wilson, 28th President of the United States (the numeral 100,000 and the ornamental phrase "One Hundred Thousand Dollars" on the back).

Note: The $500, $1,000, $5,000, $10,000, and $100,000 bills are not circulated. They are used only for currency transfers between federal banks.

# Paper Towels

Debut: 1907
Inventive American: the Scott Paper Company

The paper towel was invented because of the mandatory thickness of toilet paper and kids with runny noses.

One day in 1907, the Scott brothers received a shipment of paper that was intended to be used as toilet paper. Unfortunately, the paper had been mistakenly manufactured much too thick for toilet paper, and the Scotts prepared to ship it back...until one of the brothers heard about a local schoolteacher who was definitely ahead of her time when it came to germ theory and the avoidable spread of bacteria.

This teacher had begun the practice of handing out pieces of soft paper to every kid with a cold. The kids were told to only blow their nose with their own paper, and this effectively helped prevent the spread of colds from child to child.

The Scotts used the truckload of problem paper to create "Sani-Towels," which they then sold to Philadelphia schools.

It would be more than two decades, though, before paper towels were offered to homemakers for use in the kitchen instead of cloth towels, and even after their debut, it took awhile for them to be accepted by housewives. The idea of using a piece of paper for wiping things up and drying hands and then throwing it away was radical.

Paper towels eventually caught on, though, and now they are the norm in almost all kitchens. The microwave oven boosted their popularity when it was learned that food could be wrapped in paper towels for cooking in a microwave. Today, many paper manufacturers market a roll of plain white paper towels (no designs or inks) specifically for use in the microwave.

My wife likes Scott paper towels; I prefer another brand.

# The Parking Meter

Debut: 1935
Inventive American: Carlton Cole Magee

The invention of the parking meter made the concept of "free parking" obsolete. Cities could now rent motorists space to park on city streets. It was a no-lose situation for the municipality: If a person fed the meter, the city would realize the income; if a person chose to be a scofflaw, then the city would collect the fine when the motorist was issued a parking ticket. One single-car parking space on a city street could generate a whole bunch of money in one year.

Carl Magee invented the parking meter and received a patent for a "coin controlled parking meter" on May 24, 1938. The first parking meter was installed in his hometown of Oklahoma City. This probably did not endear Carl to his neighbors.

# The Pencil Sharpener

Debut: November 23, 1897
Inventive American: John Lee Love

The mechanical pencil sharpener brings to mind a lyric from Talking Heads: "Same as it ever was."

The pencil sharpener is one of those inventions that was perfect in its original design, efficient in its simplicity, and flawlessly utilitarian. You place a pencil in a tapered hole in the side of a small box and turn it clockwise. As you turn it, a blade sharpens the point, and the shavings remain inside the box. Perfect. There have been improvements in the size and shape of the sharpener box; as well as in the dimensions of the hole so that now thick pencils and crayons can also be hand-sharpened, but the original design that John Lee Love came up with in 1897 is still essentially the same. Portable, inexpensive, and reliable. You might even call it the perfect invention.

Love's name for his product was the "Love Sharpener."

# The Personal Computer

Debut: 1976
Inventive American: Steve Jobs and Steve Wozniak

*At $666.66 (including 4K bytes RAM) it opens many new possibilities for users and systems manufacturers.*

So read the 1976 ad for the Apple I, the world's first personal computer. My, how times have changed.

After graduating high school, Steve Jobs and Steve Wozniak both dropped out of college to take jobs in Silicon Valley. They were both interested in electronics and designing. After creating a computer with a $25 microprocessor, no memory, no power supply, and no keyboard, they conceived, designed, and built the Apple I. They started Apple Computers out of a garage in 1976, and the Apple I was their first product. In classic Apple fashion, they improved the model and released Apple II the following year. (The Macintosh faithful, of which I am one, have come to accept that the Apple machine they buy today will, in all likelihood, be usurped tomorrow by a faster, better—and cheaper—model.)

They continued to expand the company and improve their computers, releasing new models regularly. In 1984, though, they changed the world with the release of the Macintosh 128K. This was the first computer that unabashedly made the bold statement that computers were not just for offices and companies anymore. The Mac was the first personal computer—emphasis on the word "personal." Computers in the home? Of course, the release of the Mac proclaimed. And the day is coming when computers will be as ubiquitous as TVs and phones. (That day is almost, but not quite, here.)

The 1984 Mac was a desktop computer and it was very well-received. Sales were huge, and the era of the personal computer had begun. (I wrote my first two books on a Macintosh 128K, using Microsoft Word 1.0. With no hard drive, I ended up using dozens of floppies to store the book. These drawbacks aside, it was a glorious experience moving from an electric typewriter to Word. Interestingly, I had to buy a separate program—PFS File—to sort the alphabetical entries of my *Andy Griffith Show* encyclopedia, *Mayberry, My Hometown*. Word 1.0 did not yet have the ability to sort text. Again, how times have changed.)

Today, the computer has become a critically important part of everyday life. With the widespread use of the Internet and e-mail, computers have become as important to individuals and businesses as fax machines and phones.

## The Pet Rock

Debut: 1975
Inventive American: Gary Dahl

This is one of those "inventions" that makes one wonder about the intelligence of American society. Or perhaps it is the quintessential validation of America being known as the "Land of Opportunity?"

The Pet Rock was a rock in a cardboard box. It sold for $3.95. Millions were sold all over the world, making its "creator," California adman Gary Dahl, an instant multimillionaire.

One night over beers, Dahl was snarking to his friends that he considered cats, dogs, fish, and birds nothing but annoyances.

They needed attention, made messes, caused trouble, and were expensive. He then told his friends that *he* had a pet rock, and that it was not only completely maintenance-free, but it had a great personality. His friends immediately began volleying one-liners about the benefits of having a rock for a pet, and Dahl was so taken by the ridiculous idea that he spent the next two weeks writing a book he hoped to sell as a humor book.

The process of writing the book spurred Dahl to actually own a pet rock, so he went to a building supply store and bought the most expensive stone they offered, a Rosarita Beach Stone, which cost him a penny.

He concocted some clever packaging, printed up his manual, and shortly thereafter introduced it at a gift show. Neiman-Marcus immediately ordered 500 Pet Rocks, Dahl appeared on the *Tonight Show* twice, and ultimately, a goofball idea created a millionaire.

As they say, only in America.

# The Phonograph

Debut: December 4, 1877
Inventive American: Thomas Edison

Today, recorded music is one of the most taken-for-granted pleasures of society. Technology has virtually eliminated the phonograph, and CDs have replaced vinyl recordings, but the principle is the same: being able to hear what we want, whenever we want. (The pendulum has swung high, too. The current controversy over swapping and sharing digital music on the Internet takes this principle to its extreme: Being able to hear what we want, whenever we want—but not having to pay for it.)

We owe many thanks for this ubiquitous creature comfort to Thomas Edison. Edison worked in a time when the idea of recording a human voice and allowing others to hear it was considered an impossible task. Prior to audio recording and photography, the only ways of "recording" the people, places, and things of the human condition was to write about them or draw them. And these renderings were always after the fact. But then photography came along and captured a moment in time as it happened; and then audio recording captured specific sounds of life as they happened.

Thomas Edison combined the new technology of the telephone with the existing technology of the telegraph to create a device that would allow the human voice to be recorded and played back. Interestingly, very few people understood the significance of the telephone, and the device was originally planned to be used only to transmit information that would then be transcribed and delivered like a telegram. The process was conceived to consist of the following: telephone transmits info to someone operating a telegraph machine, who transcribes the info into text, which is then officially a telegram that can be delivered to the person for whom it was intended. The cumbersome, backwards use of these technologies seems obvious to us now, but in the 19th century, as inventions and breakthroughs were exploding everywhere like firecrackers, figuring out how to make effective use of some of these new tools in the marketplace took a little longer.

Edison conceived the phonograph to replace the telegraph as the transcription device for the transmittal of telegrams. Telegraphs were too slow, so he came up with the idea of a permanent record of the message that could be logged at the speed at which it was sent.

At first, Edison had tried to record electric telegraph signals using a stylus and a piece of paper. He would shout into the phone, his voice would send electrical signals to the stylus, and the vibrations would create indentations in the paper. This did not work the way Edison hoped it would, but it did prove that the human voice could—in some way—be permanently recorded.

By December 1877, Edison and his team had designed a machine that used tinfoil instead of paper to record sounds, and which was manually operated by a hand crank.

Edison was the first to try the new recording device. He said, "Mary had a little lamb, its fleece was white as snow, and everywhere that Mary went, the lamb was sure to go." Edison's new machine repeated his words perfectly.

This was the earliest version of the phonograph. Shortly thereafter, Edison demonstrated it to the public and the American

Academy of Sciences. He also gave a personal demonstration to President Rutherford B. Hayes. After he had proved that the phonograph was a viable technological breakthrough, Edison got bored with it and abandoned work it to invent the lightbulb.

Edison would eventually return to his invention and, in 1877, perhaps planning ahead, he formed the Edison Phonograph Corporation after the successful demonstration of the phonograph. Others tried to usurp his designs and work, however, and he ultimately ended up in court suing to protect the patents of his phonograph recording machines.

Edison ultimately made an enormous amount of money selling his phonographs, and he also made money from selling the recordings to play on his machines.

One cannot help but wonder what Edison would think of today's prerecorded CDs, digital MP3s, Internet file-sharing, battery-powered Walkmans, and satellite radio. The growth of the recording industry was explosive, and within decades, records and "record players"—true American Firsts—had become an important part of the world's culture—all from "Mary Had a LittleLamb."

# The Photocopy

Debut: 1937
Inventive American: Chester Floyd Carlson

A pundit I once read suggested that the worst thing that ever happened to American business was the invention of the photocopy. All it does, he waxed superciliously, is add unnecessary paper to an already overloaded office environment.

This view is, of course, ridiculous.

The photocopy changed business practices for all time. After its introduction and widespread availability, any number of people could review a single document, something that had been difficult and time consuming before the debut of the photocopy machine. The case can be made that photocopying actually changed in a big way how the world does business.

Carlson invented xerography, which is the process of making paper copies of documents without using ink. He used static electricity to charge a lighted plate, after which toner was applied to create the image of the original.

After he invented the process, Carlson tried to sell it, but he was turned down by 20 companies until the Haloid Company decided to take it on.

The Haloid Company later changed their name to Xerox Corporation.

# Play-Doh®

Debut: 1956; patented in 1965
Inventive Americans: Noah W. McVicker and
Joseph S. McVicker

Sometimes, the essence of a thing is elusive. Sometimes, what we imagine a thing to be is not what it ultimately becomes.

This is what happened with Silly Putty, and this is what happened with Play-Doh. It took a toy merchant to recognize that Silly Putty would make a great toy. Something similar happened with Play-Doh, which was originally created to be a wallpaper cleaner.

After batches of the clay were made, someone—probably the McVickers themselves—recognized the material's undeniable similarity to modeling clay. But there were differences—the wallpaper cleaner was non-toxic, and it was easy to work with for long periods of time without making a mess.

Thus, a toy was born.

Joseph McVicker was a multimillionaire before he turned 27, and to date, 350,000 tons of Play-Doh have been sold all over the world.

# Polaroid® Instant Photography

Debut: 1948
Inventive American: Edwin Land

It has long been said that the overwhelming number of Polaroid "instant" cameras were bought to take sex pictures. This suggestion is probably accurate.

Instant photography eliminated the need for developing film, and it also eliminated the self-imposed censorship of many couples who liked to have a little "photographic fun" in the bedroom. Prior to the instant photo, amateur photographers could only go so far as to what was captured on film. After the Polaroid hit the market, there were no more limits, other than what the couple themselves chose to commit to film.

Edwin Land was a physicist who came up with a process for developing film inside a camera, using a sealed compartment, pressure rollers, and developing and fixing chemicals. The whole thing took about a minute, and the earliest versions of self-developing film required peeling a cover off the finished photograph.

This was a revolutionary American First, and it wasn't long before advancements made the two-part system obsolete and the state of the art became a single developed picture that ejected itself from the front of the camera.

Today, digital cameras are slowly replacing the Polaroid for instant photos, but a great many professional photographers still shoot Polaroids of their subjects before moving on to the more sophisticated (and expensive) photographic techniques and films.

# The Polio Vaccine

Debut: 1952
Inventive American: Jonas Salk

In his first HBO special, *Curb Your Enthusiasm*, Larry David (the cocreator and writer of *Seinfeld*) does a very funny routine about Jonas Salk's mother obnoxiously bragging to all her yenta friends about her son, Jonas. The punch line was that she finally had something to throw up to the mothers who repeatedly boasted to her about their sons' accomplishments.

Whether or not Mrs. Salk did, indeed, brag about her son, she would have had every right to. Jonas Salk was a man committed to finding ways to prevent disease. While trying to develop a successful polio vaccine, he put his and his family's health on the line by testing it on himself, his wife, and their three sons. After it was proven effective, he refused to profit personally from his breakthrough.

Salk worked to put himself through college and medical school, and, while studying at New York University, he worked with the microbiologist Thomas Francis and developed an influenza vaccine later used by the U.S. military during World War II. Salk began teaching at the University of Pittsburgh in 1947, and it was there that he did the research that would lead to his development of a polio vaccine.

Salk's vaccine was made from killed polio virus, which triggered the body's immune system to create antibodies against it, but did not make people sick. In 1954, two million schoolchildren were injected with Salk's vaccine and none of them contracted polio. A few years later, Alfred Sabin developed an oral polio vaccine that, unlike Salk's, was made from *live* polio virus instead of killed virus. Tragically, some of the children who received Sabin's vaccine contracted polio from it. Today, the injected vaccine is the preferred choice for many medical practitioners.

On a personal note, I was one of those students who received Sabin's vaccine instead of Salk's when I was in the fourth grade. The school nurse had each class line up in the hall. She stood (flanked on either side by nuns, of course) behind a card table on which were dozens of small paper cups filled with, I believe, a green liquid. When we approached the table, we said our name, she checked us off on a clipboard, and she then handed us a cup. We had to drink it in front of her. I believe the entire school was vaccinated in one day with the oral vaccine. Thankfully, I suffered no ill effects, but I have lost touch with many of my grammar school classmates so I cannot speak for their ultimate fate.

# The Polygraph (Lie Detector)

Debut: 1921
Inventive American: John Larson

If lie detectors work, then why aren't the results of a polygraph test accepted in court as evidence?

The polygraph measures physiological responses to being asked questions. Through various sensors and cuffs, the machine measures marked changes in blood pressure, heart rate, respiration, and perspiration, and interprets these changes to indicate that the person is being deceptive. The polygraph examiner, by law, cannot state that a person is lying. He or she can only report "Deception indicated," "No deception indicated," or "Inconclusive" for each of the examinee's responses.

The United States Supreme Court has ruled that polygraph results are inadmissible in court, writing, "there is simply no consensus that polygraph evidence is reliable.... scientific field studies suggest the accuracy rate of the 'control question technique' polygraph is 'little better than could be obtained by the toss of a coin,' that is, 50 percent."

Some employers require a potential employee to submit to a lie detector test before being hired. Many job applicants do not know that they can legally decline to take the test and that they cannot be refused a job based on their unwillingness to take it. Many employees are also not aware that they can legally refuse to take a lie detector test, and that their employer cannot subsequently fire them. The only legally valid reason for an employer to *demand* a lie detector test of an employee is when there has been some type of embezzlement or other financial loss to the business and the employer has reason to believe that the targeted employee was involved in the loss.

The reason polygraph results are not accepted in court is because polygraphs do not record lies; they record physical changes. Consider this scenario: You work for a company at which a computer was recently stolen from your department. You happened to see who stole it, but you had nothing to do with it, and the thief doesn't even know he was spotted. Your boss decides to polygraph everyone in the department, and when you are asked the question, "Did you steal the computer?" your blood pressure and pulse skyrocket because you happen to know who stole it. You answer no because you didn't steal it, but your body responds guiltily because, first, you know who took it, and second, you know that you are considered a suspect. In this scenario, the polygraph examiner would probably tell your boss that you were being deceptive when asked about the theft of the computer. Your boss will probably then either fire you or make you submit to another polygraph test, which will likely turn out the same way, and *then* he'll fire you. You will have been branded a thief and you will have lost your job because you got nervous about being asked a question about a stolen computer.

Is this fair? Of course not, and that is why polygraph results are not accepted in court.

There are books and Websites devoted to teaching people how to beat a lie detector test. Some common tactics include taking a sedative before the test, placing a tack in your shoe and then stepping on it after each question, and placing deodorant on your fingertips.

I have also heard of people who lie for every question—even the control questions about their name and address—so that the examiner cannot get a base response reading.

John Larson's invention has been the source of endless controversy, and much of the ongoing debate has been about whether or not Larson's basic postulate—that people get nervous when they lie—is true. As we all know, some people are *incredibly* convincing liars. They can tell you that the sky is green so persuasively that they have you looking up to confirm it's still blue.

Individuals' responses to being questioned are diverse and unpredictable. This unavoidable fact is why the Supreme Court has (wisely) rejected allowing polygraph results as valid evidence in trials.

# The Popsicle®

Debut: 1905
Inventive American: Frank Epperson

One of the most beloved frozen confections of all time was invented by an 11-year-old.

Frank Epperson of San Francisco, California, accidentally left his fruit drink outside one cold night and it froze. Frank had fortuitously left a wooden stirring stick in his drink and, when he tugged at it, out popped the world's first Popsicle. Only Frank did not call it a Popsicle at first. He christened the treat an "Epsicle." In 1923, at the age of 29, Frank received a patent for "frozen ice on a stick." It was renamed the Popsicle, and Frank later went on to invent the twin Popsicle (two sticks), the Fudgsicle, the Creamsicle, and the Dreamsicle.

# The Pop-top Can

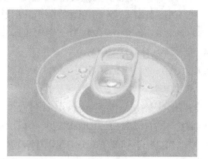

Debut: 1959
Inventive American: Ermal Fraze

Is there any worse feeling in the world than to pull up the tab of a pop-top can and have it break off without opening the can?

Be it beer or soda, you stand there dumbstruck, the can in your left hand, the amputated pop-top in your right, staring at this devastating scenario.

Now you have to find *a can opener*? One of those long things with the triangular-shaped point at one end? Is there one in your house and can you find it—*now*?

The occasional break-off is not the only potential problem with pop-top cans. Lately, people with nose piercings have reported getting their nose ring caught in the pop-top when drinking from the can.

Americans open 250 million pop-top cans a day. These cans contain beverages, of course, but also fruit, vegetables, soup, and nuts.

A pop-top can is made from a single sheet of aluminum that is shaped and formed into a can without a top. The top is made from a denser aluminum that can be scored for the hole for the pop-top and that can tolerate the rivet for the pop-top being punched into it. Have you ever noticed that the top of a pop-top can is smaller than the diameter of the can itself? Have you ever wondered why this is so? Follow the money: The aluminum used for the top is more expensive than the aluminum used for the can. Granted, the difference in size is miniscule, but the savings add up when you're making a minimum of 250 million cans every day (at 400 cans per minute per machine).

Ermal Fraze first developed the pop-top in 1959, but it was Ralph Stolle of Lebanon, Ohio, who invented the machinery that made the manufacturing of pop-top cans economically feasible. He sold his machinery and process to Alcoa in 1975, and may have been one of the few inventors who actually made some money from his creation.

Schlitz Brewing Company first sold beer in pop-top cans in 1963. These pop-tops detached (yes, intentionally) after opening the can. In 1975, the pop-top of today, known as the "Sta Tab" was introduced. The pop-top stayed on the can, which apparently saved the lives of some dumb animals that were eating the detached rings from the earlier cans. Pop-top cans from the 1964 to 1972 "pre-Sta Tab" period are highly collectible and quite valuable today.

Beverage cans are the most common use for pop-tops these days. (A variation on the original pop-top design is now used for a wide range of non-beverage products, including soups and tuna. The pop-top rings on these items remove the entire top of the container). A can costs about 4 cents to manufacture, including the pop-top. Ten cents of the price goes for advertising. The 12 ounces of beverage inside the can costs less than a penny to make.

And a six-pack of Coke is *how much?*

# The Pop-up Toaster

Debut: 1919
Inventive American: Charles Strite

There are two tried-and-true, overused, utterly predictable visual pop-up toaster jokes in movies and TV shows, and you have seen each of them countless times.

The first is the bread popping out of the toaster with such force and speed that the toast takes down a chandelier, knocks something off a shelf, or hits somebody and knocks them out. The second is the toast popping out of the toaster, flying into the air, and landing in the character's hand or on a dish, all without him or her looking up.

As in the case of the blender, if you see a toaster on a movie or TV set, there is probably a good chance that there will be a pop-up toaster joke at some point during the scene.

The pop-up toaster uses a timer to determine when a piece of bread is officially a piece of toast.

The dial on the front or side of the toaster that shows varying degrees of darkness of the toast simply changes the length of time the bread is toasted.

Interestingly, one of the all-time consumer complaints about toasters is that they never deliver the color toast that the dial claims it will. You set it to medium darkness, and when it pops up it's barely even a beige color. So now you have to push it down again, but do you change the setting to something darker? Or do you just do another cycle at your original color setting? Should you stand there and peer inside the slots, the waves of heat hitting you in the face, and try to determine when the toast is the way you want it? And if you think it's done, and you manually pop it up, and it's not done, once again, do you push it down at the same setting? Or should you change the color?

Toaster ovens made a dent in toaster sales because people could watch their toast toast through the glass door and decide when it was to their liking. Many toaster ovens also have the allegedly helpful color dial, but you really don't have to depend on it completely, because you can monitor the toasting yourself.

Originally, toasters had no timers and no automatic, spring-loaded pop-up feature. They were simple electric grilling machines that had to be carefully monitored so that the bread wouldn't burn.

Minnesota mechanic Charles Strite invented the first pop-up toaster in 1919, but it was only for commercial restaurant use. His design used a spring-loaded ejection mechanism and a clock. The first models were big and heavy. They weighed more than 20 pounds and were made of cast aluminum. They also could toast four slices of bread at one time, something that would not be possible in home kitchens for years to come.

Strite formed a company to manufacture his machines and sell them to restaurants. The company was called the Waters Genter Company. They later changed their name to Toastmaster.

In 1926, Strite introduced the first Toastmaster single-slice pop-up toaster for home use. (A few other companies had tried marketing single-slice toasters prior to the Toastmaster version, but none of them were successful.)

In 1930, the two-slice model was introduced, although the cost was much higher than the one-slice and was considered a high-end appliance for the family that had everything (including lots of money).

From there, we witnessed the evolution of the toaster. After the two-slice came the four-slice, and then the super-wide bagel toaster, and then, a new species, the toaster oven which, although it can do more than the humble toaster, has not eliminated the toaster from the American countertop.

After all, a piece of toast cannot fly out of a toaster oven and knock a plastic liter of Dr. Pepper all over the dog, right?

## Post-it® Notes

Debut: 1980
Inventive Americans: Arthur Fry and Dr. Spencer Silver

The poster for writer/director Mike Judge's cult movie *Office Space* shows a man covered head to toe in yellow Post-its. Only his shoes and hands are visible, and this poor office schlub has his glasses on over his Post-it-covered face.

The reason this poster works is because, as 3M puts it on their Website, "The Post-it Note is one of the best known of all 3M products."

In 1968, Dr. Spencer Silver discovered by accident the unique repositionable adhesive used in Post-its. It was obvious to Silver that such an innovative product should have a commercial use, but for years, no one knew how to "position" it (no pun intended). 3M scientists, engineers, and marketing people were ambivalent about the commercial market for such an adhesive, and they tried bulletin boards, tapes, spray glues, and other uses, none of which were really right.

Then, one day, in the 1970s, 3M's new product development researcher Art Fry was attending church choir practice and was becoming increasingly frustrated by his scrap paper bookmarks falling out of his hymnal. In one of those serendipitous moments of true inspiration, Fry suddenly realized that he could use Silver's adhesive on the back of different size pieces of paper to create repositionable bookmarks. As Silver had accidentally stumbled onto the adhesive formula, Fry had accidentally stumbled onto the perfect use for it.

At first, the 3M production people were skeptical. They were concerned about the costs of creating such a product, as well as the amount of waste the production process would generate. Fry's response? "That is great news! If it were easy, then anyone could do it. If it really is as tough as you say, then 3M is the company that can do it."[12]

Fry began distributing his "Pull and Peel Notes" to the 3M office staff. They loved them, and many of them remarked that they didn't know how they managed without them. 3M then began a free distribution program in Boise, Idaho, where everyone who used them said that they would buy them if they were available in stores.

In 1980, Post-it Notes officially hit the market, and, the following year, they were named 3M Outstanding New Product of the Year.

What does the now-retired Arthur Fry think about all the hubbub surrounding his church choir brainstorm? "It is like having your children grow up and turn out to be happy and successful."[13]

# Potato Chips

Debut: 1853
Inventive American: George Crum

The beloved potato chip was a sarcastic invention.

In the summer of 1853, George Crum, a half-black/half-Native American chef at the Moon Lake Lodge resort in Saratoga Springs, New York, was livid when one of the resort's most distinguished guests, railroad magnate Cornelius Vanderbilt, sent back his order of fried potatoes with the complaint that they were too thick. Chef Crum did not like food returned to his kitchen. From all reports, it not only frustrated him, it enraged him. Sometimes, he would concoct a noxious, repulsive dish for the complaining diner, which likely lost the restaurant a customer, but which must have given Crum some meager satisfaction.

When Vanderbilt sent back his potatoes, Crum probably knew it would not be wise to deliberately antagonize one of the resort's most important customers, so he decided to accommodate Vanderbilt's request. He sliced potatoes almost thin enough to see through, deep-fried them in oil, and then heavily salted them.

When Vanderbilt bit into his first potato slice, he was delighted. They were delicious, and what had originally been intended as a sarcastic culinary rejoinder to a pompous customer, turned into Saratoga Chips, a staple at the Moon Lake Lodge from then on and a favorite at Crum's own restaurant a few years later.

Potato chips became available in stores in 1895 and were served to customers in paper bags until 1926 when Laura Scudder developed the sealed wax bag for the popular snack.

Today, five billion pounds of potatoes are used for American potato chips, and the potato chip business is a $15 billion worldwide industry.

Sometimes something good *can* come from sarcasm, eh?

# PROZAC®

Debut: 1988
Inventive Americans: the Eli Lilly drug company

There are two drugs that are household names in America: Viagra (which was invented by British scientists), and Prozac, which is an American invention through and through.

Viagra is for erectile dysfunction; Prozac is for depression. What this says about the English and American people, I will leave for the reader to decide.

Prozac is the trade name for fluoxetine hydrochloride and it is what is known as a serotonin reuptake inhibitor. It was unleashed on the world in 1988, and, in what may be a revealing truth about the collective state of mind of mankind, by 1990, it was the most prescribed antidepressant in the world.

Serotonin is the bandleader of the orchestra that is your brain. It regulates your moods, your appetite, your sleep cycles, and a shortage of this extremely important neurotransmitter can create all kinds of problems, including insomnia, mood swings, loss of appetite, food cravings, and depression.

Reuptake is what happens when neurotransmitters that carry messages between nerve cells are destroyed or absorbed after delivering their message. When this reuptake is restricted, the brain, for some unknown reason, increases its production of serotonin, which makes a person feel better. Prozac inhibits reuptake, and the loved ones of depressives around the world are grateful.

The late chemist Ray Fuller, working with a team at the Eli Lilly drug company, discovered fluoxetine and figured out a way to safely use it as a medication. It does have some side effects, most notably nausea, diarrhea, insomnia, and reduced libido (for which you can take Viagra), but most patients who have achieved good results from Prozac are willing to live with the side effects.

# The Pushpin

Debut: 1900
Inventive American: Edwin Moore

Edwin Moore's first pushpin—an undeniable improvement on the thumbtack—had a round ball on the top; today's most popular type uses a barrel-type plastic "handle" with a flared bottom and round cap.

According to the Moore Push-Pin Company Website:

> In 1900, Mr. Edwin Moore founded the Company with a capital of $112.60. He rented a room and devoted each afternoon and evening to making pushpins, an article of his own invention which may be briefly described as "a pin with a handle." In the mornings, he sold what he had made the night

*before. The first sale was one gross of pushpins for $2. The next memorable order was for $75, and the first "big deal" was a sale of $1,000 to the Eastman Kodak Company.*

Moore began advertising his product in 1903; today, you will find his invention on bulletin boards in offices all over the world.

# Q

## Q-Tips®

Debut: 1920s
Inventive American: Leo Gerstenzang

Q-Tips are a great idea, but we cannot help but wonder how many eardrums have been punctured by people digging in their ears a tad too enthusiastically.

Leo Gerstenzang designed the first cotton swab because he loved his wife and child and wanted to, first, help his wife and, second, prevent his child from having his eardrum impaled by a toothpick.

Mrs. Gerstenzang was not one to tolerate dirty ears on her baby, so she routinely wrapped a piece of cotton around the end of a toothpick and used this concocted implement to clean out young Gerstenzang's infant ears. Yes, a toothpick has a point, and, yes, this homemade apparatus could have conceivably put a hole in a membrane that needed to remain intact.

Leo saw what his wife did and decided to devise something that would be easier to use and, more importantly, safer. He still used a stick, but it did not have a pointed end and the cotton was affixed so that it would not fall off and expose the wooden tip.

The swabbing instrument that Leo came up with was obviously marketable to mothers everywhere, and so he started the

Infant Novelty Company to produce and sell them. For some unknown reason, he thought that his cotton swabs should be called
"Baby Gays," and that is the name he used for their initial release.
In 1926, he changed the name to "Q-Tips Baby Gays," and then,
ultimately, to simply "Q-Tips."

Ironically, today it is *not* recommended that consumers use
Q-Tips for the purpose for which they were designed—cleaning
inside the ear. A small cotton swab can be used for many things,
but I would suspect that the vast majority of purchasers still use
them for cleaning ears, punctured eardrums be damned!

# QWERTY

Debut: 1866
Inventive American: James Densmore

The original layout of typewriter keys was designed to slow
typists (and aid marketing, which we'll discuss in a moment)
because the existing typewriting mechanisms could not handle the
rapidity with which some people typed.

I remember once owning a black, monumentally heavy, cast-
iron Remington manual typewriter. This machine, on which I
produced some of my earliest attempts at what you might charitably
call writing, is long gone, and I have zero recollection of what
happened to it. Every now and then, though, I nostalgically remi-
nisce about writing on a manual typewriter, the paper jutting up
out of the roller, the ribbon riding up and down as the keys pum-
meled it, the extraordinarily long space bar...but then I remember
what I had to go through every time I made a mistake. Then the
nostalgia flies out the window and I am happy to be working in
the age of word-wrapping, selecting a word by double-clicking on
it and then typing over it and, of course, cutting and pasting. They
say word processors increase a writer's output by at least 50 percent.
As Paul Simon said, "I do believe it...I do believe it's so..."

The problem with this black typewriter of mine (as with all of
the typewriters from the era in which it was built), was that if you
typed too fast, the return of a key to its bed would take longer
than the time the next key would strike the ribbon. Thus, any of
us who could type reasonably quick would regularly experience

typewriter key gridlock. Remember having to reach inside and pull the snarled keys apart, hoping against hope that you did not accidentally bend the key arm?

The QWERTY layout forced typists to type more slowly. How? By placing commonly used letters in out of the way places. For instance, the *A* is beneath your left little finger. *A* is one of the most used letters in English, and yet the QWERTY layout assigns it to our weakest finger.

Also, the most commonly used letter—*E*—is in the top letter row. The home row—*ASDFGHJKL;'*—holds the letters that can be reached the quickest with your fingers. So wouldn't it make sense to put the most used letters where they could be reached the quickest? Sure, but then we might type too quickly and jam the keys.

So QWERTY became the standard layout, and it stuck. There are many today who claim— "know" would be a better word here—that a different layout, designed so that the aforementioned most-used letters are closer to each other could greatly increase typing speeds.

The odds of a new keyboard layout succeeding, however, are slim to none. Such a switchover would have been difficult to implement when it would have only been used for typewriters. Now that computers are everywhere and even people who would have never bought a typewriter now own a computer, getting all those people to switch would be a gargantuan, and perhaps an impossible, task.

There was one other reason why the QWERTY layout was implemented by typewriter manufacturers (in addition to protecting themselves from complaints from consumers about jammed keys). At least the top row was designed to make it easier for typewriter salesmen to sell machines. The word "typewriter" can quickly be spelled by typing only the letters in the top row.

# R

## Radio Astronomy

Debut: 1932
Inventive American: Karl Guthe Jansky

Radio astronomy is the branch of astronomy that deals with detection and study of celestial objects and phenomena by means of the radio waves emitted by these objects and phenomena.[14]

Karl Guthe Jansky was a radio engineer who had always been interested in attempting to pick up radio waves from deep space and use them to identify and locate planetary and other cosmic objects.

In 1932, Jansky heard something: He picked up radio waves coming from the distant center of our own Milky Way galaxy. That was the beginning of the science of radio astronomy.

Today, enormous parabolic satellite dishes scan the heavens ceaselessly listening for radio waves and then plotting their source.

So far, these dishes have not picked up Kasey Kasem's countdown coming from anywhere but here. But we're still listening.

## In the Time of Edison

The following passages are from *Edison, His Life and Inventions* by Frank Lewis Dyer and Thomas Commerford Martin, originally published in 1910. They artfully describe the huge leaps that had been made in science and society by the time we met Thomas Edison. Some of the advancements they cite may have had their genesis in Europe, but all of them were improved and sublimely utilized by American inventors and thinkers; all of them were made new by American ingenuity.

*Viewed from the standpoint of inventive progress, the first half of the nineteenth century had passed very profitably when Edison appeared—every year marked by some notable achievement in the arts and sciences, with promise of its early and abundant fruition in commerce and industry. There had been exactly four decades of steam navigation on American waters. Railways were growing at the rate of nearly one thousand miles annually. Gas had become familiar as a means of illumination in large cities. Looms and tools and printing-presses were everywhere being liberated from the slow toil of man-power. The first photographs had been taken. Chloroform, nitrous oxide gas, and ether had been placed at the service of the physician in saving life, and the revolver, guncotton, and nitroglycerine added to the agencies for slaughter. New metals, chemicals, and elements had become available in large numbers, gases had been liquefied and solidified, and the range of useful heat and cold indefinitely extended. The safety-lamp had been given to the miner, the caisson to the bridge-builder, the anti-friction metal to the mechanic for bearings. It was already known how to vulcanize rubber, and how to galvanize iron. The application of machinery in the harvest-field had begun with the embryonic reaper, while both the bicycle and the automobile were heralded in primitive prototypes. The gigantic expansion of the iron and steel industry was fore-shadowed in the change from wood to coal in the smelting furnaces. The sewing-machine had brought with it, like the friction match, one of the most profound influences in modifying domestic life, and making it different from that of all preceding time.*

A final word on the creative process as it applies to technological progress...

Contrary to the general notion, very few of the great modern inventions have been the result of a sudden inspiration by which, Minerva-like, they have sprung full-fledged from their creators' brain. But, on the contrary, they have been evolved by slow and gradual steps so that, frequently, the final advance has been often almost imperceptible.

# The Revolving Door

Debut: August 7, 1888
Inventive American: Theophilus Van Kannel

Why a *revolving* door? Wasn't the ordinary, tried-and-true, rectangular hinged door that opened by turning a knob good enough? What was the inspiration that spurred Theophilus Van Kannel to invent a door that *spun*? Was it to force people to exercise more? After all, there is more walking involved when you enter a building through a revolving door. Was it to keep the kids entertained? "Ooh, look at the spinning door, Susie!" Was it to trap potential thieves by having onlookers hold one of the "spokes" and prevent escape?

The actual explanation for Van Kannel's invention is much more pedestrian (no pun intended).

It seems that as buildings got taller and taller, an air pressure anomaly occurred. Entrance doors on the first floor became increasingly difficult to open, and it was ultimately determined that this was due to an air pressure differential. Apparently, a vacuum was created by air flowing upwards through stairwells and elevator shafts and this essentially pushed air pressure against the lowest level openings, that is, the front door.

Van Kannel's revolving door design solved this problem. As it turns, the revolving door equalizes pressure in the building, thereby making it easier to push through to the interior.

Today, revolving doors are found mostly in high-rise skyscrapers. They *do* entertain the kids, too.

# The Richter Scale

Debut: 1935
Inventive American: Charles Richter

The intensity of an earthquake is expressed in magnitude using the Richter scale—numbers ranging from 1.5 to 10. These numbers indicate the severity of the quake and its subsequent damage. The Richter scale, which was developed in 1935 by American seismologist Charles Richter, is logarithmic in nature, meaning that each successive whole number represents a 10-fold increase in power and intensity. Even though the Richter scale is not really used much by seismologists anymore (today's technology allows far more specific and accurate readings of seismic activity), earthquake magnitudes are still commonly expressed using the familiar Richter scale. The damage from an earthquake ranges from a quake that is generally not felt by people but detectable by seismologists, to nearly total destruction in which large rock masses are displaced, buildings are leveled, and large objects are hurled great distances.[15]

# The Rocket

Debut: 1914
Inventive American: Robert Goddard

Physicist Robert Goddard was the father of modern rocketry and, at the time of his death in 1945, he had 214 scientific patents to his name that were related to rocketry.

He first proved the principles underlying rocket propulsion in 1907, but it took many years for him to build a liquid-fueled rocket that could be launched and sustain flight. On March 16, 1926, Goddard launched a 10-foot rocket that climbed to a height of 41 feet and traveled a distance of 184 feet. The entire flight lasted less than three seconds.

In the 1930s, Goddard lived in Roswell, New Mexico (yes, *that* Roswell), and devoted his work to developing better, faster, and more powerful rockets.

It is reasonable to say that the world's space programs owe their existence to the genius and work of American Robert Goddard.

# The Roller Coaster

Debut: 1884
Inventive American: La Marcus Adna Thompson

On Tuesday, July 1, 2003, 25 roller coaster riders were stranded for more than two hours when the *Two Face: The Flip Side* roller coaster they were riding on at the Six Flags Amusement Park outside Washington, D.C., malfunctioned. No one was injured. One man interviewed after the accident reported that he had been suspended face down the entire time, held in place by his seat belt. Many riders later admitted that they were terrified of the cars ripping free from the tracks and of them falling almost 175 feet to the ground and their possible demise.

Technicians were able to get the ride restarted a little over two hours after it stopped, and officials for the park later said that the roller coaster's safety mechanisms probably activated when a problem (still undetermined) was detected. These safety mechanisms are fail-safe and stopped the cars in what officials described as "a safe place."

"A safe place?"

They should ask the guy who was suspended upside down, held in place by his seat belt, the blood rushing to his head for two hours if *he* felt safe during that time.

Calling the roller coaster an American First requires a caveat: Technically, the roller coaster was not first invented in America, but rather in France. What we are looking at here is America's domination of the ride after its debut here in 1884. America can boast of roller coasters with the world's longest drop (400 feet), tallest height (420 feet), fastest speed (120 miles per hour [yikes]), and steepest angle of descent (90 degrees). (Are we gluttons for punishment, or what?)

The roller coaster is a very popular amusement park ride. The new, high-speed "scream machines" are quite an experience: Some of the g-forces riders experience probably make them feel like they're riding a rocket into space.

The first American roller coaster was built by La Marcus Adna Thompson and was called the Switchback Railway. It opened at

Coney Island in Brooklyn, New York in 1884 and was immediately an overwhelming success. Thompson charged five cents a ride and thousands of people rode every day, earning Thompson hundreds of dollars a day.

Today, roller coasters are in both indoor and outdoor amusement parks, and are, for the most part, extraordinarily safe. When they do fail (as in the angst-inducing story above) they fail safely and no one gets injured.

However, there are still some downsides to being sent hurtling through space at extremely fast speeds in a variety of physical positions. Two are especially disturbing. The first is the fact that a rider might become extremely nauseous. People have vomited during roller coaster rides and after. This should not be surprising. It isn't called "motion" sickness for nothing!

Also, even more alarming, a study in the January 11, 2000 issue of the journal *Neurology* reported that several roller coaster rides in a single day may trigger blood clots on the surface of the brain.

A 24-year-old Japanese woman rode three roller coasters two times each in one day and later reported severe headaches. She went to her doctor who prescribed muscle relaxants but the headaches persisted. Two months later (two *months*?), an MRI was performed on the woman and it was discovered that she had subdural hematomas (blood clots) on the surface of her brain. Surgery was performed and she recovered.

There have been three other cases of blood clots on the brain reported after roller coaster rides, including a 73-year-old man who died from his hematoma.

Researchers now believe that the constant up-and-down and back-and-forth motion of the ride can cause blood vessels to break in the neck and head and cause the blood clots.

A day of family fun, complete with cotton candy, vomiting, and blood clots. Not to mention the possibility of being suspended upside down for two hours.

Where do I sign up?

# The Rolodex®

Debut: 1958
Inventive American: Alfred Neustadter

For decades, the manual Rolodex was the mandatory office accessory. And who you had in your Rolodex was often a sign of your clout and influence.

The Rolodex is a rotating cardholder with a dome-like cover and a large knob that turns the spindle on which the removable cards are attached. Today, there are electronic versions of the Rolodex, but computers, PDAs, and other electronic digital storage devices are beginning to make the manual Rolodex a bit of an office dinosaur.

The Rolodex was invented by Alfred Neustadter of Brooklyn, New York, who went on to invent a non-spilling inkwell, a hole puncher, and a sliding phone directory device.

# The Rubber Band

Debut: 1845
Inventive American: Stephen Perry

When I was in the seventh grade, I sat in the back corner of the classroom. To my left was a large window, which was nice, and because my seat was the last one in the longest row, there was no one sitting next to me, which was also nice. On the other side of the room, also in the last seat in his row, sat Bowser. He and I were best friends and had gone through every grade of our Catholic grammar school in the same class. Remember, though, that we were also both 12 and, therefore, we were also both complete idiots.

For some reason, we became obsessed with flinging notes to each other across the room using a rubber band as a launching device. We would write something stupid on a piece of paper (*Mary Lou stinks!*), fold the note into a small square, and then, when the nun wasn't looking, slingshot it across the nine rows of desks. Sometimes it would land on our desk; sometimes we would have to make a Hail Mary grab to catch it; once, one of Bowser's notes flew right out the window.

We did this for quite some time, until we got caught.

Sister Immaculata happened to look up (it was bound to happen) as one of our missiles was in flight. Her eyes tracked it from beneath her starched, white headpiec. Adding to our ultimate doom was the fact that not only did myr airmail package not land on Bowser's desk, it hit Mary Margaret in the ear, eliciting a cry of unbearable agony that was truly remarkable for its dramatic excess. (I'm betting she went on to become an actress.)

Sister Immaculata slammed her pointer down on her desk, making a noise proportionally louder than might be expected both from the size of the pointer and the size of the nun, and then shrieked out our last names.

Bowser and I were terrified. Back then, nuns were *scary*. And they were also allowed to hit us at will.

"Up here!" she shouted, and Bowser and I reluctantly got up from our desks and marched to the front of the room.

Sister Immaculata held out her hand. Knowing what she wanted, we both dropped our rubber band into her palm.

"Hold out your arms."

We did as told and were puzzled as she slid our rubber bands onto our wrists.

With a nasty smile, she then grabbed the band on my wrist, stretched it out, and let it go. Have you ever done that? I think they use this technique for behavior modification: Every time you want to takeadrink/smokeacigarette/eatapizza/callahooker, you snap the rubber band instead. It *stings*.

When I flinched, Sister appeared to be delighted. She then repeated the snap on Bowser's wrist. He also flinched, and she was again pleased.

There were 20 minutes of class time remaining until lunch, and Sister Immaculata made us stand in front of the class and repeatedly snap the rubber band on our wrists the entire time. By the time the noon bell rang, both our wrists were bright red and hurt like hell. Bowser and I did not hurl notes across the room anymore after that.

That story would not have been possible were it not for the ingenious creativity of Stephen Perry, founder of a rubber manufacturing company. In 1845, Perry was experimenting with different rubber compounds when the idea of a thin circle of stretch-able rubber that could be used to secure bundles of envelopes or pencils came to him. The rubber band has changed little in the ensuing years. They now come in varying thicknesses, lengths, and colors, and there are even enormous rubber bands that can be used to hold together books and other large objects.

And they still make very good slingshots.

# S

## Saccharin

Debut: 1879
Inventive Americans: Constantine Fahlberg and
Ira Remsen

Okay, so now we know it causes cancer, but saccharin was heralded with accolades and ecstatic delight when it was first released to the general public.

Saccharin is 500 times sweeter than cane sugar and has no calories. Its place as king of artificial sweeteners, however, has since been usurped by aspartame.

Saccharin was discovered by Constantine Fahlberg, who reportedly spilled some white powder (an experimental concoction he was working on consisting of carbon, hydrogen, and other elements) while working in the lab of Ira Remsen and noticed its sweet taste when some of it dusted his hand. (The accessible historical record does not tell us what Fahlberg was trying to make, invent, or modify when he discovered saccharin.) He and Remsen published a paper announcing the discovery, but Fahlberg patented it on his own and became an exceedingly wealthy man. In later years, Remsen, President of John Hopkins University, described Fahlberg as "a scoundrel."

# The Safety Elevator

Debut: 1852
Inventive American: Elisha Grave Otis

The first *real* elevator was invented by an American, who went on to start a company—the Otis Elevator Company—that still bears his name today and which can be seen inside countless elevators in countless buildings all over the world.

In 1743, however, the incredibly lazy King Louis XV had a contraption known as a Flying Chair built to save him the travail of having to climb from the first floor of his palace to the *second* floor.

The modern safety elevator is as fail-safe as it can possibly be. It is essentially impossible for an elevator car to plummet to the basement of a building, no matter what Hollywood scriptwriters tell us. If power is lost or any (or even all) of the cables break, brakes in the elevator shaft stop the car almost immediately.

Elisha Otis sold his first elevator car to the A.T. Stewart department store on Hudson Street in New York City. Today, that store is long gone, and in its place is a one-story building—with no elevator.

# The Safety Pin

Debut: April 10, 1849[16]
Inventive American: Walter Hunt

Walter Hunt was a mechanic from New York who spent his spare time inventing things. He invented the streetcar bell, a knife sharpener, a flax-spinning machine, a hard coal burning stove, and even the tricycle.

Hunt was inventive, creative, and industrious, but he never seemed to make any money from his many inventions.

This situation did not change when he invented one of the most useful, ubiquitous, and lucrative everyday items of all time— the safety pin.

Hunt owed a friend $15 and he didn't have the money.

One day, Hunt was sitting at his desk, fooling around with a piece of brass wire about eight inches long and a piece of flat sheet brass. After about three hours of twisting and turning the wire and manipulating the flat piece of metal, he created a pin that, after it was inserted through an item and closed, shielded its point. He called it the safety pin.

Hunt quickly patented the idea, but then equally as fast, he sold the rights to his invention for $400. (He needed $15, remember?)

Hunt paid his debt and pocketed $385 for his work. It is probably safe to say that the safety pin has earned countless millions of dollars. Its forgotten inventor, Walter Hunt, was less successful.

# Saran Wrap®

Debut: 1933
Inventive American: Ralph Wiley (for Dow Chemical)

Saran Wrap keeps food fresh. A sheet of Saran wrapped over the top of a bowl will keep out air and moisture, and it will cling to the side of the container almost like it was glued on. The only problem most people have with Saran Wrap and all of the other copycat products that use the same polyvinylidene chloride base is trying to get it apart if it accidentally touches. Many a piece of Saran Wrap has been crumpled up in frustration and tossed away because of this problem. (Contact paper used to pose the same threat: If the sticky side of the paper touched at any point, you could kiss that piece good-bye. Today, they use a glue that does not bond instantaneously, so you can gently pull the pieces apart if they do touch.)

Saran Wrap was yet another accidental discovery. One day in 1933, at his job in the lab at Dow, Ralph Wiley was vexed by a vial that he could not scrub clean. The substance that could not be removed was vinylide chloride, which had somehow been polymerized with acrylic esters and carboxyl groups. It seemed impervious to water. Dow immediately began marketing the vile-smelling green substance as a water-repellant spray to the military. Eventually they figured out a consumer use for it, removed its stench and green color, and packaged it on rolls in a box with a razor on the edge. The home user could pull off a piece of any size. They just had to be careful not to accidentally let it touch itself (or slice their fingers open on the razor).

# Scotch® Tape

Debut: 1930
Inventive American: Richard Drew (for 3M)

Scotch tape and masking tape are two of those commonplace, everyday items that we so take for granted that it is hard to imagine a time when we did not have them around.

We do have them around thanks to Richard Drew, an engineer for the Minnesota Mining Company (later known as 3M).

Masking tape, a thin, removable paper tape, came first in 1923; the clear cellulose tape which would soon become known around the world as Scotch tape came in 1930.

One of Drew's 3M colleagues, John Borden, invented the ubiquitous tape dispenser two years later.

# Scrabble®

Debut: 1948
Inventive American: Alfred Butts

Scrabble is a very popular game, and it was an American First. There are big money Scrabble tournaments, and we can now buy computer versions of the game. (I have Mac Scrabble and I almost always cheat by looking at the hint. I'm not proud of this.)

Alfred Butts created the tile-interlocking word game in 1948, and his friend James Brunot then made some modifications that gave us the game we know today.

Butts turned to creating games after he was laid off during the Depression.

# The Sewing Machine

Debut: 1832 (Hunt); 1845 (Howe); 1851 (Singer)
Inventive Americans: Walter Hunt; Elias Howe; Isaac Singer

In the story of the sewing machine, we once again see how necessity is the mother of invention.

Prior to the Industrial Revolution—that period of rapid industrial growth that began in England in the mid-18th century and then spread to other countries over the next 150 years—there really wasn't a pressing need for a sewing *machine*. *People* were the sewing machines. In a time when cotton was harvested by hand, wool was shorn by hand, and leather was handcured, handcut, and handstitched, the making of clothing was slow-paced. It was usually done on a small scale by the women in the family, and usually only for their own family's use. Tailor shops served to fulfill whatever other needs a society had, but they were individual enterprises in which every item was a handcrafted, one-of-a-kind creation.

The Industrial Revolution launched the era of mass production, and introduced manufacturing processes that have never ceased to expand and improve. One of the major advancements was in the area of fabric production. Suddenly, cotton was picked and cleaned by machine, mills rolled out great bolts of material; companies sprang up to produce and sell garments and other items made from fabrics, such as towels, tablecloths, and curtains.

Seemingly overnight, handsewing everything became impossible.

Early versions of sewing machines were created in England and France, but they were completely unworkable as commercial machines. Thomas Saint's machine, for example, designed in 1790 to sew leather, was never even built. Barthelmy Thimonnier invented a machine in France in the late 1820s that sewed a chain stitch using a crocheting needle. He enjoyed some success with the machine sewing soldier's 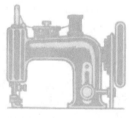 uniforms for the French Army, but his shop and machines were destroyed by rampaging tailors who believed that Thimonnier was set on putting them out of business and that any machines designed to replace human labor were sinful.

Walter Hunt, the inventor of the safety pin (discussed in this book), was the first American to invent a sewing machine. In 1832, he built a machine that worked, but it had its problems. It could only sew a straight seam, the work could not be manipulated or turned under the needle, and the seam's maximum length was only a few inches. In 1838, Hunt tried to convince his daughter to start a corset manufacturing business using his machine, but she refused, believing, as did the French, that machines that replaced humans were immoral. Hunt never patented his machine.

A few years later, Elias Howe, then working as an apprentice in a machine shop, decided to try his hand at designing and building a sewing machine; specifically a machine that could mechanically duplicate the individual motions of his wife when she was sewing by hand. After several false starts and dead ends (often unknowingly precisely duplicating Walter Hunt's trials and errors), Howe built a machine that could sew a seam. In the summer of 1845, he demonstrated the machine to a clothing manufacturer in Boston and, with his machine, sewed five seams by himself faster than five girls did working on only one each. The manufacturers were impressed, but they didn't buy any machines from Howe.

Howe went to England with a new partner, but was bamboozled by his new investor and left alone in London with no job and no money. He ultimately returned to America where he was amazed to find that his machine had become quite popular, but that his original partner had sold the patent without compensating him. After a series of contentious court trials, Howe was awarded his patent and began earning thousands of dollars a year from sales of his sewing machine. He ultimately died a rich man.

How did Isaac Singer figure into this potpourri of deception, confusion, and bitterness?

Singer was part of a team of sewing machine manufacturers who the court ruled had to pay Howe royalties for his invention. Singer had invented his own machine in 1851, but his invention used a foot pedal instead of a hand crank. Nonetheless, soon after he patented his machine, he ended up being sued by Howe for patent infringement.

As we know, the court ruled in Howe's favor. Although, in all fairness, it is a historical fact that essentially the same sewing machine was invented independently by three men: Walter Hunt, Elias Howe, and Isaac Singer.

As to who was the ultimate winner, have you seen any Howe or Hunt sewing machines in the stores lately?

# The Shopping Cart

Debut: 1936
Inventive American: Sylvan Goldman

The idea of the shopping cart is so obvious it astounds that someone had to actually conceive and invent one. People had been moving things around in wheeled containers—wheelbarrows, baby carriages—for eons, and yet before Sylvan Goldman, no one had ever put together the idea of grocery shopping and a wheeled cart.

The handbasket, which was used exclusively in grocery stores before the cart came on the scene, still survives and can be found in a metal rack at the entrances of all modern grocery store chains. But the limitations of the basket become all too clear when you start wandering through the store, putting things in the basket (veering from your list, of course). Before you know it, you're using both hands to carry it. Even a couple of seemingly innocuous items—say, a six-pack of 25-ounce bottles of water and a can of coffee—can suddenly make you want to throw the basket through the front window of the store.

Sylvan Goldman owned a chain of retail grocery stores and had trained his employees to monitor the contents of his customers' baskets and rush an empty one to them if need be. One night in his office, his eye fell on a wooden folding chair, and, in one of those amazing, inscrutable, incredibly precious moments of insight, Goldman came up with the idea that would revolutionize grocery shopping.

He soon developed the first version of a shopping cart, basically a folding chair on wheels with a basket on the seat and another hooked to the back of the chair, one level up.

At first, his customers resisted using them, but he overcame that by planting a few shills throughout his stores who blissfully shopped with the wheeled cart. Soon thereafter, in addition to his grocery business, Goldman began manufacturing his shopping carts. By 1940, there was a seven-year wait for one of Goldman's carts.

Goldman later designed the "nesting" cart—a shopping cart that fits inside of another cart when the back is lifted up, and which is the industry standard today (you've seen stockboys pushing a long row of them across the parking lot). Another common cart is the solid one, often plastic, which does not have a hinged back. Now if they could only do something about those wobbly wheels.

# Silly Putty®

Debut: 1943
Inventive American: James Wright (for General Electric)

Boric acid and silicone oil combine to form a polymer.

This particular polymer compound bounces 25 percent higher than a regular rubber ball, stretches without tearing, is impervious to rot, and copies any image on which it is pressed flat. However, engineer James Wright, while working in the New Haven, Connecticut office of General Electric, was not trying to invent a substance that would do those things. Nonetheless, he one day accidentally mixed boric acid and silicone oil in a test tube, and Silly Putty was born.

For years, though, no one knew what it was good for or what to do with it.

It was a New Haven toy merchant who realized that its purpose was not scientific, but frivolous. It was a *toy*, and, in 1949, Silly Putty hit the market.

In the past 50 years, 12 little plastic eggs of Silly Putty have been sold every second around the clock all over the world, totaling 4,500 tons of the stuff.

Not bad for an accident, eh?

# The Skyscraper

Debut: 1885
Inventive American: Major William Le Baron Jenney

Major Jenney was the architect who designed the structural frame capable of supporting a building as it soared higher and higher into the sky. What was so special about what came to be known as the "Chicago skeleton?" For the first time in architectural history, a building's weight was not supported by its walls, but by a steel frame.

The world's first skyscraper was erected in 1885 in Chicago, Illinois, at the corner of LaSalle and Adams Streets. It was the Home Insurance Building, and it consisted of nine floors and a basement. Two floors were added in 1891. The original skyscraper is no more, and its site is now occupied by the Field building.

The first skyscraper (and all that quickly followed) boosted another relatively new business: the Otis Elevator Company. Even nine floors was a trek, and when buildings started popping up with double-digit floors, an elevator became the only way to travel!

# Slinky®

Debut: 1945
Inventive Americans: Richard James and Betty James

You know the sound a Slinky makes when it's doing its thing? Well, according to the theme song, that sound is officially described as "slinkity."

Slinky was invented by Richard James, a naval engineer who, while experimenting with coiled tension springs one day in 1943, dropped one and was astonished to see it "walk" across the floor. Recognizing the spring's potential as a toy, James spent two years perfecting the length and thickness of the wire used to make a Slinky and designing the equipment to wind them.

James's wife, Betty, coined the name of the toy and they were first sold at Gimbel's Department Store in Philadelphia in 1945.

In the first 90 minutes, 400 Slinkys were sold.

Here are some Slinky facts:

- ✪ A Slinky contains 80 feet of coiled wire.
- ✪ Enough wire has been used in the production of Slinkys to circle the world over 130 times.
- ✪ The price for a Slinky in 1945 was $1.00; today, it's around $2.
- ✪ Slinkys are sold on every continent in the world except Antarctica.

# The Slot Machine

Debut: 1887
Inventive American: Charles Fey

In my home state of Connecticut, the Foxwoods Casino grosses over $1 billion each year from casino gambling, 80 percent of which is from slot machines. Thanks to a deal negotiated by the state, Connecticut taxpayers have been paid over $1.6 billion from slots revenues in the decade from 1993 to 2003.

The first slot machine, billed as the "nickel-operated machine" and called the Liberty Belle, was designed and built by 29-year-old San Francisco mechanic Charles Fey in 1887. It is an understatement to say that it was immediately popular. The machine had three "reels" bedecked with symbols—hearts, diamonds, spades, horse-shoes, bells, and stars—that were spun whenever a player put a nickel in the slot and pulled a handle. If the reels stopped spinning so that three symbols were lined up in a row, the player won. Originally, approximately 90 percent of the money played was won back. Today, the percentage (at the Connecticut casinos, anyway) is around 93 percent.

The nickel and quarter machines are the most popular among gamers, and make up 85 percent of the slot machine business every year. The next most popular are the dime, half-dollar, and silver dollar machines. Today, there are also "paper" slot machines that take $5 bills, and there are even some huge, progressive jack-pot machines that accept $100 bills.

Slot machines are now popular all over the world. The original Liberty Belle machine can be seen at the Liberty Belle Saloon and Restaurant in Reno, Nevada, which is owned by descendants of Charles Fey.

# The Smoke Detector

Debut: 1967
Inventive Americans: Randall Smith
and Kenneth House (for BRK Electronics)

The first residential smoke alarm was designed in 1967 by BRK Electronics. Their 1969 battery-powered smoke alarm was the first smoke detector to receive Underwriters Laboratory approval. BRK eventually went on to market the First Alert smoke alarm, one of the world's most recognized and biggest-selling brands.

Smoke detectors have saved countless lives, and they have probably also frightened countless people half to death. There is nothing more terrifying than a smoke alarm going off in the middle of the night—even when there is no fire. Newer models are much less twitchy than earlier models, which would start shrieking if someone in the same zip code started frying bacon.

Today, all new installations of smoke alarms are dual-powered. They are hooked to the house's electricity, and also have a battery for back-up.

Smoke detectors have become such a ubiquitous part of American (and global) daily life that they have received one of modern society's highest accolades: They appear in movies. Usually, the scene involves a smoke alarm going off either for no reason or because someone burns something on the stove, and then the frustrated movie person taking a baseball bat, or some such deadly implement, and bludgeoning the offending siren to death. Sometimes a character will actually shoot a smoke detector. (I wouldn't want to be living in the apartment upstairs!)

Today, inexpensive smoke detectors are available everywhere, and some even come with built-in carbon monoxide detectors.

Routinely these days, one of the first facts a television journalist will report when covering a house fire is whether or not the residence had functioning smoke detectors.

# Sneakers

Debut: 1917
Inventive American: Keds

Keds were the first canvas shoe ever marketed as a "sneaker." (The preferred name, "Peds," was already taken.) They were designed for athletes, but quickly became popular as an everyday shoe.

An advertising agent named Henry Nelson McKinney came up with the name "sneakers" because they were completely silent when people walked. Yes, the sneaker is an American First, and yet now a great many of the most popular brands are manufactured anywhere *but* America. The Keds brand is now owned by Stride-Rite.

# The Space Shuttle

Debut: 1981
Inventive Americans: The fine folks at NASA

The glories of the space shuttle have been tainted by two tragedies in its proud history, the losses of the *Challenger* in 1989 and the *Columbia* in 2003, and both their crews. Nonetheless, the monumental achievement of designing and building a reusable spacecraft that takes off like a rocket and lands like a plane is one of the crowning glories of the American space program.

The first space shuttle—the ultimately doomed *Columbia*—was launched on April 12, 1981, and the spacecraft was in orbit for two days and six hours.

There have been a total of 113 shuttle missions, with two losses of vehicle and crew—a 98.23 percent success rate.

Following the loss of *Columbia* during its 28th flight on February 1, 2003, the shuttle program has been put on hold indefinitely. (In July 2003, there was some talk that NASA might be able launch a shuttle again within a year.)

Although the *Columbia* was the first space shuttle to orbit the Earth, the shuttle *Enterprise* (which was mentioned in the first *Star Trek* movie) was the first space shuttle built. It was only used for atmospheric and landing tests in 1977, and is now in storage.

# The Sprinkler Head

Debut: 1874
Inventive American: Henry S. Parmalee

Henry Parmalee's sprinkler head was a clever contraption that used water pressure and gravity to spray water. He ran a pipe off a main water pipe in the ceiling of his piano factory in New Haven, Connecticut, and then installed a perforated cap at the end of this short pipe. Once the water was turned back on, water would shoot out of the holes, though, so he had to figure out a way to cut off the water, yet somehow allow it to flow if a fire ever broke out in the factory. He came up with the perfect solution. He lightly soldered a cap onto the perforated spray head. The solder was strong enough to keep the cap in place and stop the flow of water, but it would melt easily in the case of fire. The solder seam would break, and the water pressure behind the cap would then push the cap off and the spraying water would put out the fire.

Parmalee patented his sprinkler head in 1874 and installed them in his factory with the hope of lowering his insurance premiums. It worked. Parmalee sprinkler heads were the first anti-fire sprinkler devices to be accepted by insurance companies as a safety device that would lower loss in the case of a disaster.

To this day, insurance companies offer discounts and credits for sprinkler systems and burglar alarms, etc.

# T

## The Tampon

Debut: 1929
Inventive American: Dr. Earle Haas

The tampon introduced a revolutionary idea: absorb menstrual blood while it is still inside the woman instead of allowing it to flow out of her body.

Yet this was not a new idea. The ancient Egyptians came up with the idea of wetting papyrus—paper made from grass-like plants—and inserting the softened material into the vagina to absorb menstrual flow.

The Greeks wrapped lint around sticks and inserted them for the same purpose.

But until Dr. Earle Haas designed and produced the first modern tampon in 1929, women wore thick pads between their legs to soak up menstrual blood.

On November 19, 1931, Dr. Haas filed a patent for his "catamenial device." Shortly thereafter, Gertrude Tendrich bought the patent and the rights from Dr. Haas and formed the Tampax Company.

# The Tape Measure

Debut: July 14, 1868
Inventive American: Alvin J. Fellows

The first tape measure was designed and invented by a neighbor of mine, Al Fellows. Well, that's actually a bit of a stretch because Alvin Fellows lived in the 1800s and at that time my parents were decades away from even being considered by *their* parents. But Alvin Fellows was from New Haven, Connecticut, my hometown, and that is where he did his work and came up with one of the most useful inventions of all time.

The first tape measure was a cloth tape with inches and feet markings, encased in a metal circular shell with springs to rewind the length of tape after it was used.

Prior to the tape measure, rulers and guesses were the rule of thumb. Today, tape measures are metal, can measure great lengths accurately, and have locks to keep the tape from flying back into the housing and slicing your hand open. Tell the truth: That's happened to you, right? Thought so.

# The Tea Bag

Debut: 1908
Inventive American: Thomas Sullivan

This one's a surprise, isn't it? The tea bag an *American* First? Tea has been drunk on earth since approximately 2,500 B.C. (it is, in fact, the most popular drink on earth). But, yes, the tea bag is an American First.

In 1908, Thomas Sullivan "accidentally" invented the tea bag without even knowing that he had invented it.

Sullivan was a tea merchant in New York City who came up with the idea of offering samples of his teas in little sewn silk bags. This was obviously for the convenience of his customers and also an attempt to boost business. If a customer liked a single cup of one of Sullivan's samples, he would probably come back for more.

Sullivan probably assumed people would empty the tea out of the bag into a pot and boil it in the traditional way for drinking.

Some people certainly did prepare it in the usual manner, but some customers simply poured boiling water over the silk bag that they had placed in a cup. The tea brewed just fine, and the tea bag was born. When customers began specifically ordering tea in tiny bags, Sullivan knew of that which he hath wrought. Paper quickly replaced expensive silk, and, in 1909, Thomas Lipton, capitalizing on Sullivan's invention, patented the "flow-thru tea bag."

# Teflon®

Debut: April 6, 1938
Inventive American: Dr. Roy Plunkett (for DuPont)

Teflon is actually polytetrafluoroethylene, the solid form of tetrafluoroethylene, a gas related to Freon®. One day, Dr. Plunkett, while working at DuPont, discovered that freezing and compressing the tetrafluoroethylene gas created a thermoplastic resin that was resistant to heat and chemicals, and that would eventually be recognized as one of the slipperiest substances known to man. Dr. Plunkett had accidentally discovered Teflon, and today it is used around the world on cookware, gaskets, seals, and hoses. Good thing they changed the name of the stuff to something with less than nine syllables, eh?

# The Telegraph

Debut: 1835
Inventive American: Samuel Finley Breese Morse

Samuel Morse's telegraph sent electrical signals over a distance using wires strung between two locations. (We would have to wait for Guglielmo Marconi for true wireless communication.)

In 1837, Morse patented a working telegraph machine; the first machine that could conceivably be used for commercial, military, and even, perhaps, social use. Because the machine did nothing but send electrical signals that could trigger a tone at the other end, Morse needed to invent a system for communicating using this new invention. Morse code was his solution, and it used a series of short tones (dots), long tones (dashes), and silence (spaces) to send letters and numbers. The military made good use of Morse code, and it wasn't long before there were telegraph operators who could "read" and "write" Morse code with impressive rapidity. (See page 154)

Prior to the telegraph, communication was carried out by mail and by semaphore. Communicating by semaphore utilized flags or lights to send signals over a distance. Ships would send details of their cargo by semaphore to the harbormaster. The system worked, but it was time consuming, tedious, and, of course, limited by the two signalers being within each other's sight line.

Morse's invention eliminated these problems, and within a short time after the telegraph was introduced, America was wired and we would never be the same.

Wires strung across great landscapes were not always welcomed with open arms. It is known that many wires were deliberately cut by farmers. Why? They couldn't stand the sound of the wind humming through the wires.

# The Telephone

Debut: 1876
Credited American: Alexander Graham Bell
Actual Inventor: Antonio Meucci

---

A TELEPHONE

Complete—$3

Guaranteed to work 1 mile. One guaranteed to work 5 miles $5.
State where you saw adv't. Kent, Woodman & Co.
25 Congress St. Boston.

---

*A 19th-century newspaper ad offering a private circuit telephone.*

American Alexander Graham Bell did not invent the telephone; Italian-American Antonio Meucci did.

On June 15, 2002, the United States Congress officially recognized Meucci as the true inventor of the telephone. The complete text of the resolution is on pages 226–227. It makes for fascinating and sobering reading.

Many Americans know that Bell received the patent for a telephonic device mere hours before a patent for a similar device by an inventor named Elisha Gray was filed.

What many Americans do not know is that it has now been proven that Bell probably stole the idea for the telephone from designs and drawings by Antonio Meucci that were stored in the laboratory where Bell worked.

What many Americans also do not know is that the United States Supreme Court annulled Bell's patent in 1887 on the grounds of fraud and misrepresentation.

None of this changes the fact that the telephone was an American First (although many Italian-Americans insist on calling it an Italian First) and its invention changed the world. The telephone patent is considered today to be the most valuable patent ever issued by the U.S. government.

Meucci was born in Florence, Italy in 1807 and emigrated to America in 1845. Between 1850 and 1862, Meucci developed at least 30 different models of working telephones. (The German inventor Philip Reis, who has sometimes also been credited as being the true inventor of the telephone, invented a voice-transmitting device in 1861, more than a decade after Meucci's earliest models.) However, Meucci was too poor to pay the fees required to patent his inventions (around $250), and he had to settle for a document called a Caveat, which was a formal legal notice that stated that he had invented the telephone. The caveat was meant to be temporary until official patent papers could be acquired, but Meucci did not even have the money to renew the caveat. In 1874, he turned over some of his models to the vice president of Western Union Telegraphs, and, two years later, read in the newspaper that Alexander Graham Bell (who, remember, had been working at the Western Union Labs), had patented a telephone and taken full credit for its invention. Even though this patent was annulled, Meucci never profited from his invention and he died poor in 1889.

As a sixth-generation Italian-American, I am proud to set the record straight, at least in this small way, in this book.

107th CONGRESS

1st session

H. RES. 269

Expressing the sense of the House of Representatives to honor the life and achievements of 19th Century Italian-American inventor Antonio Meucci, and his work in the invention of the telephone.

_____

IN THE HOUSE OF REPRESENTATIVES

Mr. FOSSELLA

submitted the following resolution;

which was referred to the Committee on June 15, 2002

RESOLUTION

Expressing the sense of the House of Representatives to honor the life and achievements of 19th Century Italian-American inventor Antonio Meucci, and his work in the invention of the telephone.

Whereas Antonio Meucci, the great Italian inventor, had a career that was both extraordinary and tragic;

Whereas upon immigrating to New York, Meucci continued to work with ceaseless vigor on a project he had begun in Havana, Cuba, an invention he later called the 'teletrofono,' involving electronic communications;

2

Whereas Meucci set up a rudimentary communication link in his Staten Island home that connected the basement with the first floor, and later, when his wife began to suffer from crippling arthritis, he created a permanent link between his lab and his wife's second floor bedroom;

Whereas, having exhausted most of his life's savings in pursuing his work, Meucci was unable to commercialize his invention, though he demonstrated his invention in 1860 and had a description of it published in New York's Italian language newspaper;

Whereas Meucci never learned English well enough to navigate the complex American business community;

Whereas Meucci was unable to raise sufficient funds to pay his way through the patent application process, and thus had to settle for a caveat, a one year renewable notice of an impending patent, which was first filed on December 28, 1871;

Whereas Meucci later learned that the Western Union affiliate laboratory reportedly lost his working models, and Meucci, who at this point was living on public assistance, was unable to renew the caveat after 1874;

Whereas in March 1876, Alexander Graham Bell, who conducted experiments in the same laboratory where Meucci's materials had been stored, was granted a patent and was thereafter credited with inventing the telephone;

Whereas on January 13, 1887, the Government of the United States moved to annul the patent issued to Bell on the grounds of fraud and misrepresentation, a case that the Supreme Court found viable and remanded for trial;

3

Whereas Meucci died in October 1889, the Bell patent expired in January 1893, and the case was discontinued as moot without ever reaching the underlying issue of the true inventor of the telephone entitled to the patent; and

Whereas if Meucci had been able to pay the $10 fee to maintain the caveat after 1874, no patent could have been issued to Bell: Now, therefore, be it Resolved, That it is the sense of the House of Representatives that the life and achievements of Antonio Meucci should be recognized, and his work in the invention of the telephone should be acknowledged.

# The Telephone Book

Debut: February 1878
Inventive American: the New Haven
District Telephone Company

This will sound like a joke, but it's all true: The first telephone book did not have any phone numbers in it.

In February 1878, the New Haven District Telephone Company published a one-page "book." There were only 50 names in it, and, as noted, no phone numbers. The 50 names were organized into four categories: Residential, Professional, Essential Services, and Miscellaneous. The few telephone service subscribers used the book by picking up the phone and asking the operator to connect them with someone listed in the book. With only 50 people and businesses with a phone (minus city and service numbers), couldn't the Elm City residents simply have done that without looking anything up in the book? Just asking.

Today's New Haven and environs phone book (I happen to have one handy because I live in New Haven) is in two volumes: Residential and Business White Pages, and the Yellow Pages. The White Pages are close to 900 pages long, and contain approximately 350,000 listings. The Yellow Pages are an inch-and-a-half thick, and, in addition to more than 75,000 business listings, contain maps, government directories, coupons, and even Hispanic "Orange Pages."

The phone book certainly has come a long way since the days of the one-page book and operator–dialed calls, eh?

# Tetracycline

Debut: 1952 (patented in 1955)
Inventive American: Lloyd Conover (for Pfizer)

After Lloyd Conover earned his Ph.D. from the University of Rochester in 1950 at the age of 27, he gave serious thought to becoming a professor. He had always believed he would teach at the university level after completing his education, but things sometimes do not always work out the way we plan. He was offered a job in the research department at Pfizer Laboratories, and he accepted the position. A mere two years later, Conover, working with a team of Pfizer researchers, figured out a way of altering the molecular structure of existing antibiotics to create new, more powerful broad-spectrum antibiotics.

Conover "took apart" the existing antibiotics Terramycin® and Aureomycin® and, by chemically altering certain individual components of the drugs, discovered/created tetracycline (which, for the chemically-minded of you out there, is $C_{22}H_{24}N_2O_8$).

Conover patented tetracycline in 1955 and, by 1958, it was the most-prescribed broad-spectrum antibiotic in the United States.

Today, there are more powerful antibiotics—highly potent "superdrugs"—than tetracycline, but its creation served as an example to other pharmacologists and launched an era of research into creating new, more effective drugs by modifying existing medications. Tetracycline is still used in the treatment of Rocky Mountain spotted fever and Lyme disease.

# Toilet Paper

Debut: 1857
Inventive American: Joseph Coyetty

To put this as indelicately as possible, people have been wiping their butts for as long as we have had butts, so how can toilet paper be an American First?

Simple: Until American Joseph Coyetty invented the soft paper for "personal cleaning," people used anything *but* paper to wipe themselves.

There is very little extant information about the noble Mr. Coyetty, and some sources doubt the authenticity of his story, yet enough sources credit him as the father of TP for us to give him the encomium.

The very first paper marketed specifically for wiping appeared in 1880 in England, but the paper was not on a roll. Small individual sheets of paper were sold in a box.

What was used before paper? Mussel shells, coconut shells, wool, lace, clods of earth, stones, wet sponges, and, of course, the bare hand.

The voluminous Sears catalog was popular around the turn of the century in rural America (people were horrified when Sears switched to a glossy paper), and corncobs were the gold standard for Colonial-era Americans.

Today, it is commonly accepted that America has the softest toilet paper in the world.

# Touch-Tone® Dialing

Debut: 1941
Inventive American: The fine folks at Bell Systems

Remember how long it used to take characters in movies to dial a phone before Touch-Tone phones?

And remember how moviegoers sat patiently as the seven dialed numbers click-click-clicked around the circular dial? I always hoped that the number had a lot of twos and threes in it. The numbers with zeros and nines in them were sheer torture.

The first Touch-Tone telephone system was installed in Baltimore, Maryland in 1941. The new system used tones instead of the pulses that were generated by dial phones, but the technology was so exorbitantly expensive that only the operators could push the buttons to dial calls. There was no way people could afford to have Touch Tone technology in their homes.

In 1948, William Shockley and John Bardeen invented the transistor, a tiny electronic device that could be used as a circuit in a switch or in an amplifier. In 1952, the transistor was used in a hearing aid for the first time. Over the next decade, the Bell engineers were able to take advantage of miniaturization technology to manufacture Touch-Tone technology at a much lower cost, and, in 1962, Touch-Tone phones for the general public were introduced at the Seattle World's Fair. (Interestingly, the Seattle World's Fair got a few things right about "the future," i.e., *now*. It was pre-dicted that computers would be commonplace today and that they would be used for paying bills, writing checks, and "possibly" send-ing messages. They also got a few things wrong, though, such as predicting that traffic would be virtually eliminated by the year 2000 thanks to personal helicopters and jet backpacks. And I don't think the idea of a personal hydroelectric dam in every backyard for electricity generation is coming anytime soon.)

As is often the case with cultural evolution, there are people alive today who lived with dial technology *and* Touch-Tone technology; and there are young people who have never known anything but Touch-Tone phones. Many of them I've spoken to find it inconceivable that it took so long to dial a phone. And they're only referring to dialing a call by pushing the keys with their finger. We didn't even get into speed dialing!

# The Traffic Signal

Debut: 1923
Inventive American: Garrett Augustus Morgan

Necessity is the mother of invention, the adage goes; the invention of the traffic signal is a classic example of this paradigm.

The car was invented in the first decade of the 20th century. Shortly after the first cars hit the road, the first cars hit each other...and carts, and animals, and bicycles.

Garrett Morgan was an extremely successful African-American businessman and inventor. He only had an elementary school education, but had hired tutors to further his schooling. He invented the gas mask, the traffic sign, and started a personal products company that offered hair-straightening creams and combs, and he launched a newspaper, the *Cleveland Call*.

Thanks to his financial prosperity, Morgan was able to buy a house and a car, and it was while driving through the streets of Cleveland one day in 1923 that he came up with the idea of some kind of signaling device installed at intersections to prevent accidents.

Morgan had witnessed a collision between an automobile and a horse-drawn carriage and realized it could have easily been prevented if one of the vehicles had simply stopped and allowed the other to pass.

Because there was no one or nothing in control of traffic, each driver assumed he had the right of way, and, thus, collisions in the 1920s were frequent and disruptive on the streets of America.

Morgan designed a T-shaped pole that was manually controlled and had three positions: stop, go, and all stop. All stop
halted traffic coming from all directions so pedestrians could cross
the street safely.

In his patent application, Morgan wrote, "This invention
relates to traffic signals, and particularly to those which are
adapted to be positioned adjacent the intersection of two or more
streets and are manually operable for directing the flow of traffic...
In addition, my invention contemplates the provision of a signal
which may be readily and cheaply manufactured."

Morgan's traffic signal was immediately accepted and put
into use all over America until red, yellow, and green
traffic lights replaced them. Nowadays, traffic lights are
controlled by computers and by sensors placed beneath
the streets. (This still doesn't prevent backups or traffic
jams, though.)

The three color system is now used around the
world. Red means stop, green means go, yellow means
caution, or as Jeff Bridges's alien visitor character in
*Starman* put it, "Yellow—drive very fast."

Garrett Morgan was awarded a citation for his traffic signal
invention. He died in 1963.

# Tupperware®

Debut: 1947
Inventive American: Earl Silas Tupper

Tupperware containers are plastic bowls and other containers
with airtight lids that "seal in the freshness." When Tupperware
was first introduced to the market shortly after Earl Tupper, a
New Hampshire tree surgeon and plastics worker, invented it in
1947 (using a leftover piece of polyethylene slag given to him by
his boss at DuPont), sales were terrible. Originally offered in stores,
people were confused as to how to work the patented burp system
in which you press down on the center of the cover, slightly lift an
edge, and vent all the air out of the container.

Earl decided that he needed to demonstrate how the containers
worked, and, by 1951, Tupperware was no longer being sold in

stores, but through in-home Tupperware Parties. (Tupperware later returned to high-volume retailers such as Target®—temporarily.) The party system proved so successful that, today, a Tupperware Party reportedly begins every two seconds somewhere in the world. Tupperware's yearly sales are in excess of $1.2 billion. Tupperware has become so ubiquitous, there was even a *Seinfeld* episode written in which Kramer almost had a nervous breakdown when the homeless person he gave some food to refused to return his Tupperware bowl. *"It locks in freshness, Jerry!"*

In 2003, Tupperware canceled its contract with the Target department store chain—but not because they weren't happy with the sales. Quite the contrary. Tupperware sales were so healthy in Target that Tupperware party sales dropped, and individual party reps were losing income. The company knew that party sales were the source of the majority of their Tupperware income and they did not want to further jeopardize their unique marketing system.

So we can no longer buy Tupperware at Target. But we can go to a Tupperware party and indulge to our heart's content. Kramer would be so pleased.

# The Tuxedo

### Debut: October 1886
### Inventive American: Griswold Lorillard

One of the indicators that you have made it in this world is having a tuxedo in your closet. If you need to wear a tuxedo often enough that you need one of your own, then you are clearly traveling in lofty circles—certainly outside the orbits of the unwashed masses and hoi polloi. Also, if you can afford a decent tuxedo of your own, you have probably gone a ways beyond "getting by."

How did the tuxedo come to symbolize affluence and celebration? How did a specific type of formal wear attain an *identity*? And how could James Bond wear a rubber diving suit over his tux and not get the pants and jacket wet?

A tuxedo is actually two things: a jacket and a suit.

According to the *American Heritage Dictionary*, a tuxedo is "a man's dress jacket, usually black with satin or grosgrain lapels,

worn for formal or semiformal occasions. Also called dinner jacket."
A tuxedo is also defined as "a complete outfit including this jacket,
trousers usually with a silken stripe down the side, a bow tie, and
often a cummerbund." (I always hated the cummerbund. They
look great if you're standing still, but if you sit or dance or bend, it
rides up and looks like a back support brace bizarrely strapped to
your midsection.)

The tuxedo is named after a country club in Tuxedo
Park in southeast New York. The story is told that in
October 1886, Griswold Lorillard and his friends
showed up at the very first Autumn Ball at the Tuxedo
Park Country Club wearing a satin-lapelled jacket. This
should not have raised eyebrows except for the fact that
the jacket did not have tails, and every other male at
the ball was in traditional white tie and tails.

Since Lorillard and posse's memorable entrance
that cool autumn night, the tuxedo has become the
outfit de rigueur; the *definitive* wedding suit (except for
nude weddings and City Hall weddings, of course), and the delight of formal wear purveyors everywhere who look forward to
prom season each year with visions of tuxedo rentals (and dollar
signs) dancing in their dreams.

(On a personal note, I wore an all-white tux at my own wedding.
I was a few pounds lighter and had much longer hair back then,
but man, oh man, was I stylin'. They don't call it "timeless" for
nothing.)

## The TV Dinner

Debut: 1953
Inventive American: Gerry Thomas (for Swanson)

In 1953, the homes that had TVs had *one* TV, and it was
always in the living room.

Today, TVs are everywhere.

There's one in the living room, the family room, every bedroom,
often the kitchen, and sometimes even the bathroom. People watch
TV while they eat in the kitchen, and, in many homes, it is on
while they sleep.

Back then, TV watching was new: 10 percent of Americans owned TVs, and the demand was high among the rest of the country for TVs, but television as a societal force had not reached anywhere near the level of cultural saturation it commands today.

It wasn't long after TV's debut that people began to do other things while they sat in front of the big glowing box—specifically, *eat*. And even though bringing plates and serving dishes into the living room was a nuisance, people still did it so they could watch TV while they ate.

In the winter of 1952, the Swanson company had a problem. They had 10 refrigerated railroad cars containing 520,000 pounds of frozen turkeys traveling back and forth across America because they couldn't sell them.

Sales manager Gerry Thomas challenged the Swanson employees to come up with a way to sell the turkeys and, even though he received many suggestions, it was Thomas himself who came up with the winning idea.

One day on a business trip, he noticed that the Pan Am food serving trays had individual compartments. The lightbulb went on and the idea of the TV dinner came to Thomas in a heartbeat.

The result of his brainstorm was the first Swanson frozen "television dinner," packaged in a box that looked like a TV set.

The dinner initially had three compartments. The largest held slices of turkey on top of cornbread stuffing, covered with brown gravy. The two smaller sections held a serving of potatoes and a serving of peas, each of which had its own pat of butter. After 20 minutes in the oven, dinner was served.

The first TV dinners were incredibly expensive at the time: They sold for 98 cents, which would be comparable to $6 in today's dollars. Even the most expensive frozen dinner of today doesn't come close to that price.

Thomas initially ordered production of 5,000 dinners. This was somewhat less than they ended up needing: Swanson sold 10 million turkey TV dinners the first year they were introduced. They eventually added a fourth compartment for dessert and expanded the line to include Salisbury steak, meatloaf, and fried chicken.

The TV dinner simplified American's beloved pastime of watching TV while eating. The folding TV tray soon followed, which made every living room chair a dining room chair.

Would Gerry Thomas's idea of a complete frozen meal have been so readily accepted if he had not linked it with television? Probably. The TV dinner was introduced at a time when more and more women were working outside the home and yet still held the responsibility of providing a complete meal for the family every evening. The TV dinner's success might have taken a little longer, but the popularity of frozen prepared foods today (greatly bolstered by the invention of the microwave oven) speaks to Americans' love of anything quick and easy.

This trend is, to some extent, paradoxical. Cookbooks are one of the biggest-selling category of books in America. And yet the frozen prepared food business expands greatly each year. This means that people are buying cookbooks, but nobody's cooking.

Maybe everyone's looking longingly at the pictures?

# The TV Remote Control

Debut: 1950 (Zenith); 1955 (Polley for Zenith)
Inventive American: Eugene Polley (for Zenith)

The TV remote control made an enormous contribution toward the shortening of the American attention span. Today, channel-surfing TV viewers can view a program for—literally—a fraction of a second, decide if they want to watch it, and then move on to the next channel. And commercials can now be instantly muted, or not watched at all by flipping to another channel for the four minutes or so of advertising on the channel the viewer was watching.

Imagine watching television before the remote control.

You looked through the TV listings, you picked a program, you turned the TV's mechanical tuner (with its funky, deep-throated click) to the right channel, you adjusted the volume (and maybe the rabbit ears if you did not have an antenna), and then you sat down. The volume remained at the level at which it was set; the channel remained where it was (yes, even during commercials), and if the phone rang or someone walked into the room, you all had to talk over the sound of the TV, because the mute button had not yet been invented.

Yes, I know. What a royal pain in the patootie. And to all my younger readers who have never known anything but a remote-control-life, this was not—believe it or not—considered a royal pain in the patootie back then. In fact, most people were thrilled with being able to sit in their living rooms and watch TV. Getting up to change the channel or adjust the volume was a small, insignificant price to pay for such a technological wonder in their own home.

Then, into these halcyon days came the remote control. In 1950, Zenith offered the first TV remote control. It was called the Lazy Bones (an unintentionally insightful slur against future generations) and it was connected to the TV set by a wire that ran across the living room floor. A motor attached to the TV's tuner turned the channels when the viewer worked the remote. The Lazy Bones was very popular but, you guessed it, people kept tripping on the wire. Why didn't people just step over it? Perhaps they were mesmerized by the wonders flitting across their TV screen: *The Marshall Plan in Action* (Sundays at 9:30 p.m. on ABC); *Life Begins at Eighty* (Mondays at 10 p.m. on ABC); *The Court of Current Issues* (Tuesdays at 8 p.m. on DuMont); *Wrestling from Columbia Park* (Mondays at 9 p.m. on DuMont); or *The Horace Heidt Show* (Mondays at 9 p.m. on CBS). (Horace Heidt was actually a big band leader who still has a following.)

TV watchers had to deal with the Lazy Bones (and the programming of the time, but that's a whole other book) for a few years as Zenith worked on developing a wireless remote control. In 1955, they came out with the Flashmatic, a wireless remote control that worked by sending a beam to four photoelectric cells, one installed in each corner of the TV cabinet. This was a definite improvement, except for one major glitch. If the sun shown on the TV at just the right angle, the TV tuner would start turning wildly. (One cannot help but wonder how many devoted Catholics called priests in to bless their houses after their TV started changing channels by itself.)

The Flashmatic was replaced by the Zenith Space Command remote control. This device used aluminum rods that emitted specific high-frequency sounds when struck by a trigger-like device. It added 30 percent to the cost of a TV, but people loved it and it was an overwhelming success.

In the 1960s, transistor technology became available, and Zenith began manufacturing smaller, lighter, battery-controlled devices that could create the ultrasound frequencies needed to control the tuner.

Ultrasound remotes were the state of the art for more than two decades until the 1980s when infrared technology became available. IR technology uses an infrared light beam that is invisible to the human eye but which can be "seen" by a receiver in the television set. Infrared is the universal standard today, and electronics manufacturers have greatly expanded the remote control's capabilities.

Universal remotes can now control several devices at once; digital cable remotes are interactive and allow the user to access onscreen programming guides, interactive news services, and other features simply and quickly.

What is the future of the remote control, the device that had its genesis because people did not want to get up off the couch to change the channel?

Experts believe that the day is coming when every home will have one remote control that will allow complete control over everything that goes on in the house. Lighting, heating, air-conditioning, cooking, communications, computers, security systems, sinks, tubs, and more will all be controlled from one device. A homeowner could be sitting on the sofa and, with the push of a few buttons, turn on the lights in a certain room, start the water running in the tub, activate the alarm system, turn on the house-wide sound system (and pick the music they want to hear), answer a phone call through the TV, and check their computers for e-mail.

Guess "Lazy Bones" wasn't too far off the mark, eh?

# The Typewriter

Debut: 1867
Inventive American: Christopher Latham Sholes

The first author to submit a typed manuscript to a publisher was none other than Mark Twain, who obviously knew a good thing when he saw one. (It was *Tom Sawyer*.)

Imagine: Prior to the late 1800s, all the great books that existed had been written in longhand. Writers 'o yore certainly did have a work ethic, eh? Many writers of today, however, consider a typewriter too primitive a tool for their efforts. "You mean I have to retype a page if I want to move a paragraph from one place to another? What kind of nonsense is that?!"

Christopher Sholes, a printer and editor, invented the first true typewriter in 1867 using an old telegraph key and a flat plate coated with carbon. The letters could not be spaced and the paper had to be positioned by hand.

Carlos Glidden and Samuel Soulé worked with Sholes, and, after he built his initial working prototype, they helped add features and improvements until it was ready for patenting and commercial sale. The first typewriter patent was issued on June 23, 1868, and, within a few years, the rights were bought by the Remington gun-making company.

The typewriter was one of the most important and influential breakthroughs in the field of written communication in mankind's history. And yes, there are still writers who will only work on a typewriter—Harlan Ellison among them. It is not farfetched, however, to envision a coming day when typewriters will still be available, but will be as hard to find as LPs.

# V

## Vacuum Cleaner

Debut: 1899
Inventive American: John S. Thurman

The vacuum cleaner is a useful piece of equipment, but everyone (including non-humans) hates the sound of the infernal machine.

What a bloody, godforsaken racket! A hellish, relentless roar at what seems to be the perfect frequency for maximum annoyance.

The first vacuum cleaner was, if you can imagine, gasoline powered. So not only were homemakers subjected to the noise of the thing, they also had to contend with gasoline fumes, which probably would be comparable today to having a gasoline-powered lawn mower running full-bore in your living room.

After inventing his "pneumatic carpet renovator," Thurman went door-to-door in a horse-drawn cart, providing a carpet vacuuming service in St. Louis, Missouri. He charged $4 per visit, which would be close to $100 today.

# Valium®

Debut: 1963
Inventive American: Dr. Leo Sternbach

How well-known ("popular" might be the better word) is Valium?

No less than the Rolling Stones writing a song about the drug called "Mother's Little Helper." (Mick and company specifically wrote about the 5 milligram tablet—"the little yellow pill.")

Elizabeth Taylor admitted to a Valium and alcohol habit; TV producer Barbara Gordon ended up in an insane asylum when she quite the drug cold turkey. In its early years, it was known as "Executive Excedrin," due to its popularity among high-powered business types.

Valium is the trade name for the drug diazepam, which is used in the treatment of anxiety and tension and as a sedative, a muscle relaxant, and an anticonvulsant. It is quickly addictive, and as little as 4 to 6 weeks of use can create physical dependence. No doubt a large part of Valium's appeal is its ability to "smooth the edges" (as some users have described its effects) and help people ignore or cope with many of the daily stresses of their lives.

Valium was created in 1963 by Dr. Leo Sternbach, a Polish-born émigré to America, while he was working for the Hoffman-LaRoche pharmaceutical company in New Jersey. For many years after its introduction, Valium was the most prescribed drug in America. It has since been usurped by newer nostrums such as Prozac, Paxil, and Zoloft.

# Volleyball

Debut: 1895
Inventive American: William G. Morgan

Nudists seem to love volleyball. Those nudist magazines from the 1950s that Hawkeye Pierce enjoyed, uh, "reading" on *M*A*S*H* were always loaded with pictures of naked people playing volleyball. Why volleyball? Why not basketball? Or softball? Or touch football? (On second thought, I know why not touch football.)

Was it the sporadic jumping followed by lengths of time standing still and bending slightly forward? Perhaps a research study should be mounted, eh?

Volleyball is an American First, and yet it was more popular elsewhere in the world for decades before taking off in the good ol' U.S. of A. For ages, only soccer was more popular around the world.

In 1895, William Morgan invented the game of volleyball by combining elements of tennis, baseball, basketball, and handball. He raised a tennis net to 6 feet, 6 inches above the ground and wrote rules for the game, which required a team to ground the ball on their opposing team's side of the net in no more than three tries. Fifteen points (originally 21) won the game.

Today, close to 50 million people in America play volleyball at least once a week; 800 million around the world also play regularly. Volleyball is an Olympic sport, both in team and 2-man play (the U.S. men's team won their first gold medal in volleyball at the 1984 Olympics in Los Angeles; the U.S. women's team took home a silver medal), and beach tournaments are broadcast regularly on ESPN.

And from what I hear, volleyball is still popular among nudists. Maybe it's the jumping?

# W

## Waterskiing

Debut: 1922
Inventive American: Ralph Samuelson

If there is anything that flawlessly illustrates the concept of a "no-brainer," it is the "invention" of the sport of waterskiing.

Did its originator conceive it out of whole cloth, concocting scoring procedures, working with different approaches, scrapping the ones that didn't work until he was satisfied that he had a valid, appealing, exciting sport?

Nope.

The sport of waterskiing was created by Ralph Samuelson, an 18-year-old sports enthusiast from Minnesota, who one day got the idea of skiing on water while he was skiing on snow.

With very little effort, we can easily duplicate Samuelson's Eureka moment: "This would be so cool on water."

And voilà, a sport was born.

# WD-40®

Debut: 1953
Inventive American: Norm Larsen
(for Rocket Chemical Company)

Does "WD-40" actually stand for something, or was it just a catchy phrase somebody came up with to give the product a no-nonsense name?

WD-40 stands for "Water Displacement, 40th attempt."

Before WD-40 was perfected, there were 39 prior versions of the petroleum-based lubricant that did not pass muster.

After its development, WD-40 was first used to protect the exterior of the Atlas missile, and was mainly manufactured for the aerospace industry. In 1958, the lubricant was packaged for consumer use and is now one of the most well-known brand names of all time.

The top five household uses for WD-40 are:

✪ Removing crayon marks from walls, countertops, and tables.

✪ Removing the adhesive left behind when a price tag or some kind of label is removed from an item.

✪ Dissolving grease splatters in the kitchen.

✪ "De-squeaking" doors.

✪ Getting Silly Putty out of carpets.

# The Weather Channel

Debut: May 2, 1982
Inventive Americans: The fine folks at the Weather Channel

Weather junkies leave the Weather Channel on all day long, much like the food junkies who leave the Food Channel on, and delight in the intricacies of recipes they will never, in a million years, make.[17] WC addicts know the names of the channel's meteorologists, can explain the movements of the jet stream to their friends, and some of them even collect the music played on the channel during the six-times-an-hour local weather updates.

When the Weather Channel debuted on Sunday, May 2, 1982, they described themselves as "the non-ending weather telethon." It has since become much more than that, and the Weather Channel is now available on basic cable in more than 85 million American homes. It has metamorphosed into one of those American Firsts that probably could only have come into being in America. Only in America could watching the weather for hours on end become a hobby. Americans are not satisfied with a grocery store; we must have a superstore. We are not satisfied with a corner package store; we must have a liquor "warehouse." And we are not satisfied with a few minutes of the weather two or three times a day; we must have non-stop weather, around the clock—with local updates every eight minutes.

The Weather Channel's style can be described as "calm," and the forecasters often come across as really smart professors taking the time to be sure all of his or her students fully understand the material. The Weather Channel takes the time to explain in detail what is going on with the weather. (Although with 24 hours a day to fill, it is not surprising that their coverage can be—actually, *must* be—more expansive and in-depth than local weather broadcasts.)

The Weather Channel embraces technology (don't you just love that Doppler radar?), and nowhere is this more evident than on their Website (*www.weather.com*), which gets a staggering 350 million hits each month and is rated in the top 20 Websites in America. Their site is much more than just a place to get your weather (or the weather of Jakarta, if you so desire); it is a full-service weather resource. The site boasts comprehensive features on hurricanes, blizzards, tornadoes, and other weather events, and its information is accurate and complete. They also now regularly run informative documentaries on historical storms and weather-related topics, often with a focus on preparedness. (On a personal note, when I was writing my book *The 100 Greatest Disasters of All Time*, I found the Weather Channel's Website a godsend for accurate information about hurricanes and other major disasters I was covering in the book.)

The Weather Channel also has international Websites in the United Kingdom, Brazil, Latin America, Germany, and France. There is also a "Weather Channel" TV station and Website in Australia, but they are not related to the Atlanta-based Weather Channel.

There is something intriguing about knowing what kind of weather is happening somewhere else. I learned this firsthand when I started including the New Haven temperature, and later, the New Haven weather on my own Website, (*stephenspignesi.com*). I heard from people in Arizona, California, Britain, and elsewhere who visited my site because of interest in one of my books and, believe it or not, greatly enjoyed knowing what the weather was like in New Haven, Connecticut on the particular day they stopped by. Why is this so? Perhaps it relates to the adage that there are more ways to travel than physically...?

## The Weather Map

Debut: Late 1700s
Inventive American: Benjamin Franklin

A weather map is a map or chart depicting the meteorological conditions over a specific geographic area at a specific time.[18]

Benjamin Franklin seems to have been the first person to collect weather reports and then draw maps detailing the weather for specific areas. Franklin did not have any means of compiling this information other than through the mail, and that is precisely how he accomplished it. Franklin asked many of his friends to keep journals in which they would record the local weather—the temperature, the precipitation, cloud cover, storms, for example—and then mail them to him. Using the data, he would draw maps for each day of recorded information.

Granted, these were not the predictive maps of today, nor even of the type used later by the U.S. Army Signal Corps (later the National Weather Service), but they were the first true weather maps.

## Windows® Operating System

Debut: 1983
Inventive American: Douglas Engelbart (for Microsoft)

When the history of the computer in the 20th century is written, Microsoft's Windows operating system will be the main character. Will it be the villain or the hero? Ask 100 Windows users and you'll get 50 villain and 50 hero responses.

Douglas Engelbart oringally invented Windows for computers in the 1960s at Stanford Research Institute. It was put into development for mainstream application in the 1970s and Apple was the first to use it for its personal computers. The Macintosh was the first computer to use the Windows interface—a rectangular area of a computer screen that allows a user to use and see several operations, programs, and documents at once.

The system was purchased by Microsoft and patented under the "Windows" name, and several new versions have since been developed and released over the years.

Nonetheless, it is the definitive computer interface and it was, indeed, an American First.

# Windshield Wipers

Debut: 1903
Inventive American: Mary Anderson

It wasn't long after the invention of the motor vehicle that, again, necessity—that demanding mother of invention—reared her head. The first windshield wipers were invented by Mary Anderson around 1903, patented by her in 1905, and initially only used on streetcars. Her friends in Alabama apparently mocked her idea, but she continued to work on it, and a few years later, they were on many cars of the time. By 1915, they were standard equipment on all automobiles.

Anderson never sold her idea, and thus, never profited from her creativity and enterprise. Automobile manufacturers began designing and manufacturing their own versions of the windshield wiper, and they were apparently different enough from Anderson's version as to not infringe on her copyright. In a sense, the idea became public domain as soon as companies began making their own "wiping blades."

Today, windshield wipers are even available on many vehicles for rear windows, although they are not standard. One cannot help but wonder why.

# The Wire Coat Hanger

Debut: 1903
Inventive American: Albert J. Parkhouse
(for Timberlake Wire and Novelty Company)

The first wire coat hanger was invented in 1903 as a response to workers' gripes about too few coat hooks at the Timberlake Wire and Novelty Company.

In 1932, Schuyler Hulett added cardboard tubes to the shoulders of the hanger and patented this modification.

In 1935, Elmer Rogers came up with the idea of using a cardboard tube on the lower wire. This idea was later improved by replacing the lower wire with hooked ends which are inserted into each end of the cardboard tube. This hanger is now used by dry cleaners all over the world.

# The Written National Constitution

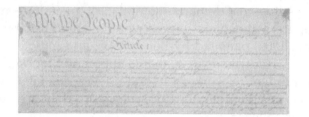

Debut: 1789
Inventive Americans: the Founding Fathers
of the United States

The Constitution of the United States—the oldest and shortest of all national constitutions—is a masterpiece of economical language that brilliantly addresses universal human concerns.[19] The Constitution is the written codification of the fundamental law of the United States and may be the landmark legal document of all time. The Constitution replaced the Articles of Confederation, which did not allow for a Chief Executive. The Constitution was drafted in Philadelphia in 1787, ratified in 1788, and went into effect in 1789.

The Constitution established a strong central government and was unique in requiring that the government must abide by the rule of law.

The Preamble to the Constitution stated, in a single, simple paragraph, the purpose of the Constitution:

- ✪ To form a more perfect union.
- ✪ To establish justice.
- ✪ To ensure domestic tranquility.
- ✪ To provide for the common defense.
- ✪ To promote the general welfare.
- ✪ To secure the blessings of liberty.

Simple words with profound reach.

The Constitution, written by the members of the Constitutional Convention, established the three branches of the United States government: executive (the presidency and state governorships), Judicial (the courts system), and legislative (Congress).

There have been 27 amendments added to the Constitution since 1789.

### BENJAMIN FRANKLIN ON MORAL PERFECTION

Moral perfection—actually the goal of *achieving* moral perfection—is not, of course, an American First. Virtuous people have been trying to lead moral lives since time immemorial. Yet America's Founding Father Benjamin Franklin took this goal to a higher level. This paragon of wisdom and inventor of the bifocal lens, the catheter, the odometer, and the writer of *Poor Richard's Almanack*, was relentlessly self-critical, as were many of the achievers and visionaries profiled in this book.

Franklin set out to live 13 moral virtues on a daily basis—all while working on his many creative projects and his writings. His words hold wisdom for us even today. (His advice regarding "Industry" defined, in a few words, the motivations of probably all the inventors and thinkers in *American Firsts*.)

**Note:** Purists will be horrified, but I have slightly edited Franklin's piece for clarity, specifically adding the "e" in past tense verbs like "wished," which, in Franklin's time, was written as "wish'd", and changing the archaic spelling of "cloaths" to "clothes."

## An excerpt from
### *The Autobiography of Benjamin Franklin*

*It was about this time I conceived the bold and arduous project of arriving at moral perfection. I wished to live without committing any fault at any time; I would conquer all that either natural inclination, custom, or company might lead me into. As I knew, or thought I knew, what was right and wrong, I did not see why I might not always do the one and avoid the other. But I soon found I had undertaken a task of more difficulty than I had imagined. While my care was employed in guarding against one fault, I was often surprised by another; habit took the advantage of inattention; inclination was sometimes too strong for reason. I concluded, at length, that the mere speculative conviction that it was our interest to be completely virtuous, was not sufficient to prevent our slipping; and that the contrary habits must be broken, and good ones acquired and established, before we can have any dependence on a steady, uniform rectitude of conduct. For this purpose I therefore contrived the following method.*

*In the various enumerations of the moral virtues I had met within my reading, I found the catalogue more or less numerous, as different writers included more or fewer ideas under the same name. Temperance, for example, was by some confined to eating and drinking, while by others it was extended to mean the moderating [of] every other pleasure, appetite, inclination, or passion, bodily or mental, even to our avarice and ambition. I propose[d] to myself, for the sake of clearness, to use rather more names, with fewer ideas annexed to each, than a few names with more ideas; and I included under thirteen names of virtues all that at that time occurred to me as necessary or desirable, and annexed to each a short precept, which fully expressed the extent I gave to its meaning.*

*These names of virtues, with their precepts, were:*

1. *Temperance. Eat not to dullness; drink not to elevation.*
2. *Silence. Speak not but what may benefit others or yourself; avoid trifling conversation.*

3. *Order. Let all your things have their places; let each part of your business have its time.*

4. *Resolution. Resolve to perform what you ought; perform without fail what you resolve.*

5. *Frugality. Make no expense but to do good to others or yourself; i.e., waste nothing.*

6. *Industry. Lose no time; be always employed in something useful; cut off all unnecessary actions.*

7. *Sincerity. Use no hurtful deceit; think innocently and justly, and, if you speak, speak accordingly.*

8. *Justice. Wrong none by doing injuries, or omitting the benefits that are your duty.*

9. *Moderation. Avoid extremes; forbear resenting injuries so much as you think they deserve.*

10. *Cleanliness. Tolerate no uncleanliness in body, clothes, or habitation.*

11. *Tranquility. Be not disturbed at trifles, or at accidents common or unavoidable.*

12. *Chastity. Rarely use venery but for health or offspring, never to dullness, weakness, or the injury of your own or another's peace or reputation.*

13. *Humilty. Imitate Jesus and Socrates.*

*My intention being to acquire the habitude of all these virtues, I judged it would be well not to distract my attention by attempting the whole at once, but to fix it on one of them at a time; and, when I should be master of that, then to proceed to another, and so on, till I should have gone through the thirteen; and, as the previous acquisition of some might facilitate the acquisition of certain others, I arranged them with that view, as they stand above.*

# Y

## The Yellow Pages

Debut: 1886
Inventive American: Reuben H. Donnelly

The term "yellow pages" was not used commercially until 1886 when Reuben H. Donnelly published a directory of business names and phone numbers, organized categorically, exactly as the book is published today. (R.H. Donnelly continues to be an important printer, and, until recently, was based in Old Saybrook, Connecticut.)

The first actual use of the term "yellow pages," however, occurred in 1883 when a printing firm working on a residential telephone directory (the typical "white pages" directory) ran out of white paper and had to use yellow paper to finish the job.

So, ironically, the first time a "yellow pages" directory was offered to the telephoning public, the listings were for residential phones.

# Z

## The Zamboni®

Debut: 1949
Inventive American: Frank Zamboni

It's cheap and juvenile, but the name of this machine always gets a laugh. Charles Schultz once based a whole *Peanuts* story line on the Zamboni. (Snoopy's birds used one on their frozen birdbath.)

The Zamboni ice-resurfacing machine was invented by Frank Zamboni, an auto repairman turned refrigeration specialist. After moving to California in 1922 to work for his brother George in his car repair business, Frank and his younger brother Lawrence started a refrigeration company that built and installed refrigerators in dairies.

It wasn't long before Frank realized that his expertise with ice could be put to more lucrative use than simply selling blocks of ice and installing refrigerators.

At the time, ice-skating was increasing in popularity, so Frank and his brothers, seeing an opportunity, built a 20,000-square-foot ice-skating rink in Paramount, California. The rink quickly became very popular and Frank realized that his current system for maintaining smooth ice—dragging a scraper behind a truck, sweeping up the shavings, spraying the ice with water, and letting it freeze—

took too much time, and was much too inefficient. He turned his attention toward designing a machine that would do all that was necessary to maintain flat ice, but quicker and with much less manpower. In 1949, Frank patented the Model A Zamboni Ice Resurfacer.

Shortly thereafter, professional ice-skater Sonja Henie took one with her on a European tour; then the Ice Capades ordered them, and soon the Zamboni became the one and only way to resurface skating surfaces.

Frank Zamboni died in 1988, but his company is still manufacturing Zambonis and still testing them out at the nearby Paramount rink.

## THE ZIPPER

Debut: August 29, 1893
Inventive Americans: Whitcomb Judson;
Gideon Sundbach

When Whitcomb Judson invented the zipper, he did not call it a zipper. On August 29, 1893, Judson, a Chicago inventor, patented his "clasp-locker" and introduced it as an alternative to the lengthy, time-wasting, and truly annoying laces that were being used at the time to close men's and women's boots.

Judson and his partners showed their new invention at the 1893 Chicago World's Fair, but no one seemed to care. Judson and company were not especially savvy marketers and, even though they formed a company to distribute their clasp-locker (United Fastener), they did not have much success. One of the main reasons for the lack of acceptance was the fact that their creation frequently jammed and clothing manufacturers did not want to switch over from laces to the new fastener until it was perfected. Changing manufacturing equipment from punching holes for laces to sewing in zippers would be a major expense and no one wanted to commit to the investment until it was perfect.

The improvements necessary to make the zipper a mainstream convenience were eventually realized, but it was too late for Whitcomb Judson to enjoy the fruits of his creativity. Judson died in 1909, four years before a Swedish-American named

Gideon Sundbach smoothed out the rough spots of the clasp-locker and created the zipper as we know it today. By 1913, the zipper was a huge success and what added to its popularity was the U.S. military's use of zippers in its gear and clothing for World War I troops. The timing was fortuitous. The truly efficient and easy-to-use zipper was perfected in 1913, and World War I started in 1914. Suddenly, the War Department had to sign contracts for all manner of material for the troops, and here was this innovative new way of closing jackets, pouches, and pockets.

But what about the name? How did the zipper become known as the zipper?

The name was created by the B.F. Goodrich Company in 1923 when they started using the fastener in their rubber boots. They wanted something, uh, "zippy" (sorry) for their promotional material, so they created a name based on the sound the clasp made when it was opened and closed: Zip!

And in a zip, Whitcomb Judson's clasp, now known as a zipper, became a part of the American lifestyle.

# APPENDIX

## All-American Lists

American Firsts That Changed the World

- ✪ Air-conditioning.
- ✪ The airplane.
- ✪ Anesthesia.
- ✪ The assembly line.
- ✪ Audiotape recording.
- ✪ The cotton gin.
- ✪ E-mail.
- ✪ Express delivery service.
- ✪ FM radio.
- ✪ The lightbulb.
- ✪ The microprocessor.
- ✪ The motion picture.
- ✪ The nuclear power plant.
- ✪ The personal computer.
- ✪ The phonograph.
- ✪ Polaroid photography.
- ✪ The rocket.
- ✪ The sewing machine.

- ✪ The skyscraper.
- ✪ The telegraph.
- ✪ The telephone.
- ✪ The typewriter.
- ✪ The written National Constitution.

## American Firsts That Were Invented By Accident

- ✪ Bubble gum.
- ✪ Instant replay.
- ✪ Ivory soap.
- ✪ Kevlar bulletproof material.
- ✪ The popsicle.
- ✪ Post-it Notes.
- ✪ Saran Wrap.
- ✪ Silly Putty.
- ✪ Slinky.
- ✪ The tea bag.
- ✪ Teflon.

## American Firsts That Are Good for Our Health

- ✪ Activase.
- ✪ Alcoholics Anonymous.
- ✪ Anesthesia.
- ✪ Angioplasty.
- ✪ The Apgar scale.
- ✪ The artificial heart.
- ✪ Band-Aids.
- ✪ The blood bank.
- ✪ The cardiac pacemaker.
- ✪ The CAT scan.
- ✪ ChapStick.
- ✪ The Coronary Bypass Operation.
- ✪ Cortisone.
- ✪ Dental floss.
- ✪ Enovid.

- Fluoride toothpaste.
- The MRI.
- Norplant implantable contraceptive.
- Novocaine.
- The Polio vaccine.
- Prozac.
- Tetracycline.
- Valium.

## American Firsts That Make Life Easier

- Air-conditioning.
- The ATM.
- Barcodes.
- The bifocal lens.
- Brillo Pads.
- The calculating machine.
- Caller ID.
- The can opener.
- The collapsible ironing board.
- Condensed milk.
- Contact lenses.
- Cruise control.
- The Dewey Decimal System.
- The dishwasher.
- The disposable diaper.
- The drinking fountain.
- The drinking straw.
- Earplugs.
- The electric razor.
- The escalator.
- The flyswatter.
- Liquid Paper.
- Liquid soap.
- The microwave oven.

- ✪ Pantyhose.
- ✪ Paper towels.
- ✪ The personal computer.
- ✪ The photocopy.
- ✪ The pop-top can.
- ✪ The pop-up toaster.
- ✪ Post-it Notes.
- ✪ The pushpin.
- ✪ The Rolodex.
- ✪ The rubber rand.
- ✪ The safety pin.
- ✪ Saran Wrap.
- ✪ Scotch tape.
- ✪ The shopping cart.
- ✪ Teflon.
- ✪ The telephone.
- ✪ The telephone book.
- ✪ Toilet paper.
- ✪ Touch-Tone dialing.
- ✪ Tupperware.
- ✪ The TV dinner.
- ✪ The TV remote control.
- ✪ The typewriter.
- ✪ The vacuum cleaner.
- ✪ WD-40.
- ✪ The wire coat hanger.
- ✪ The Yellow Pages.
- ✪ The zipper.

## American Firsts That Help Us Know More

- ✪ CNN.
- ✪ The Dewey Decimal System.
- ✪ E-mail.
- ✪ Free public schools.

- ✪ Instant replay.
- ✪ Junior high school.
- ✪ The motion picture.
- ✪ The personal computer.
- ✪ Radio astronomy.
- ✪ The Weather Channel.

## American Firsts That Protect Us

- ✪ Air bags.
- ✪ The cylinder lock.
- ✪ The gas mask.
- ✪ Kevlar.
- ✪ The safety elevator.
- ✪ The smoke detector.
- ✪ The sprinkler head.

## American Firsts That Changed the Way We Shop

- ✪ Amazon.com.
- ✪ The assembly line.
- ✪ The ATM.
- ✪ Bar codes.
- ✪ The cash register.
- ✪ eBay.
- ✪ E-mail.
- ✪ Express delivery service.
- ✪ Frozen foods.
- ✪ The grocery bag.
- ✪ The shopping cart.

## American Firsts That Changed the Way We Dress

- ✪ Blue jeans.
- ✪ The brassiere.
- ✪ Nylon stockings.
- ✪ Panty hose.
- ✪ The sewing machine.

- Sneakers.
- The tuxedo.
- The zipper.

## American Firsts That Changed the Way We Eat

- The bread-slicing machine.
- Cheerios.
- Cheese in a can.
- The chocolate chip cookie.
- Coca-Cola.
- Condensed milk.
- Cornflakes.
- The donut.
- Fig Newtons.
- Frozen food.
- The graham cracker.
- Jell-O.
- Kool-Aid.
- Life Savers.
- The MoonPie.
- The popsicle.
- The pop-top can.
- Potato chips.
- Saccharin.
- The Tea bag.
- The TV dinner.

## American Firsts That Are Nothing But Fun!

- Bubble gum.
- Cheerleading.
- The Chia Pet.
- Crayola crayons.
- The crossword puzzle.
- The drive-in theater.
- The Ferris wheel.

- The Frisbee.
- The golf tee.
- "Happy Birthday to You."
- The jukebox.
- Monopoly.
- The Pet Rock.
- Play-Doh.
- The roller coaster.
- Scrabble.
- Silly Putty.
- Slinky.
- The slot machine.
- Volleyball.
- Waterskiing.

## Runners-Up

- Aerial photography.
- Air brakes.
- The all-mechanical cotton picker.
- AM radio.
- Atomic energy.
- The Automat.
- Automation.
- The ballpoint pen.
- The balloon catheter.
- The biplane.
- Blood vessel cauterization.
- The candy bar.
- The cellular phone.
- The Clapper.
- Cloud seeding.
- Comic strips.
- The commercial passenger plane.
- The compact disk.

- The compression ice-making machine.
- The computer.
- Conveyor belts.
- The cork-lined bottle cap.
- Correspondence courses.
- The cotton mill.
- The crash test dummy.
- The cyclotron.
- The dental plate.
- Dial telephones.
- The dumbwaiter.
- Earmuffs.
- The electric dental drill.
- The electric iron.
- The electric motor.
- The electric oven.
- The electric sewing machine.
- The electric starter.
- The electric trolley car.
- The electric washing machine.
- The electrical transformer.
- The electrical transmitter.
- The elevated railway.
- Erector Set®.
- The foot-operated sewing machine.
- The Gatling machine gun.
- Genetically-engineered human insulin.
- Genetic engineering.
- The grain elevator.
- Graphite.
- Guarantees of freedom of speech and religion *in writing*.
- The Hale telescope.
- The halftone photo-engraving process.

✪ The hepatitis vaccine.

✪ The hideaway bed.

✪ Homogenized milk.

✪ The Hubbell Space Telescope.

✪ The Influenza antiviral drug Amantadine.

✪ The Intellectual Property Patent System.

✪ The interlocking-stitch sewing machine.

✪ The jet plane.

✪ The jet-powered backpack.

✪ The Jet Ski®.

✪ The Joy Machine Tunnel Cutter.

✪ Kerosene.

✪ Kindergarten.

✪ Kraft Paper.

✪ The Laser.

✪ Legal aid.

✪ The Liquid-Fuel Rocket.

✪ The locomotive.

✪ Machine shorthand.

✪ The magnetic observatory.

✪ The mail-order catalog.

✪ Margarine.

✪ The Mars Orbiter.

✪ The Mercury-Vapor Electric Light.

✪ The metal lunchbox.

✪ Miniature golf.

✪ The mobile home.

✪ The modern hotel.

✪ Moldable cast iron.

✪ The Moon Lander Vehicle.

✪ The mumps vaccine.

✪ The necktie.

✪ Nuclear chain reaction.

✪ The nuclear-powered submarine.

- The orthopedic traction device.
- The outboard motor.
- The paper cutter.
- The pay telephone.
- Pentothal.
- The petroleum oil well.
- The Phillip's Head screw.
- The pipe wrench.
- The platform scale.
- The plow.
- The prefabricated home.
- Probation®.
- Public relations.
- The radio broadcasting station.
- The radio telescope.
- The railroad steam engine.
- The RAM memory chip.
- The rapid-fire Gatling gun.
- Ready-to-use paint.
- The reaper.
- The refrigerated car.
- The repeating rifle.
- Rice Krispies®.
- The rotary printing press.
- The science of polling.
- Scuba gear.
- The single porcelain tooth.
- The six-shooter revolver.
- The 16-millimeter camera, projector, and film.
- The Springfield flintlock musket.
- Standardized jigs.
- The steamboat.
- The subatomic particle accelerator.
- The submarine.

- The suburban neighborhood.
- The superhighway.
- Suspenders.
- The suspension bridge.
- Synthetic rubber.
- The teddy bear.
- The telephone switching system.
- Television broadcasting.
- The toothpick.
- Touch-screen technology.
- The tractor.
- The train air brake.
- Transatlantic telephone service.
- The two-cylinder automobile.
- The two-tiered train sleeping car.
- The typesetting machine.
- Uranium enrichment.
- Vacuum canning process.
- Virology.
- Virus culturing.
- Vulcanized rubber.
- The walkie-talkie.
- The washing machine (drum).
- The water-tube boiler.
- The wheelchair.
- The wood frame house.
- The wooden coat hanger.
- The wrench.
- The zinc-lidded mason jar.

# NOTES

1. According to the Website *http://home.att.net/~jnozum/ Energy.htm*, the equation is **Vf** $=(M1V1+M2V2)/(M1+M2)$. For those of you so inclined to understand the equation, the site continues: **Speed of Entangled Vehicles Immediately After Inelastic Collision (Vehicles Cannot Separate):** This is a collision equation. Vf is the speed immediately after an inelastic collision (in M/s). M1 is the mass (in kilograms) of one object hitting or being hit by another object. V1 is the speed of the first object in M/s. M2 is the mass of the second object in this equation. V2 is the speed of the second object in M/s. An example use of this equation would be when one car rams into another. Please note that in a head-on collision, one vehicle must be assigned a negative velocity (due to moving in the opposite direction).

2. © 2003 Alcoholics Anonymous World Services, Inc. All Rights Reserved.

3. Thanks to *Smithsonian Magazine* for the research for this entry.

4. Dr. Thomas A. Preston, Professor of Medicine at the University of Washington School of Medicine and Chief of Cardiology at Pacific Medical Center, Seattle, Washington; *Journal of Holistic Medicine*, Vol. 7 No. I. Spring/Summer 1985, Pages 8-15.

5. *The New Haven Register*, June 10, 2003.

6. *New York Recorder*, June 15, 1891; *Wizard*, p. 111.

7.  Writing Instrument Manufacturers Association, *www.wima.org*.

8.  A different version of this list appeared in the author's *The Hollywood Book of Lists* (Kensington, 2001). Used by permission. All rights reserved.

9.  From a 1918 Parks Service policy letter.

10. Stephen Spignesi, *The 100 Greatest Disasters of All Time.* (Kensington, 2002.)

11. Ibid.

12. *www.3m.com*.

13. Ibid.

14. *American Heritage Dictionary*.

15. Stephen Spignesi, *The 100 Greatest Disasters of All Time.* (Kensington, 2002.)

16. This is the date it was patented by Hunt.

17. "Single-subject" cable channels were a natural evolutionary outgrowth of the expanding cable television channel line-up. (Other single-subject cable channels include cartoons, history, news, sports, golf, Congress, entertainment, comedy, court, game shows, science fiction, and animals.)

19. *American Heritage Dictionary*.

20. The first actual Constitution, the Fundamental Orders of Connecticut was written in 1639, but it was for a state, not a country.

# BIBLIOGRAPHY

Axelrod, Alan. *The Complete Idiot's Guide to American History*. New York: Alpha Books, 1996.

Carey, John, editor. *Eyewitness to History*. New York: Avon Books, 1987.

Flexner, Stuart with Doris Flexner. *The Pessimist's Guide to History*. New York: Avon Books, 1992.

Garner, Joe. *We Interrupt This Broadcast: Relive the Events That Stopped Our Lives—from the Hindenburg to the Death of Princess Diana*. Naperville, Ill.: Sourcebooks, 1998.

Garraty, John A. *1,001 Things Everyone Should Know About American History*. New York: Main Street Books, Doubleday, 1989.

Gove, John. *Made in America: The True Stories Behind the Brand Names That Built A Nation*. New York: Berkley Books, 2001.

King, Norman. *The Almanac of Fascinating Beginnings*. New York: Citadel Press, 1994.

Lee, Min, editor. *Larousse Dictionary of North American History*. New York: Larousse, 1994.

Loewen, James W. *Lies My Teacher Told Me: Everything Your American History Textbook Got Wrong*. New York: The New Press, 1995.

Nash, Bruce and Allan Zullo. *The Misfortune 500*. New York: Pocket Books, 1988.

Ochoa, George and Melinda Corey. *The Timeline Book of Science*. New York: The Stonesong Press, 1995.

Panati, Charles. *Panati's Browser's Book of Beginnings.* Boston, MA: Houghton Mifflin, 1984.

———. *Panati's Extraordinary Endings of Practically Everything and Everybody.* New York: Harper & Row, 1989.

———. *Panati's Parade of Fads, Follies and Manias.* New York: HarperPerennial, 1991.

Seifer, Marc. *Wizard: The Life & Times of Nikola Tesla.* New York: Kensington Books, 2001.

Shenkman, Richard and Kurt Reiger. *One-Night Stands with American History.* New York: Quill, 1982.

Spignesi, Stephen J. *The 100 Greatest Disasters of All Time.* New York: Kensington Books, 2002.

———. *The Hollywood Book of Lists.* New York: Kensington Books, 2001.

———. *The USA Book of Lists.* Franklin Lakes, NJ: New Page Books, 2001.

# Suggested Reading and Websites

*Hartford Courant*
*Journal of Holistic Medicine*
*Los Angeles Times*
*New Haven Register*
*New York Post*
*New York Recorder*
*New York Times*
*Washington Post*
*Writing Instrument Manufacturers Association, www.wima.org*
*www.amnestyusa.org*
*www.driveintheater.com*
*www.stopatmfees.com*
*www.thedeathhouse.com*
*www.weather.com*

# INDEX

# ABOUT THE AUTHOR

STEPHEN J. SPIGNESI is a *New York Times* best-selling author who writes about historical biography, popular culture, television, film, American and world history, and contemporary fiction. He is also a published novelist and poet.

Spignesi—christened "the world's leading authority on Stephen King" by *Entertainment Weekly*—has written many authorized entertainment books and has worked with Stephen King, Turner Entertainment, the Margaret Mitchell Estate, Andy Griffith, Viacom, and other entertainment industry personalities and entities on a wide range of projects. Spignesi has also contributed essays, chapters, articles, and introductions to a wide range of books.

Spignesi's more than 35 books have been translated into several languages and he has also written for *Harper's*, *Cinefantastique*, *Saturday Review*, *TV Guide*, *Mystery Scene*, *Gauntlet*, and *Midnight Graffiti* magazines, as well as the *New York Times*, *New York Daily News*, *New York Post*, *New Haven Register*, the French literary journal *Tenébres*, and the Italian on-line literary journal, *Horror.It*. Spignesi has appeared on CNN, MSNBC, Fox News Channel, and other TV and radio outlets, and has also appeared in the 1998 E! documentary, *The Kennedys: Power, Seduction, and Hollywood*, as a Kennedy family authority, and in the A & E *Biography* of Stephen King that aired in January 2000. Spignesi's 1997 book *JFK Jr.* was a *New York*

*Times* best-seller. Spignesi's *Complete Stephen King Encyclopedia* was a 1991 Bram Stoker Award nominee.

In addition to writing, Spignesi also lectures on a variety of popular cultural and historical subjects and teaches writing in the Connecticut area. He is the founder and Editor-in-Chief of the small press publishing company, THE STEPHEN JOHN PRESS, which recently published the acclaimed feminist autobiography *Open Windows*.

Spignesi lives in New Haven, Connecticut, with his wife, Pam, and their cat, Carter, named for their favorite character on *ER*.

# Other Books by Stephen J. Spignesi

April 1987

*Mayberry, My Hometown* (1987, Popular Culture, Ink.)

1990

*The Complete Stephen King Encyclopedia* (1990, Contemporary Books)
*The Stephen King Quiz Book* (1990, Signet)

1992

*The Second Stephen King Quiz Book* (1992, Signet)
*The Woody Allen Companion* (1992, Andrews and McMeel)

1993

*The Official "Gone With the Wind" Companion* (1993, Plume)

1994

*The V. C. Andrews Trivia and Quiz Book* (1994, Signet)
*The Odd Index: The Ultimate Compendium of Bizarre and Unusual Facts* (1994, Plume)
*What's Your Mad About You IQ?* (1995, Citadel Press)
*The Gore Galore Video Quiz Book* (1995, Signet)

1996

*What's Your Friends IQ?* ( 1996, Citadel Press)
*The Celebrity Baby Name Book* (1996, Plume)
*The E.R. Companion* (1996, Citadel Press) 1997
*J.F.K. Jr.* (1997, Citadel Press; originally titled *The J.F.K. Jr. Scrapbook*) – New York Times best-seller
*The Robin Williams Scrapbook* (1997, Citadel Press)
*The Italian 100: A Ranking of the Most Influential Cultural, Scientific, and Political Figures, Past and Present* (1997, Citadel Press)

1998

*The Beatles Book of Lists* (1998, Citadel Press)
*Young Kennedys: The New Generation* (1998, Avon; written as "Jay David Andrews")

*The Lost Work Of Stephen King: A Guide to Unpublished Manuscripts, Story Fragments, Alternative Versions, & Oddities* (1998, Citadel Press).

*The Complete* Titanic: *From the Ship's Earliest Blueprints to the Epic Film* (1998, Citadel Press)

## 2000

*How To Be An Instant Exper*t (2000, Career Press)

*She Came In Through the Kitchen Window: Recipes Inspired by The Beatles & Their Music* (2000, Kensington Books)

*The USA Book of Lists* (2000, Career Press)

## 2001

*The UFO Book of Lists* (2001, Kensington Books)

*The Essential Stephen King: The Greatest Novels, Short Stories, Movies, and Other Creations of the World's Most Popular Writer* (2001, New Page Books)

*The Cat Book of Lists* (2001, New Page Books)

*The Hollywood Book of Lists* (2001, Kensington Books)

*The Essential Stephen King: The Complete & Uncut Edition* (2001, GB Books)

## 2002

*Gems, Jewels, & Treasures: The Complete Jewelry Book* (2002, QVC Publishing)

*The 100 Greatest Disasters of All Time* (2002, Kensington Books)

*In the Crosshairs: The 75 Most Famous Assassinations and Assassination Attempts, from Julius Caesar to John Lennon* (2002, New Page Books)

## 2003

*Crop Circles: Signs of Contact* (with Colin Andrews) (2003, New Page Books)

*The Weird 100* (2003, Kensington)

## 2004

*The Husbands of Coventry* (2004, The Stephen John Press)

*What's Your Red, White & Blue IQ?* (2004, Kensington)

*The 100 Best Beatles Songs* (with Michael Lewis) (2004, Black Dog & Leventhal)